D1639677

'What do we do now?'

Sophie looked up at him, her eyes wide with anxiety and curiosity, and he realised that nothing would ever be the same again. Her question was so naïve as to be almost absurd. He knew he should answer her purely on a formal level, because there was indeed a great deal to do now.

'We seal our bargain,' he said instead, as his baser self elbowed its way to the front of the stage.

'How do we do that?' she asked seriously, and he laughed—more at himself than at her—swamped by relief that it was done, that she had agreed, and that he could now finally do what he had been waiting to do since that day in the gardens.

'Like this,' he said, raising her chin and bending to brush his lips across hers.

Lara Temple was three years old when she begged her mother to take the dictation of her first adventure story. Since then she has led a double life—by day she is a high-tech investment professional, who has lived and worked on three continents, but when darkness falls she loses herself in history and romance…at least on the page. Luckily her husband and two beautiful and very energetic children help her weave it all together.

Books by Lara Temple

Mills & Boon Historical Romance

Lord Crayle's Secret World
The Reluctant Viscount
The Duke's Unexpected Bride

Visit the Author Profile page at millsandboon.co.uk.

THE DUKE'S
UNEXPECTED
BRIDE

Lara Temple

First published in Great Britain 2017
By Mills & Boon, an imprint of HarperCollins*Publishers*
1 London Bridge Street, London, SE1 9GF

Large Print edition 2017

© 2017 Ilana Treston

ISBN: 978-0-263-06787-3

Our policy is to use papers that are natural, renewable and recyclable products and made from wood grown in sustainable forests. The logging and manufacturing processes conform to the legal environmental regulations of the country of origin.

Printed and bound in Great Britain
by CPI Antony Rowe, Chippenham, Wiltshire

THE DUKE'S
UNEXPECTED
BRIDE

To Tom and Lia,
who taught me the beautiful tension
between chaos and creation
and who would have loved Marmaduke…

Chapter One

London—1819, summer

Sophie inspected her prey. The stout pug lay in the middle of an enormous chartreuse-velvet cushion placed strategically close to the fireplace in Lady Minnie's back parlour, which was known as Marmaduke's Parlour—though never within the hearing of the lady of the house.

'It's just you and me, Marmaduke. And I'm not backing down.'

Nothing. Not a quiver of his pudgy body. She knew he was awake because his eyes were open, but otherwise he might have been in a trance, his frog-like eyes fixed on the faded gold and crimson wallpaper, his backside defiantly pointed in her direction.

'It's very simple, Duke. Either you let me walk you as per doctor's orders or Aunt Minnie will probably put me on the next coach back to Ashton Cove and Awful Arthur will get to keep his record of longest sojourn in Aunt Minnie's mausoleum, and what is more to the point, I will have to go home and I really, *really* don't want to go home just yet. This may have been a version of hell for Augusta and Mary, but even if I can't explore London, it is sheer and utter bliss to be absolutely on my own with no one criticising me, or expecting anything of me, other than Aunt Minnie's once-a-day read-aloud session, of course. You obviously have no idea what it is like to live in a small house with nine people, not to mention being surrounded by Papa's parishioners, most of whom are convinced you're a changeling. Now do you understand why I need your help?'

His jaw opened and a curling pink tongue lolled out, dancing slightly with his panting breath. She knew he had no idea what she was talking about so he could hardly be laughing at her, if dogs even laughed. To be fair, she might be laughing at herself if it wasn't so serious. She had been ecstatic when her turn to be summoned to Aunt Minerva Huntley's London mansion had arrived, despite her older siblings' reports about the horrors of their own visits. They had been forbidden to go further afield than the gardens across the road, spoken to no one but the servants, eaten their meagre meals in their rooms while evidence of some serious feasting took place in Aunt Minnie's chambers and been sent packing again after only a few days. Not one of them had lasted more than a week. And no one, not even Cousin Arthur, had had any luck with Marmaduke.

Aunt Minnie's very sympathetic butler had managed to convey to her that though the two other, less-favoured pugs in Aunt Minnie's menagerie were quite docile, no one in the house dared approach Marmaduke since he had an unfortunate habit of producing such heartrending high-pitched squeals that the last servant who had tried to exercise him had been sacked on the spot. Sophie knew her chances were poor, but aside from her own considerations she really believed it would do Marmaduke a world of good.

'It's not that I hate Ashton Cove, Duke,' she told Marmaduke's behind. 'But we have to face the facts. I'm not much use to my family as I am. Even if I had wanted to accept the offers of any of the men who showed an interest in me, which I didn't, I still managed to scare them all off before they actually took the leap. And Augusta always said my one contribution to Papa's parish work is that I'm good with eccentrics and animals because we think alike and I know not even that really makes up for my peculiarities. And here I am in London with an animal and a reclusive eccentric, apologies to Aunt Minnie, and I am making no headway. If you would only make a little, a teeny-tiny effort so I could prove I have some use? If I can show Aunt Minnie I am actually helping you follow doctor's orders, I might be allowed to stay a little longer and perhaps even explore the town. What do you say, Duke? Just a little stroll? I promise it will be fun!'

Her bright statement followed its friends into the silence and she stood eyeing the Buddha-like canine. Clearly matters required more than words. With an indrawn breath of resolution she scooped him up from his pillow and strode out into the hallway and towards the front door. Her move, worthy of Wellington's finest surprise attacks, so confounded Marmaduke he didn't react even when she strode across the busy road into the gardens. Safely inside, she looped a sturdy curtain cord through the velvet bow at his neck, deposited him on the grass and looked down at her captive. He stared back, eyes wide, mouth closed.

Then his head did a strange little turn, taking in the sights of the garden, a brace of pigeons picking at the gravel, a nursemaid leading two young children briskly down the path, the trees gently swaying in the spring breeze.

'See? It's not so bad, is it?' Sophie said encouragingly and was rewarded by a low growl as a pigeon moved threateningly nearby. Marmaduke hauled himself to his feet and the pigeon spread its wings and fluttered upwards. That was encouragement enough and Marmaduke, who Sophie had never seen move more than a yard at a time, mostly from his cushion to his silver food bowl, now proved he could move very quickly indeed. Sophie laughed and tightened her hold on the cord and hurried after her pudgy charge as he set about ridding the garden of all forms of fowl. After ten minutes of this sport he was panting heavily, his tongue out and jaw spread in an alarming grin, and Sophie judged she had done well enough for the day and scooped him up again, heading back towards Huntley House.

He lay so confidingly and comfortably in her arms, wheezing gently, that it never occurred to her he might have more energy left in him. But just as they crossed the street, he spotted another bird at the kerb and gave a mighty leap out of her arms, setting off in pursuit. Sophie was so surprised she did not even manage to grab the cord and watched in dismay as it snaked along in Marmaduke's wake.

After a second of shocked panic she sprang after him.

'Duke! Heel!' she called out sharply, with more hope than conviction, but though Marmaduke paid no heed, a man and woman stopped abruptly on the pavement ahead and the pug hurtled into the man's Hessian boots. This moment's check was enough for Sophie. She grabbed the trailing cord before he could recover and looped it about her wrist.

'There—it's back to St Helena's for you, you traitorous little dictator. That's the last time I take you for a walk if this is how you repay me!'

Marmaduke directed a very supercilious stare at her and bent to sniff at the boots that had been his Waterloo.

Sophie looked up, directing an apologetic glance at the couple who had been her unwitting accomplices.

'I'm dreadfully sorry about that, but thank you for stopping him. Aunt Minerva would have never forgiven me if he had run off. He's her favourite, though I don't know why. Most of the time he does nothing but sit on his cushion and stare at the wall. I hadn't even realised until today he could do more than shuffle.' She glanced down at the offender. 'To be fair, that was a very fine show of spirit, Marmaduke. But perhaps a bit too much of it all at once. We shall try it in stages, no?'

The woman, her dark hair tucked into a fashion-able bonnet lined with lilac silk and dressed in a very dashing indigo military-style walking dress with silver facings, looked slightly shocked, but then she glanced up at the tall man beside her and giggled, an incongruous sound from someone so elegant. Sophie, having fully and rather enviously surveyed her fashionable clothes, turned her attention to the man and had the strange sensation of standing before a carefully and magnificently crafted statue of an avenging warrior. Everything about him was powerful and uncompromising and would have graced the portals of the temple of a particularly vengeful god quite adequately. He stood motionless other than his intense dark grey eyes, which narrowed slightly as she met his gaze, and she was thrown back to a memory of getting lost in the gardens of their Cornish cous-

ins in St Ives at night and stumbling into a Greek
sculpture of Mars. She had frozen, dwarfed by
the moonlit, frowning and half-naked god of War,
too scared to move until rationality had prevailed
and she had run back to the house.

He bowed slightly and the strange impression
dissipated, leaving only a peculiar echoing feeling, like the silence after stepping out of a rau-
cous assembly, a sense of being alone and very
separate.

'That's quite all right,' he said in a deep, languid voice that hardly masked his impatience. 'We
were happy to be of service. I think a leash might
be more effective than that cord, though.'

Sophie shook herself and tumbled into embarrassed speech. 'I know, but Aunt Minnie doesn't
believe in going out of doors and refuses to buy
leashes. It is quite sad because it's clear he needs
exercise. Look at the poor thing.'

They all glanced down at Marmaduke, who
was now seated, as solid as a small boulder, his
pink tongue hanging out of his mock grin, and
the man's hard, uncompromising face relaxed into
a faint smile. A very nice smile, Sophie thought,
surprised by its transforming effect, and the sensation of being set apart increased.

'I am not sure he qualifies as a poor thing in my book. He looks about as indulged as humanly possible. Is Aunt Minnie by any chance Lady Minerva Huntley?'

'Yes, do you know her?'

The couple glanced at each other and there was an easy, laughing communication in the glance that connected them and Sophie thought, with a twinge of uncharacteristic envy, that they must be a very loving couple.

'Not really,' the woman answered. 'She doesn't go out much any more. But we used to see her often when we were children and before Lord Huntley passed away. She was always very grand. Are you staying with her?'

'Yes. I'm her niece and her latest pet.'

The lady's grey eyes sparkled with laughter.

'Pet?'

Sophie flushed in embarrassment at her slip. She was letting her embarrassment tumble her into just the kind of informal talk that sent her parents cringing.

'That's awful of me, isn't it? She is really being…considerate, in her way. Well, thank you again, I should return Marmaduke before we are missed. Good day.'

She smiled and turned in the direction of Huntley House, tugging at the leash, but Marmaduke had apparently expended all his energy for the day and merely allowed himself to be dragged a few inches. There was a moment of awkward silence and heat licked up Sophie's cheeks as she bent down to scoop him up.

'You are a master of contrariness, Duke. That innocent gaze doesn't deceive me in the least!' she informed him and with a last nod towards the couple, which she hoped was at least a facsimile of dignity, she headed towards Huntley House, closing her eyes briefly as she realised just how ridiculous she must have appeared to that beautiful, elegant couple. No doubt they were laughing at her behind her back. It was lucky her parents weren't there to see how predictably she had put her foot in it in her first interaction with human beings outside Aunt Minnie's domain. Well, she was unlikely to ever see them again. She tucked Marmaduke more closely to her, comforted by his rapid panting. At least she had done some good today, even if only to a pug.

Chapter Two

Max watched the young woman until she disappeared into the entrance of Number Forty-Eight and then glanced down at his sister with the remnants of amusement in his eyes.

'That proves it. Madness is clearly heritable, Hetty.'

His sister laughed again and shook her head as they turned and continued heading eastwards towards Brook Street.

'Nonsense, Max, I doubt that girl or Lady Huntley are any madder than I. Lady Huntley has just given herself over to the enjoyment of being a famous recluse and eccentric. From what I gather from my maid she is kept fully up to date on all London gossip. And that young woman is probably just bored to tears and happy to talk with anyone if she is the latest of Lady Huntley's relatives commandeered to attend to her. Really, that woman seems to have more cousins and indigent relatives than anyone I have ever seen. Even with her fortune, if she ever does have to divide it up among them, there won't be more than a pittance apiece.'

'Perhaps this latest helpmate is hopeful Mad Minnie's canines will win her exclusivity on the Huntley fortune. She certainly seems quite happy conversing with that…dog, if you can even call it that. She almost had me convinced he knew what she was talking about.'

'You are such a cynic, Max. I don't doubt I'd be reduced to talking to the dogs if I had to spend more than a day in there. I heard Lady Huntley sometimes doesn't speak to these relations at all, just sends them commands through her butler. And once she sent one of them away on the night mail with only twenty minutes' warning! I can't imagine what would happen to that poor child if she lost Mad Minnie's favourite pug.'

'She'd probably find herself locked in the cellars, or worse. But I would think she would be grateful to be evicted, even if it is by the night-mail coach. And she's hardly a child. I would say twenty-three or four.'

Hetty snorted in a very unladylike manner. 'Of course I wouldn't dispute the verdict of the connoisseur of all things female. Are you certain you cannot fix the date more accurately? Or wasn't she beautiful enough to merit that degree of examination?'

'Don't be snide, Hetty. She was tolerable, but I don't favour pert little country misses, not even ones of her undisputed originality. Far too tiring.'

Hetty sighed.

'You don't favour anyone, Max dear. Please try and be a bit more positive when we reach Lady Carmichael. She and Lady Penny won't know what to do with your biting comments. Do behave!'

Max stopped himself from uttering just such a comment about his sister's current offering for potential spouse. He should really learn to reserve judgement. After all, he had only spoken to Lady Penny once, at a very tedious evening at Almack's, and he should hardly be surprised if all she had to say for herself was a sampling of the same inanities which young women felt were expected of them in such occasions. And to be fair, she did appear to be, as Hetty pointed out, a pretty, sweet and modest young woman from an excellent family. She would do very well as Duchess of Harcourt and mother of his heirs. And if she really was too boring, Hetty had promised she had three other candidates in mind.

And most of all he should show Hetty some gratitude for being willing to help him fulfil his highly regretted but inescapable promise. The thought of going through the forest of debutantes and potentially marriageable women on his own was more daunting than any military campaign he had ever undertaken. He would almost be willing to face Napoleon again rather than an endless row of Wednesday evenings at Almack's. And that meant he needed Hetty's help. She had been by far the most socially adept of his five sisters and until her marriage six years ago she had known everyone who was anyone in the upper ten thousand of London.

'That is twice I've been called to heel today, Hetty. Have pity,' he replied with a rueful smile.

She chuckled.

'That *was* funny! And she did manage to bring a Duke to heel even if it was only you and not the pug. If I ever feel the need to take you down a peg, I shall share that story with your friends. Everyone takes you far too seriously.'

'If you do, I might be forced to remember some of your more embarrassing escapades from our childhood,' Max warned. 'That was bad enough, but to liken that fur ball to Napoleon on St Helena is carrying eccentricity too far. That peculiar girl obviously has no town sense to be talking to strangers like that. She'll get into trouble.'

Hetty waited until they had crossed Mount Street before replying.

'I do feel sorry for her. She seemed so eager to talk. Perhaps I should be brave and introduce myself while I am in town. You know I always wanted an excuse to cross the portals of the Huntley mausoleum.'

Max smiled down at her.

'You've a soft heart, Hetty. But remember what happened to Mother when she went to visit Mad Minnie after Lord Huntley died? Are you sure you want to risk a similar rebuff?'

'Pooh, that was years and years ago. And Mama never had the slightest notion of tact and certainly no sympathy so I'm hardly surprised she was sent packing. You're just scared of Mad Minnie.'

They stopped in front of the elegant town house on the corner of Brook Street and Max sighed with resignation.

'Frankly, I would prefer to spend the afternoon with Mad Minnie rather than at Lady Carmichael's. I wish I had never promised Father I would marry within ten years. Thirty-one seemed like a hell of a long time away back then and a fair price to pay to get his approval to join Wellington in Spain.'

Hetty considered. 'I think he might have let you enlist even if you hadn't. I know what Harcourt meant to Papa, but he was a stickler for duty and he saw nothing wrong in your wanting to serve your country. He just wanted to make certain you married eventually. I think he was afraid you might not…after what happened with Serena…'

Max stiffened involuntarily and her voice trailed off.

'Sorry, I shouldn't have mentioned her,' she said contritely.

He shrugged, trying to relax the tension that always took hold when anything brought back memories of Serena. He would have happily traded quite a bit of his worldly goods for a magical remedy that could slice off that year of his life. His father, as stiff as always, had made one of his rare attempts at being paternal and supportive when he had offered him the trite 'time heals all wounds' aphorism. But though time had dulled the pain and guilt and all the other emotions he had tried to escape by drowning in the horrors of war, he didn't feel healed. Just muted. Older and wiser. Another cliché.

He could vaguely remember the excitement that Serena's beauty and vivacity had sparked in him, but just as he remembered his favourite childhood books—intense but distant, not quite real. More powerful were the feelings that gradually took their place—confusion, resentment, helplessness. Hatred. She had definitely widened his emotional repertoire. And each time something evoked her memory he still flinched involuntarily and the throb of guilt came back, proof that there was still a core of poison inside him that refused to dissipate. He grimaced at the thought. A poor choice of words...

'It was a long time ago. It almost seems as if it happened to someone else. As for Father, whatever his motives, I was too shocked that he agreed to let me go to Spain to even consider negotiating his terms.'

'You know, you don't *have* to marry if you don't want to. I mean...surely he wouldn't expect you to hold to a promise if it is something you—' She broke off as she met his gaze. 'Oh, dear, of course he would. Poor Papa. But he's dead and so—' She broke off again. 'I forget who I am talking to. Of course you will hold to it.'

Max forced a smile. He wished he had it in him to break his promise as she suggested, but he knew himself well enough to know that he wouldn't. It hadn't been an idle, arbitrary promise. He might never have felt very close to his father, but the previous Duke of Harcourt had done a very good job inculcating him with a sense of what they owed to their position and the people who depended on them. The Duchy was not theirs individually, but theirs in trust. Fulfilling his duties wasn't just a matter of honour; it was a matter of practical concern for hundreds of people who depended on their properties. His father had allowed him to put that on the line by joining the army because he had been clever enough to understand that Max had needed to get away from the setting of his tragedy, but he had made it clear that every indulgence came at a price and he had chosen this particular price with a sense of evening out the scales.

And Max couldn't really find fault with his father's concern. He might have chafed at his parents' constraints as a child and even fantasised that he had been stolen as a baby from the Shepstons, a warm family of fishermen from Port Jacob on Harcourt land who had often taken him fishing with them, but he was a Harcourt after all. He would not let something as important as the succession be completely subverted by his and Serena's mistakes. There was nothing wrong in principle with a marriage of convenience. He and his parents had just miscalculated, royally, about Serena's suitability.

Max hadn't even wanted to get engaged so young, whatever his father's concerns about the succession, but his father had cleverly not pushed the point, merely invited Lord Morecombe and his daughter to join them in London. The first time he had seen her she had been dressed in a bright yellow dress, bursting with excitement at finally being released from school, her dark eyes hot and focused with an intensity that was completely foreign to him. He had agreed to the engagement the very next day and had sealed their fate. Serena had gulped at life and kept demanding more and at first it had been exhilarating, utterly different from anything he had ever allowed himself. He should have known they were just too different.

Part of him had, but by the time he had stopped to think it was too late. This time he would be more careful. What was the point of making mistakes, especially monumental ones, if you didn't learn from them?

'It's not so bad, Hetty,' he said at last. 'I have to marry eventually; I might as well get it over with.'

'It isn't something one can simply get over with!' she said with unusual asperity. 'You will be stuck with your choice for the rest of your life, you know!'

'Only too well. So I will do my best to choose someone comfortable and conformable. Even if it weren't for the promise, I think I would have a very hard time leaving the succession to Uncle Mortimer and Cousin Barnaby and they certainly wouldn't thank me for it.'

'They would make dreadful Dukes, wouldn't they? How did Mortimer put it? That the Duchy was hanging over them like a swarm of locusts about to descend upon his beloved gardens.'

Max sighed and headed up the stairs to strike the knocker.

'Right now it does feel like one of the plagues of Egypt. Or one of those fairy tales with a cursed treasure where the genie informs you you've had your fun and must now pay the piper. But you're right; I can't have the whole of the Harcourt estate depending on them. No steward would be able to withstand the destructive capabilities of those two well-meaning idiots. They'd have all the tenants put off so they could grow a dozen different breeds of lilies and roses instead of grain and feed. Couldn't Mother have supplied Father with another male heir so he wouldn't have forced me into that promise? I don't really need five sisters, you know.'

Hetty laughed.

'I won't ask which of us you can do without, Max dearest. Now do try at least to be charming. I know you can, if you would only put some effort into it—'

She broke off as the door opened and Max clenched his jaw and followed his sister and the butler to meet one of his potential future wives.

Chapter Three

Sophie picked up the small package which was waiting for her on the escritoire when she came down from reading Aunt Minnie the latest chapter of Mrs Pardoe's novel.

Scrawled across the wrapping paper was the message 'To be delivered to Lady Huntley's niece'. And below: 'For the safety of the residents of Grosvenor Square.' Sophie frowned and unwrapped the package and burst into laughter. A brown-leather leash and collar lay curled in the wrapping paper. She picked up her sketching bag and went in search of Marmaduke.

She found him in his favourite position on his cushion, rump to the room and nose an inch from the wall, panting faintly.

'Behold, fair Marmaduke. I have been delivered the means of your undoing!' she declared dramatically, but with absolutely no effect. She sighed and went to slip on the new collar. It took Marmaduke a moment to realise the offense against him, but by the time he surged to his pudgy feet and shook his head vigorously it was too late. Before he managed to descend into yowls she flapped one hand suggestively in front of his face and the shaking stopped, his gaze intent.

'That's right. Remember what fun you had chasing the birds? Well, they're outside, waiting for another round.' She began carefully moving towards the door and, to her surprise and amusement, he followed. They made a stately exit under the shocked stares of the butler and the doctor who had just entered the house.

'Good gracious,' said the doctor. 'He can walk!'

'And run, with the proper avian incentive. And now, if you will excuse us, I really don't want to stall our momentum.' She nodded, proceeding down the steps, and Marmaduke followed, thumping down each step ponderously but with resolution.

The collar and leash worked perfectly, and after a vigorous campaign against the winged invaders, Marmaduke allowed her to lead him to a bench in

the shade of a chestnut tree and settled content-
edly at her feet as she pulled out her sketch pad.

'And now I will commemorate this auspicious
moment, Duke,' she informed him grandly, but
he merely snuffled the grass in front of him and
grinned.

She sketched rapidly, capturing the lumpy body
and the beatific expression on his frog-like face.
He looked amazingly content and she laughed a
little at how content she herself felt at her minor
victory.

'There. I shall title it "Duke Reposing" and be-
stow it on Aunt Minnie so she can enjoy your fair
smile even when you are sulking downstairs. Do
you think she will like it?'

'Undoubtedly,' said a deep and vaguely familiar voice behind her and she turned in surprise.
The tall man who had stopped Marmaduke the
day before was standing a little behind the bench.
His grey eyes were on her sketch, but there was
no expression on his beautifully sculpted face.
More than ever he made her think of a statue of a
guardian of the gods, expertly crafted but without
emotion. But though he seemed utterly cold, she
was uncomfortably aware of a tingling heat that
was pricking at her cheeks and she could think

of nothing to say. The silence stretched and, as she struggled to think of anything that would not compound the embarrassing impression of yesterday, he surprised her by sitting down on the bench and taking the sketch pad from her hands. She looked away, but her gaze only settled on his hands and she noticed he was not wearing gloves and that his hands might have been formed by the same meticulous sculptor who had shaped the rest of him and with the aim of conveying strength and skill. But the perfection of his left hand was marred by a jagged and puckered white scar along the side, curving under towards the heel of his palm. She curled her own fingers into her palm against the need to touch it.

'That is quite good,' he said finally, handing it back to her.

The casually delivered comment finally woke her to the peculiarity of the situation and her confusion faded in annoyance at the very mild nature of his compliment on an issue of some importance to her.

'It is *very* good, for a rough, impromptu sketch,' she corrected him and his eyes narrowed and she could not tell if he was amused or annoyed by her correction.

'So it is. I apologise for not showing the proper degree of appreciation. It is certainly well outside the usual fare of young ladies' sketches, which are usually just a sight more bearable than their endeavours on the pianoforte. Do you play?'

'Even if I did, I wouldn't dare admit to it now,' she replied primly. 'Do you? Or are we proceeding on the assumption that only young ladies are expected to be execrable in artistic endeavours?'

'I have no artistic skills whatsoever. The difference is I don't try.'

'Is that an observation about yourself or a suggestion to me?' she asked suspiciously.

'I wouldn't presume. I did say the sketch was quite good, didn't I? You are overly sensitive.'

His voice was deep but without inflexion, but something in the narrowed slate-grey eyes that were watching her made her wonder if he was laughing at her. It was like looking into the night, trying to make out shapes in the varied shades of black. It was easy to imagine monsters in the dark and she wondered if she was imagining that echo of amused warmth in his eyes. Probably. But it still teased at her, like a late summer breeze, disorienting her. She would never be able to capture that particular grey, a shade lighter than the sea off the bay in winter. But she would love to try to sketch his face, with its strongly chiselled features, all definite lines and planes, and the tightly held mouth that she wished would relax into the smile she had seen the day before.

'May I sketch you? You have a very sketchable face,' she blurted out before she could stop herself.

She had not thought his face could get any stonier, but she had been wrong. There was a flash of surprise in his eyes, like a glimmer of faraway lightning, then his brows drew together, accentuating the resemblance to a very annoyed deity.

'No, you may not!' he said curtly and she turned away with a shrug, leafing through her sketchbook to mask her mortification.

'Fine,' she said as indifferently as possible, fully expecting him to get up and leave, but he didn't move. She came to the sketch she had made yesterday of his wife and stopped. The lovely, smiling face was a sobering reminder that she should not be looking at a married man or frankly at any man in quite that manner. Though to be fair, he *was* an amazing specimen. She had thought him handsome but rather cold yesterday, but now she realised it was much more than that. He was utterly, utterly male. And utterly out of her sphere.

Augusta would have made mincemeat of her had she been present and probably rightly so. Sophie breathed in resolutely, determined to redeem herself with a gesture of goodwill.

'I made a sketch of your wife, though. She has a lovely face. In fact, she looks like you a little. I find that married couples often look a little alike. Perhaps it is because we try to find people who remind us of ourselves so we can love ourselves better. Here it is. It is quite like her, don't you think?'

She forced herself to look up at him with all the calm unconcern she could muster, trying to mirror his lack of expression. He stared at her and then down at the sketch, a three-quarters' face of a woman and part of the shoulder of her gown. Sophie had sketched her smiling, which had been hard, but that was all she could remember. She waited, peculiarly tense, for his reaction.

He took the pad from her again and she didn't resist. She watched his profile, trying to memorise its strong lines so she could sketch him later, but she found it hard to focus on the whole, distracted instead by the details she usually considered later when doing a portrait—the way the skin stretched taut from his cheekbone, the small groove at the side of his mouth, the shadow below the strong line of his jaw. Her hands tingled with the need to reach out and touch his face as she might a sculpture. She clasped them tightly and forced herself to look down at Marmaduke, now snoring calmly at their feet.

'May I have my drawing pad back, please? I should go back.'

He looked up at her and there was something in his gaze as the dark eyes moved over her face that increased her already significant discomfort by a notch. And then his mouth relaxed slightly into a smile that brought to the surface the warmth she had glimpsed the day before.

'Would you consider giving this to Hetty? I think she would love to have it. And she is my sister, not my wife, by the way, hence the resemblance.'

Sophie felt her face heat with a sudden burning blush and she pressed her hands to them unconsciously.

'Oh, dear, I'm so sorry. I always say more than I ought. And of course you may give it to her. In gratitude for the collar and leash, which I was so impolite as to forget to thank you for. Here.'

She pulled the sheet from her pad and held it out to him, wishing the blush would fade.

He reached out to take it just as Marmaduke awoke with a snort and she started and dropped the sheet. Marmaduke, his eye catching the fluttering page, readied himself to leap, but before he could move she managed to capture it just as the man grabbed for it as well. His hand closed half on the page, half on her hand and she drew back abruptly, slightly shocked by the heat of his touch. The contact had been only for a second, but her arm felt like it had been dipped in hot water and her skin tingled uncomfortably, retaining the imprint of his fingers. She clasped her hands together again, as if she could blot it out. He merely regarded the sketch and stood up.

'Thank you for this. Good luck with... Duke.'

She nodded and busied herself with her pad and with Marmaduke. The man hesitated for a moment and then strode off without another word and she could finally breathe. She picked up Marmaduke and headed back to Huntley House rather blindly, forcing a man driving a tilbury to pull up sharply and bark out at her as she almost stepped directly on to the road in front of him. She glanced up at the angry driver, mumbled an apology and rushed across the road and into her temporary home. Once inside she deposited Marmaduke on his cushion and hurried up to her little nursery-like room on the third floor. In its small quiet space there was nothing to come between her and her disturbing thoughts, and the memory of that moment in the park kept recurring, of his hand, strong and firm and warm, grasping hers and the way her nerves had flared, a striking of a tinder-box. It was absurd and unwanted. This abrupt, unpredictable man came from a very different world from hers, no matter how respectable her birth. Everything about him spoke of wealth and influence and a degree of comfort in this foreign world that she would never understand. She should not be foolish enough to let herself be drawn to him simply because she was lonely and he and his sister were the only people who had treated her with any degree of sympathy, though on his part quite a cold and sardonic sympathy.

This was not the first time she had been attracted to a man, after all. Why, she had spent three whole months thoroughly enthralled with the squire's middle son John when he had come down from Cambridge before realising he was a pompous, oily snake, hardly any better than Cousin Arthur. Her fascination with him had then sputtered and faded pretty quickly which had been

very lucky since he had actually considered offering for her until he, too, had come to accept
his parents' viewpoint that she was completely
unsuitable. No doubt this silly attraction would
fare just the same as soon as she found out a little
more about this strange man.

It was just that he was so very handsome. And
then there was that contrast between the cold
mask and his sudden, almost intimate smile. No
doubt it had done very well for him with dozens
of gullible women. Well, she might not know London rules, but she was *not* gullible and she knew
when a man was very used to commanding attention and getting what he wanted from women.
In fact, now that she thought about it, she could
hardly believe she had actually asked if she could
sketch him. What must he think of her? His abrupt
withdrawal made it quite clear what he thought of
her offer. She should remember she was not back
at home with people who had already come to
terms, of sorts, with her strange ways. She would
never find her way in this town if she did not learn
to mind her tongue. Not that there was any chance
of finding her way here in any event. In a matter of days she, too, would be sent packing back
to Devon and all this would seem nothing more

than a passing dream. She should do her best to just enjoy the remaining days of blessed solitude. It would be over all too soon.

Max walked into the drawing room where Hetty was seated at the escritoire, writing a letter.

'Here, this is for you.' He handed her the sketch and watched her face light up in delight as she scanned the simple, evocative drawing.

'Max! What on earth? Where did you get this? Oh, I look quite lovely!'

'Lady Huntley's madcap niece drew it. I came across her sketching that pug in the park and she made me…or rather you, a gift of this, in recognition of the collar and leash we sent. It is good, isn't it?'

'It's marvellous, though I suppose I shouldn't say so since it is almost a compliment to myself. It is certainly more like me than that stiff portrait Mama commissioned before Ned and I married. Now I certainly must go and storm the mausoleum and thank her. How sweet of her!'

Max sat down, his eyes on the drawing. The absurdity of the whole encounter was still raw and he had no idea whether to be annoyed or amused by the girl. It had been many years since anyone had managed to disconcert him. Her voice and even her proper but outmoded dresses might mark her as another of the multitude of well-born young women who invaded London from the country, but the resemblance stopped there. Women of her birth and age usually knew how to conduct themselves with proper modesty and certainly did not engage strange men in conversations that were not only peculiar, but bordered on an unspoken intimacy, as if she knew and trusted him. It was absurd that for a brief moment he had taken her at face value and had been imprudent enough to even sit down beside her in the first place. He couldn't imagine doing that with someone like Lady Penny without having been properly introduced. And Lady Penny would not be wandering alone in the gardens in the first place with no better chaperon than that pug. Or asking if she could draw a man's face, even had she been introduced to him with all formality. It was little wonder he had been so disconcerted.

'She asked to sketch me. She said I have a "sketchable" face.'

Hetty's giggle caught on a little hiccup as she tried to rein it in.

'My goodness, she is an original, isn't she? Did you agree?'

He frowned.

'Of course not!'

'Oh, why not? You could send it to Mama; you know she has always wanted you to sit for a portrait. And by the looks of it she would do a very creditable job.'

For a moment Max contemplated the possibility. It was true their mother had begged him repeatedly to sit at least for a watercolour she could hang in her drawing room in the Dower House alongside the portraits she had commissioned of his five sisters. A quick sketch would be much less painful. Or should be. But the thought of sitting while the girl's expressive blue eyes surveyed and catalogued him wasn't something he was comfortable with. There was something too…intimate in it. If he had to be painted by someone, he preferred it to be someone who knew how to respect boundaries.

There had been no reason to even stop to speak with her and he still didn't understand why he had. He certainly hadn't intended to when he had seen her while crossing the gardens, but her total concentration on her sketch had made him curious. And once he stopped behind her it had been hard to move, as if doing so would disturb some unfamiliar wild animal he had come across in the parks on the Harcourt estates. Or one of the wood sprites his sisters had insisted appeared at dusk in the deepest reaches of the woods. He had watched her hand moving lightly but firmly over the page, her head slightly canted, the sun casting a warm line down the side of her neck and along a strand of light brown hair that had escaped her bonnet and curved round her neck and downwards. It was only when she had spoken to that dog of hers that he had shifted back into reality. But not enough to continue on his way.

It was his own foolishness that he had spoken with her, but it had been just curiosity. At least until he had touched her hand. It was ridiculous that such an accidental and inconsequential contact had sparked the same kind of sensation like those galvanic contraptions he had seen at the Royal Academy. He was too old and experienced for such a raw physical reaction. It was probably the surprise and that peculiar sensation of having a place as familiar to him as the gardens transformed into something where he was the interloper and not she. Yes. That must be it.

'Are you coming to the Carmichael soirée to-night?' Hetty asked as the silence stretched.

Max knew what she was asking and sighed.

'I can't do it, Hetty. Lady Penny is everything you said she would be, but she is just too…compliant. I would wish her at the devil before the ceremony was over. Who's next on the list? There has to be someone who can have a conversation without deferring to everything I say.'

Hetty sighed as well.

'You are probably right. Lady Penny's first impression is unfortunately her best. Perhaps Clara Bannerman, she is very sweet and…'

'No.'

'Why not?'

'Her laugh.'

'Oh, dear. You're right, that *would* be hard to bear day in and day out. Then what of Lady Melissa Arkwright?'

Max considered Lady Melissa, his gaze straying to the sketch Hetty held in her lap. She might do. She was certainly beautiful and poised and already showed signs of becoming a very skilful hostess. She could preside quite easily over his properties. It was worth examining.

'She is suitable on the face of it. Why didn't

you suggest her before Lady Penny? She seems more the part.'

'I know, but Penny is...nicer. I thought she might be a better mother. I don't know. It's not easy choosing a sister-in-law for my only and very dear brother, you know!' she said severely and Max laughed, relaxing.

'And I appreciate your help very much, Hetty. I know it's not easy taking time from your family because I have been putting off dealing with my promise to Father all these years. There always seemed to be plenty of time to get round to it. I should have done something about it sooner.'

'Nonsense, I'm having a grand time. This is my first time on my own in six years. Ned and the children will eventually benefit from a much refreshed wife and mother. Which gives me an idea—I shall have this framed and send it to Ned to keep him company until my role here is played out. It really makes me look lovelier than I am, doesn't it? I wonder if she paints...'

Max shrugged. He had had enough of the eccentric blue-eyed sprite for one day.

'I have no idea. Will Lady Melissa be at the soirée tonight as well? Perhaps we should go after all.'

Chapter Four

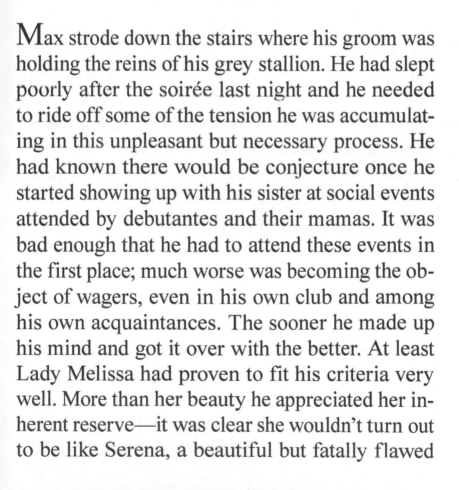

Max strode down the stairs where his groom was holding the reins of his grey stallion. He had slept poorly after the soirée last night and he needed to ride off some of the tension he was accumulating in this unpleasant but necessary process. He had known there would be conjecture once he started showing up with his sister at social events attended by debutantes and their mamas. It was bad enough that he had to attend these events in the first place; much worse was becoming the object of wagers, even in his own club and among his own acquaintances. The sooner he made up his mind and got it over with the better. At least Lady Melissa had proven to fit his criteria very well. More than her beauty he appreciated her inherent reserve—it was clear she wouldn't turn out to be like Serena, a beautiful but fatally flawed vessel, just waiting for the right amount of pressure to crack it. And he certainly wouldn't have to worry whether his children were really his. Lady Melissa was as cool and controlled as Serena had been fiery and volatile. He would let it sit a day or to and then take the plunge. There was no point in prolonging the agony.

He had just taken the reins and dismissed his groom when he saw the Huntley girl walking her ungainly pug. He hesitated, wishing he had held off for a couple minutes so he could have avoided her. Still, there was nothing for it but to be civil. He held his stallion easily as it fretted at the in-action and nodded to her.

'Good morning. I see he has come to accept his fate with equanimity.'

She stopped, smiling up at him, but perhaps she sensed his diffidence because her smile lacked the openness of yesterday and her voice was a shade more like a society miss.

'Good morning. He actually walked down the stairs himself after his morning visit with Aunt Minnie. He is becoming quite alert, aren't you, Marmaduke?'

Max eyed the near-dormant pug dubiously. Alert was not an adjective that sprang to mind.

'Impressive. What did Lady Huntley have to say about the introduction of a dreaded leash into her home?'

'I hadn't meant to tell her, but the doctor tattled on me and it has had a most alarming effect on her.'

'Is she angry?'

She laughed and he had to actively resist the urge to smile in reflexive response.

'Not at all. After the doctor gave such a glowing report of Marmaduke's performance, and I gave her Marmaduke's sketch, she actually pinched my cheek. And apparently her spies among the servants told her the leash had been delivered anonymously and she demanded to know where it had come from, but I said I don't know you and your sister's name, merely that you probably lived near here and she said I was being very sly and good for me. That is by far the longest conversation I have had with her thus far.'

Max gave in and laughed. This strange girl seemed to see the positive or at least the amusing in everything. It really wasn't quite proper or wise to be talking to her like this in the middle of the street, but as Hetty had pointed out someone as lively as she must be terribly bored with only

Minerva and the pugs for company. A few moments of conversation would make no difference.

'For how long are you captive in the Huntley hold?'

'That is wholly up to Aunt Minnie. My other siblings lasted between a two days at the shortest to six days at the longest. That was Augusta, but she said Aunt Minnie almost never spoke to her, it was just that she liked the way she played the pianoforte. Then there was Cousin Arthur— he held on for a whole two weeks and was completely hateful and unctuous about it and I would dearly love to break his record.

'I see. And what skill does the length of your servitude depend on aside from reforming her pugs?'

She twinkled up at him.

'I am not quite certain. She has me read to her a great deal, the most amusing books and certainly nothing we are allowed at home. And now that she has discovered I am a fair artist she has decided she wants me to paint a full portrait...' her voice wavered slightly '...of Marmaduke.'

'Good God.' Max glanced down at the object of the conversation and Marmaduke scratched himself absently. 'In a heroic pose?'

Her laugh was joyful and infectious, but it caught on the end, as if she was used to reining it in.

'Exactly. On a pedestal, with a landscape behind, or perhaps a castle. And both the Huntley and Trevelyan family arms. I told her I would be happy to, just so I can get her to buy me the painting supplies. I am to go to Reeves in Cheapside and buy what I need, which shall be very exciting, and also to the Royal Academy so I can get some ideas for the proper composition of a portrait. My dear Marmaduke is proving very useful, aren't you, love?'

Marmaduke's curly pink tongue lolled out and he directed her a look which was surprisingly adoring. Max smiled at the absurdity of it all—of the girl, the dog, the conversation and especially of his part in it.

'So it looks like it is going to be a protracted stay. Have you ever been to the Royal Academy before?'

'No, I have been pining to go see the Summer Exhibition, but one of the conditions of our stay has been that we not enjoy ourselves or at least not stray from Grosvenor Square. But now that I have a legitimate excuse to roam, I intend to take full advantage of it. The Royal Academy is this way, isn't it?'

'It is, but…do you intend to walk there? With the dog?'

'Is it too far?' she asked, concerned.

'It is. He would expire before you made it halfway. And besides, you can't take a pug into Somerset House!' he said sternly. 'And you also can't go there on your own. You should at least take a maid with you.'

'Aunt Minnie would never allow me to commandeer her maid and I can't very well have James the footman trailing me around an art exhibition. I refuse to let this opportunity slip by simply because I don't have a chaperon. I would never forgive myself. Besides, what on earth could happen to me there?'

'That is not the point. Young women…well-born young women…do not wander around town unaccompanied.'

'Oh, please don't make me feel any guiltier than I already do. It is not as if I am known in London, so there is no reason anyone would ever know or even notice me. I simply *can't* not go.'

Max told himself to take a firm step back. This was none of his business. And she had a point—

no one knew her in London. But the thought of her wandering alone and unprotected through an unfamiliar city...

'Take that misbegotten canine for his walk and then meet me in the garden in an hour. I will take you there,' he said abruptly.

Her eyes widened in surprise, subjecting him to the full pressure of her sea-blue gaze. She was almost too expressive. He could see surprise and wariness and wistfulness in their multi-hued depths and he hoped no one would find out he was actually choosing to play chaperon for this peculiar girl.

'That is kind of you, but it is really not necessary for you to put yourself out on my account,' she said properly and some of his tension faded, giving way to amusement at what was clearly an uncharacteristic show of propriety on her part.

'You sound like you are impersonating someone,' he replied and her warm tumbling laugh, like the sound of water in a brook, evoked the same surge of proprietary heat as when he had accidentally touched her hand the previous day in the garden. It was short but sharp, unmistakable. Not that there was anything particular about her that merited this unwanted tug of desire. She was mildly pretty but unexceptional aside from her eyes which reminded him of the colours of the sea at summer off the coast near Harcourt. It was something that went beyond her looks, a vividness that was magnetic—an unconscious invitation to enjoy life.

'Oh, dear, I *was*. My Aunt Seraphina, Arthur's mother. She's dreadful. I wasn't at all believable, was I? But I do mean you needn't go with me. I shall be perfectly fine on my own, really.'

'Probably. We shall compromise then. I shall just make sure you get in safely and then leave you to explore while I continue on to the City. I have a meeting there later. And then you can take a hackney directly back home afterwards.'

He swung on to his horse before she could argue.

'I will see you in an hour,' he repeated and rode off, wondering if she would be there or whether even she would back down before such unconventional behaviour.

Somehow, when he entered the garden an hour later he was not very surprised to see her standing just inside the gates. For once she was not wearing a simple countrified white-muslin dress and spencer, but a walking dress of a pale smoky blue under a darker blue pelisse. And though the style was perhaps a few years out of fashion, it was well tailored and for the first time he could see she had a very appealing and well-proportioned figure. She also looked more her age and dignified, but contrarily that just made it clearer he should not be doing this, no matter how chivalrous his motives. Then he met her eyes which were sparkling with suppressed excitement and he relented. It was such an inconsequential thing for him and such a great deal for her, there surely was nothing very wrong in merely seeing her safely into the Academy.

'Come,' he said, holding out his arm and she moved towards him with her peculiar brand of pent-up energy, following him out to the street where he hailed a passing hackney cab.

She gave a breathy laugh as she settled on to the seat.

'I feel like I am escaping from the Bastille! This is quite ridiculous. I have been here less than two weeks and already I am losing perspective on reality.'

Max smiled. He should have known she would treat this with her usual irrepressible enthusiasm.

He settled back and waited for her next outrageous comment. It was not long in coming.

'Thank you for offering to take me there. It makes it seem so much more...commonplace.'

'That sounds disappointing. Should I apologise for taking the adventure out of it?'

'Oh, I didn't mean it like that... Just that I am trying to convince myself that it needn't be such a to do. That it is quite normal for me to go to see some of the most amazing painters alive in England today. Part of me doesn't want to go.'

'Why not?'

'Well, I am bound to discover that an unbridgeable chasm lies between my puny talent and real artistic skill. I am quite prepared to suffer some mortification before I can free myself from vanity and enjoy real genius.'

'That is very...broad-minded of you,' Max replied after a moment's struggle not to laugh, reminding himself this was a serious issue for her, after all.

'Are you laughing at me?' she asked, her gaze both questioning and accusing.

'Is that terrible?'

Her eyes slanted again in the amusement that never seemed far from the surface.

'I did sound terribly pompous, didn't I? But I mean it. Back in Ashton Cove I was always by far the best artist, not that anyone really cares about that over there unless they need me for the church decorations. But I know today I will see real talent. There are so very, very few and some of them will have their paintings on those walls. And I will know, for certain, that I am not and never will be of that calibre. I know that I am going to feel something in me die today and even though it will hurt, I wouldn't avoid it even if I could, because the other side of that coin is the experience of witnessing genius. It's still pompous, but I can't help it—that is what I feel. Oh, look, is this Piccadilly?'

Max assented, absorbing what she said. He was acquainted with several artists because of his uncle and this was a very mature and quite unusual approach among those gifted, or cursed, with artistic talent. She didn't speak again, aside from occasional questions about the buildings they passed as they made their way towards the Strand. Finally they drew towards St Mary le Strand and pulled up in front of the neoclassical façade of Somerset House where the Royal Academy was housed.

'Oh, here we are! That was so very quick! Oh, come!'

She almost jumped from the hackney, waiting with clear impatience as Max paid the driver, her hand straining on his arm as he led her through one of the three tall arches into the Somerset House complex and towards the winding staircase leading to the Exhibition Room at the top of the building. Her eyes moved hungrily over the decorations that marked their passage, the sculptures by Wilton and Bacon, and the ornamented landings with occasional benches for the visitors to rest as they climbed the long staircase.

'It's a good thing you didn't bring Marmaduke,' he remarked halfway up and she looked up at him, laughter chasing away some of her intentness, but she didn't reply. She didn't flag on the stairs, as did many women who had stopped to rest and fan themselves and gossip, for which Max was grateful since it meant that beyond nodding at his acquaintances, he did not have to speak to anyone, though he was aware of the curious stares directed at them.

'Aren't you tired?' he asked her, curious about the seemingly boundless energy she radiated.

The question cut through her concentration.

'Tired?' she asked in obvious confusion and he indicated the steep stairwell.

'You're going up these at breakneck speed.'

She flushed guiltily.

'Sorry, but I am so excited. And I am very used to climbing up and down the cliffs near Ashton Cove. My favourite place to draw is a little bay just to the west of where we live and there is quite a steep ascent. These stairs don't really compare. I will slow down if it is too fast for you, though.'

'Don't be cocky,' he said easily and she laughed. They had just made it to the final landing and he turned her to him.

'Before we enter the Exhibition Room and I lose your attention utterly, you should probably tell me your name in the event we have no choice but to speak to someone. It would be a bit embarrassing to introduce you simply as the girl with the pug.'

She was straining forward like a racing horse against the gate, but that checked her and her eyes widened.

'You are quite right. How foolish, but I hadn't realised…still, we haven't been introduced formally so it is not at all surprising. I am Sophie Trevelyan. And you?'

He hesitated. He had initiated this, after all.

'Max…'

'Harcourt!'

Max squared his shoulders and turned towards the exquisitely dressed dandy who was approaching them from the Exhibition Room. His shirt points were so high his amiable face seemed to bloom from the middle of a tight white flower. He stopped and bowed to Sophie, raising one brow expectantly. Max resigned himself.

'Miss Trevelyan, this is Lord Bryanston. Bry, this is Miss Sophie Trevelyan.'

'Trevelyan! That's a West Country name, isn't it? Do you live near Max?'

Before Max could respond, she extended her hand properly and answered with a warm smile.

'Yes, we are neighbours. How do you do, Lord Bryanston?'

He assessed her with a practised eye and bowed gallantly over her hand.

'Much better now, Miss Trevelyan,' he replied, his eyes wide and appreciative. Her captivating laughter rolled out and two men who had been inspecting the Carlini sculpture at the top landing turned, one of them raising a curious quizzing glass towards them.

'I hadn't realised the exhibition began out

here,' she remarked with such a mixture of inno-cence and mirth that Max wasn't surprised to see Bryanston's gaze sharpen, like a dog catching the scent of prey.

'Neither had I,' Bryanston responded. 'And to think I almost managed to find an excuse not to accompany my aunt here today. My luck is defi-nitely in. I should go lay a wager while it lasts. Max, be a good fellow and bring Miss Trevelyan over to join our party.'

'Not this time, Bry.' Max replied firmly.

'Here, what kind of friend are you?' Bryanston protested and turned to Sophie. 'I don't know why I put up with him. He's as stiff-necked as those statues over there and about as warm.'

'At least I'm not as gaudy as a potted plant. Where the devil did you get that atrocity of a waistcoat, Bry? It reminds me of one of my grand-mother's dressing gowns.'

'Have you no discrimination, you heathen? I personally designed this with Stultz! That's what your parents get for naming you after some ma-rauding Welsh warrior.'

'He was a Roman, he just married a Welsh-woman.'

'That's worse. They wore sheets.'

'I think your choice of colours is very creative, Lord Bryanston,' Sophie interceded. 'Not many people would have thought of putting saffron together with puce like that.'

'Thank God for small mercies,' Max muttered. 'I think your aunt is trying to catch your attention, Bryanston, so run along now.'

Bryanston half-turned in alarm, restricted by his high shirt points.

'Have some pity, man. Between my aunt and Lady Pennistone I am being reduced to emotional rubble. You clearly have a kind heart, Miss Trevelyan, convince the cold brute to join us.'

He grinned appealingly at Sophie, but before she could respond Max took her elbow, urging her towards the entrance of the Exhibition Room.

'Go charm your aunt before she writes you out of her will, Bry.'

'Good day, Lord Bryanston,' Sophie said properly as they moved forward, but the laughing smile she directed at Bryanston was so vivid Max wasn't surprised that his friend remained standing on the steps with his hand held dramatically to his breast in what might have been a very successful Byronic pose if not for his irrepressible grin. Max considered enlightening Sophie as to the lack of wisdom in encouraging the likes of Bryanston when he realised it was too late, he had clearly lost her attention.

They had entered the great Exhibition Room and she stared in awe around the enormous space, her head back and lips slightly parted. He had been here so often, he had forgotten how powerful the impact of entering the enormous hall could be during the Summer Exhibition. For someone like her it must be overwhelming. Hundreds of gilt-framed paintings jostled each other on the walls of the enormous space, lit by the wide, arced skylights that dominated the ceiling. Dozens of fashionable men and women were moving idly around or seated on the low olive-green sofas in the centre of the room. The cavernous buzz of voices swallowed her gasp of surprise. She took a step forward and then, as if suddenly conscious of his presence, she turned back to him.

'Oh, thank you for bringing me here. You needn't stay, I know you would prefer not to. I shall be just fine now. Good day, Mr Harcourt.'

Max hesitated, wondering if he should correct her, but since he had suffered under one title or another from the day he remembered himself there was an appeal in being just plain Mr Harcourt. This woman knew nothing about him but that he lived near her and had a sister, and unlike most of the young women he met she didn't seem to have an agenda for him other than wanting to sketch him. Being Mr Harcourt made everything simpler, lighter. In a few days she would probably be back on her way home and he would never see her again. What was the harm in taking just a few more minutes to enjoy one of his favourite places in London in the company of someone who actually appreciated the artwork itself rather than the spectacle of people on the strut? Ten minutes and he would be on his way. There was no harm in that.

'Come. I will show you my favourite,' he said.

She directed a questioning look at him and then gave a little nod and he took her hand and placed it on his arm again and led her towards the other side of the enormous room. As they walked her gaze swept over the paintings, drinking them in, her lips parted as if on the verge of a smile, but he could feel the tension of her hand on his arm. He drew her to a halt just where the room led off into another corridor where a silk cord marked a barrier.

The light from the skylight was not as pronounced here, but Turner's painting still stood out from among the more ponderous landscapes and portraits. It was labelled *Venice, looking east from the Giudecca, Sunrise* and its deceptive simplicity and limited palette also made it stand out. It was mostly washed sky and sea in pale pink and golden yellow and a long line of Venice's skyline traced in purplish blue in the distance. She drew away from him, moving towards the painting, taking it in and then moving back again, forcing a portly couple to make way for her without even noticing them. Max moved so he could watch her face, the smile that bloomed slowly, suffusing her face with joy. Finally she turned to him, her eyes filled with pleasure and even some sadness.

'I had no idea anyone could do that. He is utterly unfettered. It is quite unfair to have him crowded here like this. There is nothing here like it. I see why you love it,' she said, her gaze locked back on the painting.

She stood there for a long moment and then with a sigh she turned away to examine the other paintings. She hardly seemed to notice that he placed her hand on his arm again, her attention fully on the paintings. Surprisingly he didn't mind being taken for granted. Her face was so expressive of enjoyment and awe, it was enough to just watch her revelation and to answer the questions she occasionally directed at him about the artists and the paintings which became more frequent as they advanced.

When they had completed the circuit of the room he led her down a corridor to the Academy's Council Chambers.

'Come, I want to show you something.'

Guests could not usually enter this part of the Academy, but she would appreciate seeing Angelica Kauffman's allegorical murals, as much for their quality as for the artist's gender. But they had barely entered the chamber when a portly man who had been standing talking with a small group of men and women turned and noticed them and promptly gave a shout of greeting and headed in their direction.

'Oh, hell,' Max said ruefully under his voice. 'It's a good friend of my uncle's and a relentless gossip. Once he starts asking questions, we will never escape. Wait here, I'll get rid of him.'

He moved forward to intercept the man, grasping his elbow and deflecting him from his trajectory. As they moved towards the other end of the room, the man's voice rang out merrily.

'Max, old boy! What have you been up to? How is Charles? Still having a high time out with the ladies in Venice? The old dog!'

Max answered the barrage of questions about his uncle's activities in Italy as best he could and drew the conversation to a close with a promise to remember him to his uncle. Then he turned around to an empty room.

'You looking for that pretty little thing you came in with? Saw her head to the inner rooms.'

'What?' Max exclaimed and without even bothering to say goodbye he headed towards the doorway at the other side of the room. Damn the girl. It was just like her to go to the one place in the whole Academy she was absolutely forbidden to enter.

He found her easily enough the moment he entered the inner room. She was staring in wonder at the tightly packed nude paintings and studies that covered most of the wall space.

'For heaven's sake, you can't come in here!' Max said sternly, grasping her arm and drawing her towards the door at the other end of the corridor.

'Why not?'

'Why not? I would have thought that was obvious! This part of the Academy is not for well-bred young women.'

She turned to him with the amused twinkle in her eyes he was becoming very familiar with and which did nothing to lower his guard.

'I know that's what people say, but that is rather ridiculous, isn't it? There's hardly anything here a woman hasn't already seen. If anything, I would have thought this wasn't a room for well-bred young men.'

Max had to make a considerable effort not to laugh at this rather original view of the matter. She really was absurdly peculiar.

'Besides, I just saw two very nicely dressed young women pass through here,' she pointed out.

'They may have been nicely dressed, but I doubt they were well bred.'

'Oh! Do you mean they were…lightskirts?'

'I mean that unless you want to find yourself classified alongside them, we should return to the main exhibition,' Max said, exasperated as much at himself as at her.

She glanced back with a rather wistful look at the painting of the reclining woman.

'It is such a pity. There are some amazing paintings in here, though I don't know what I think about this one. There is something not quite right about her, something in the eyes. Though other than that it is one of the best paintings I have seen today, aside from Mr Turner's…'

'Why, thank you, miss. Though I do not know what I feel about being classified alongside Turner's increasingly eccentric oeuvres.'

A man dressed almost entirely in deep grey and black moved towards them. He was extremely handsome, his hair was a deep shade of chestnut and his brown eyes gleamed amber around the iris, but his expression, which was calculating and faintly malicious, did not match his features. He bowed slightly towards Max and the malice became more apparent.

'Harcourt.'

Max cursed their ill luck. Of all the men in London to run into…

'Wivenhoe,' he acknowledged and took Sophie's arm, guiding her towards the door.

'Going so soon, Harcourt? Aren't you going to introduce me to your…friend?'

To Max's surprise Sophie burst out laughing.

'Oh, dear, you are right!' she said to Max, chuckling. 'He thinks I'm your…what is it called? *Chère amie?* Do you really think I look the part?'

she asked Wivenhoe curiously. 'I wouldn't have thought so with my looks and clothes, judging by the two lovely ladies I just saw. Did you really paint this amazing painting? Frankly, you don't look the part either.'

That speech seemed to shake even Wivenhoe's world-weary pose and he inspected her with a look unusually devoid of cynicism.

'I find myself quite afraid to enquire into the meaning of that comment,' he said at least.

'Yes, I think that beast is best left dormant,' Max said caustically. 'Now if you don't mind, I will take Miss Trevelyan back to the main room. She is unacquainted with Somerset House and has strayed into this area by mistake.'

Sophie allowed Max to propel her out of the room and back down the corridor to the main hall, her gaze scanning the paintings as she went. Once in the corridor she sighed.

'It really is quite unfair of men to keep such lovely paintings to themselves. I am beginning to suspect that London is a great deal more strait-laced than the countryside. After all the dire warnings I received from the squire's wife I thought it would be a great deal more exciting than it is.'

Wivenhoe gave a soft breathy laugh as he followed behind them.

'It depends on the company you find yourself in, my dear. Harcourt is not the right escort if it is excitement you are after. Or at least not if you are gently born. I cannot speak for his other relationships since he chooses women as discreet as he.'

Sophie glanced from Wivenhoe to Max with a slight frown and Max wished he had Wivenhoe across from him in Jackson's Boxing Saloon right now. Or preferably as they had been almost a decade ago, in a dark alley, just the two of them. He would not mind repeating that experience and hopefully doing a bit more damage this time around.

'Wivenhoe is enjoying himself at your expense, Miss Trevelyan. You would do best to ignore him.'

'Quite right, my dear,' Wivenhoe replied, unabashed. 'I am not a very dependable fellow. You see, I freely admit my vices. Max here is more circumspect about his, though to be fair they are probably milder than mine, but one can never know what such a controlled façade harbours. Certainly he is more generous, as his last high flyer would attest judging by the very lovely bauble I saw her wearing when he was done with her.'

Sophie glanced back at Wivenhoe with a sudden frown.

'You actually sound contemptuous of people who are generous towards the women who depend on their patronage. I can't imagine that kind of approach gets you very far, Mr Wivenhoe,' she said with blighting coldness.

Max struggled between shock at this very improper but principled condemnation of Wivenhoe's ethics and amusement at the stunned expression on Wivenhoe's face. But Wivenhoe swiftly recovered his characteristic expression of jaded ennui.

'I compensate, my dear, I assure you.'

'If you say so.' She shrugged, clearly unconvinced. The corridor had led back to the Exhibition Room, which was still as crowded as before, and she turned to Max. 'And now I really should return to Grosvenor Square or Aunt Minerva will start baying for my blood. Thank you very much for showing me these lovely paintings, Mr Harcourt.'

'I will see you home—' Max began, but she cut him off.

'Nonsense. You said you had business in the City and that is quite the other direction. I shall do very well with a hackney cab, I noticed there are plenty outside. Thank you. Good day, Mr Wivenhoe.' She nodded briefly in the artist's direction and headed towards the staircase.

'*Mr* Harcourt?' Wivenhoe enquired softly. 'Does that original young lady have something against titles or is she in ignorance of the identity of her very obliging cavalier?'

'She is merely an acquaintance of my sister's. I saw her wandering into this room and thought it prudent to extract her before she came across someone like you. She's not in your league, Wivenhoe.'

'Oh, clearly beyond it. And not in your usual line either, my dear Harcourt. Far too outspoken. And so very refreshing. Trevelyan. That name rings a bell. Who did she say…? Ah, Aunt Minerva in Grosvenor Square… Could she possibly be related to Lady Minerva Huntley, *née* Trevelyan?'

Max didn't bother answering, but merely turned and left as well. Wivenhoe's veneer of cynical affability did not deceive him. Almost a decade had passed since the incident, but neither of them had forgotten or forgiven. He rubbed the scar on his hand unconsciously. Wivenhoe's appearance was a sharp reminder that his idea of escorting that pert and uncontrollable country miss to the exhibition had been very ill conceived. He should have known it would only lead to trouble. Now that she was gone he couldn't even understand why he had gone in with her. He had been drawn along in the wake of her enthusiasm like that pug of hers. Whatever the case, he would do well to stay out of her way in future. There was some quality to her that attracted trouble like bees to a flower. He had had enough of that in his life. He should know better.

'I met Lord Bryanston at Lady Jersey's last night. He asked me who your latest flirt was. A young woman from Devon with a pair of delightfully smiling blue eyes, in his words,' Hetty said blandly as she sifted through the pile of invitations Gaskell had brought in on a tray as they sat at the breakfast table.

'Bryanston is an idiot,' Max replied, not looking up from his newspaper.

'True. But then there was Mrs Westminger. She asked me the identity of the animated young woman you were so attentive to in the Exhibition Rooms for close to an hour. Since she is Lady Penny's godmama I presume it was by design that she said this very loudly next to Lady Melissa now that the betting appears to have swung in her favour. She was somewhat more careful about communicating the information you had been seen with the same young woman conversing with Lord Wivenhoe, of all people. That little titbit she passed along in a stage whisper to only three of her cronies in the dowagers' corner.'

Max folded the newspaper and laid it down.

'Is there a question in there?'

Hetty nodded, undaunted by his cool tone.

'There is indeed. I presume they were referring to Lady Huntley's niece? Is any of this true? Did you really take her to Somerset House? And introduce that young woman to the likes of Wivenhoe?'

Max held on to his temper by a thread, mostly angry at himself. At least Hetty did not know the full extent of Wivenhoe's infamy. Thankfully his parents had never told his sisters the truth about Serena.

'Yes, I took her. Because she was about to head there, on foot, on her own, in the company of that dratted pug. But do you really think I would introduce her to someone like Wivenhoe? That was her own doing. I turned my back for one minute and she wandered off into the private rooms where she proceeded to make mincemeat of Wivenhoe. Besides, this whole thing is your fault!'

'*Mine?*'

'Yes, you were the one who said she must be bored on her own in the mausoleum. I felt sorry for her. That's why I offered to see her there safely. My mistake, but acquit me of either taking advantage of her or exposing her to someone like Wivenhoe!'

Hetty sighed.

'No, I know you wouldn't. But really, Max, it wasn't very wise to take her there at all. Naturally people are curious when you are seen squiring an unchaperoned, unknown and personable young woman.'

'I would think my credit is sufficient to make clear I have never shown an interest in toying with virtuous young women,' he bit out.

'Well, precisely, it is out of character, which is why it drew so much attention. Now that it is clear to everyone that you finally intend to marry you know the gossips are having a fine time speculating who will be the next Duchess of Harcourt. I can hardly step outside the house without someone coyly asking me who you are favouring. Fine, I won't say another word. Just do be careful.'

'That was four more words. And don't worry; I've satisfied my chivalrous instinct for the next decade. I will stay well away from that trouble-some pixie.' He picked up the newspaper again, as much to block out his sister's anxious frown as to prevent himself from venting his resentment on her. It was just typical that the moment he did anything that was one step out of character everyone was up in arms. All his life he had walk a fine line between his independence and his parents' confining criticism, couched always in un-arguable terms of duty, but to have to put up with it from Hetty as well when all he had done was take pity on that aggravatingly buoyant girl was putting a serious strain on his civility. Suddenly he wished Hetty and everyone at the devil.

Chapter Five

'Lady Henrietta Swinburne, Miss Trevelyan.'

Lambeth's voice was a blend of surprise, approval and curiosity. Lady Henrietta entered the parlour as he stood aside, approaching Sophie with a smile, her hand extended.

'I do hope you don't mind my showing up like this, Miss Trevelyan, but I had to come and thank you for that lovely sketch.'

Sophie stood up, still holding her paintbrush, and extended her hand automatically. Then they both glanced at her paint-covered fingers and to Sophie's relief Lady Henrietta burst out laughing.

'Never mind. May I stay for a moment? This is all very unusual; we haven't even been introduced properly. I am Lady Henrietta Swinburne as your butler pointed out, but please call me Hetty,' she announced, glancing around the room. 'Goodness, I don't think this place has been redecorated since Bonaparte was chased out of Egypt!'

Sophie relaxed at Hetty's easy informality.

'This is quite mild. There is a brocade sofa with gilded crocodile-claw legs in the Green Salon. Aunt Minnie never comes down here, but she insists that nothing is to be put under holland covers which means the colours have all sadly faded. Still, it is rather grand, isn't it?'

'Very grand. But then your aunt was very fashionable when we were children. What are you working on? May I see?'

Sophie turned with some embarrassment to the canvas she had been working on and nodded nervously as Hetty moved towards it.

'Oh, he's adorable!' she exclaimed. 'And you paint as well as you sketch!'

Watching the woman's animated face, Sophie succumbed to impulse.

'Do you know, Marmaduke's portrait means I am fully equipped with artistic supplies and it would be a pity to waste all of this on a mere pug. Would you mind if I tried to paint you?'

'Mind? I would be delighted! But I really don't want to impose…'

'Oh, I promise you it would be my pleasure.

With all due respect to Marmaduke, he isn't the most inspiring model. Please say yes. I really don't have much else to do while I am here...' She flushed. 'I didn't mean to sound self-pitying. I really would like to paint you, if you don't mind.'

'I would love it. When?'

'The light is perfect right now, if you sit in that seat by the window...'

Hetty smiled and moved toward the window.

'So be it. On condition you tell me how you like being in town.'

Sophie hurriedly picked up her sketch pad, wondering what on earth she could say. She could hardly reveal that her most memorable experience in London involved this woman's brother. Not that her fascination with him was surprising. He was so very different from any of the men she knew back home. In fact, she rather thought he was unlike most men in London, too. She would hardly be the first or the last to be so drawn to him. His virility and unconscious air of command were bad enough, but much worse was the guarded humour in his dark grey eyes, and the fact that unlike so many people he actually appeared to sometimes find her peculiarities vaguely interesting rather than merely regrettable. That was perhaps the greatest danger of all.

Somehow, no matter how stony the façade he presented, he radiated an underlying curiosity that she felt was an unconscious invitation to be herself, an invitation she so rarely encountered it was bound to be intoxicating. It was probably completely fictitious, but it was so tempting to believe in it. She looked down at the blank paper in her hands and resolutely began sketching.

'There's not much to tell. I haven't seen much, aside from gardens outside and the exhibition yesterday. Still, I am revelling in being on my own. There are nine of us at home and very little privacy and quite a lot of…meddling, you see. So, forced solitude has its advantages. Could you please raise your chin a little?'

Hetty complied.

'Nine! I can see why this might be considered a holiday. Still, it is a pity your aunt hasn't provided you with any entertainment at all.'

'Aunt Minnie is convinced there isn't any to be had any more. From her tales, London society used to be exciting, scandalous, and very licentious when she was in her prime. But it has become sadly dull and she derives much more enjoyment from her books than from reality.'

'That's a bit unfair. Society can still be all that, though mostly behind closed doors today. There is an unspoken agreement that if one is suitably discreet and respects the rules of the game, they can do pretty much as they please. But the moment one steps outside the bounds of the game there is no more brutal jungle. What happened to Lord Byron is just one dramatic example of what happens even to society's darlings if they transgress.' She hesitated, tracing the elaborate brocade pattern of the sofa with one long, elegant finger. 'My brother, Max, is probably a fine example of how to play the game to perfection. One of his friends once told me he had never seen anyone with quite that talent for driving their horses so well up to their bits so that it looks like they might be bolting, but they are never out of control. He is just the same in society—he makes his own way, but he never transcends the rules.'

Sophie paused, but did not look up. It was clear Lady Hetty's comment was anything but casual. Coming on the back of her own internal lectures Hetty's words stung and she spoke before she could censure herself.

'Are you by any chance warning me not to develop any expectations regarding your brother based on his charitable impulse yesterday? I assure you I am not so naïve.'

'No, it's not that!' Hetty flushed. 'You seem a very…sensible young woman. Surprisingly so, since you don't know London and just how it works. It is just that…oh, dear, this is difficult… it is just that young women often…because of his looks, and his war exploits and all that…they tend to think him…heroic and develop quite the wrong ideas about him. It's not that he encourages it. He is not in the least romantic or gallant, you know. In fact, he hasn't a romantic bone in his body,' she said with some exasperation. 'If he did he would hardly have asked me to find him a wife—' She broke off in confusion. 'My wretched tongue. I always say too much when I am nervous. Max will have my head.'

'Never mind. I shouldn't have spoken so bluntly myself,' Sophie said apologetically. She should not blame this woman for her own foolishness in being attracted to Max. Sophie chose a different pencil from her box, wondering what her father would make of her performance in London so far. She could imagine the lecture.

'Poor Papa,' she murmured.

'I beg your pardon?'

'Nothing. I was just thinking of my father. He is a vicar and has never known quite what to make of my ways or my love of painting. He shares your brother's view that ladies should be adequate sketchers, but that anything else is a presumption against nature. Not that I am in any way extraordinary, but painting is more than just another accomplishment to be acquired as far as I am concerned. It really gives me pleasure.'

'Max?' Hetty asked, surprised. 'You are quite wrong. Max might be very rule bound himself, but he has very few prejudices when it comes to other people and certainly not against female artists. I suppose that's my Uncle Charles's doing because our papa was quite narrow-minded and Mama is…well, she means well, but… Anyway, Charles was very close with Angelica Kauffman and Mary Moser who were both amazing artists and he used to take Max with him to the Academy all the time. He's off painting somewhere in Italy at the moment which is a pity because I think you would like him.'

Sophie absorbed this, embarrassed by her curiosity and the need to know more about Max. She really could not quite make out the contradictions in his character. Max! She should not be calling him that even in her mind, she told herself sternly and leaned back, inspecting her work.

'I think that will do for now. It's a pity to stop now, but it's time for me to go read to Aunt Minnie. Could you come again once or twice so I can decide on the colours and shading?'

Hetty nodded and came to inspect the drawing and Sophie tensed as she always did when someone saw her work for the first time, no matter how much she tried to be sophisticated and unconcerned.

'It's even lovelier than the first,' Hetty said quietly. 'I look…joyous, though I'm hardly smiling. It is such a pity Max doesn't want you to even sketch him. Mama is always trying to convince him to sit for a portrait, but he has something against them. Do you think you could do a drawing of him sight unseen like you did for me before or is that too hard?'

Sophie bent over her box of charcoals and pencils to hide her flush. She knew she had to say something that would satisfy Lady Hetty. Certainly not the truth.

'It's easier with some people than others. I don't

know if I could, from memory. It is not just the structure of the face, but there must be something I can…base myself on, an idea of the person.'

Lady Hetty nodded, shaking out her crumpled skirts.

'He is a bit hard to read. Mama always complains of it. But it's not because there's nothing there, like some people.'

'No. I don't think it is that. Perhaps there is just more than people expect or even want and he knows it.'

She wished she hadn't spoken, aware of Hetty's eyes on her, but she kept her own down as she wiped her fingers clean and then extended her hand with a smile.

'All clean now. Could you come tomorrow, then?'

'With pleasure! Thank you, Miss Trevelyan.'

The moment the door closed behind Hetty, Sophie's shoulders sagged. Under other circumstances she would have been ecstatic about meeting someone so genuine. But it was a strain, having to make believe that all these references to Max had no effect on her. And the strain just made it obvious that something had changed yesterday. She hadn't realised at the time, but she had felt so right walking with him around that immense room. Even knowing it was nothing more than the polite courtesy of a gentleman for the lady he was escorting, and even through the layers of her glove and his coat, she had been aware of the strength of his arm beneath her fingers and a radiating heat that had accompanied her as they inspected the paintings. It had heightened her senses and dimmed her judgement, like wine. After her initial protest she had not had the will to release him to his business, at least not until his anger at her about her mistake in entering the forbidden room. Then the folly of succumbing to the fantasy that there was actually something more keeping him at her side than civility became clear. She might be socially clumsy, but she wasn't naïve. She knew she was in danger of liking him too much and it did not take his sister's warning to point out she had no chance with someone like him. She had managed to repel men with far fewer endowments and expectations; there was no future for her with Max.

Chapter Six

Max climbed into his phaeton and took the reins from his groom who jumped up on his perch behind. He had promised to take Lady Melissa for a ride in the park, but at the moment he would have happily just headed west until he was clear of the town and all its inhabitants. His plans of identifying, courting and securing a wife, which had seemed so straightforward a month ago when he had commandeered Hetty for the campaign, were becoming mired in the mud of his flagging resolution.

He was just about to set his team of matched bays in motion when he saw Lord Wivenhoe coming leisurely down the stairs of Huntley House, his ebony cane swinging in his hand. Wivenhoe caught sight of Max and nodded, his eyes gleaming.

'Well met, Harcourt. Are these your famous bays? Beautiful beasts. I forgot you are neighbours with the wealthy Lady Huntley. And by extension with Miss Trevelyan.'

'What are you doing here, Wivenhoe?'

Wivenhoe raised one chestnut brow at Max's curt tones.

'How very dog-in-the-manger of you. Is it my visit to the fair Trevelyan that excites your formidable frown or is that just your habitual greeting to yours truly? I didn't think country misses were in your line, no matter how original. And she is, isn't she? Quite refreshing. Not a classic beauty, but such an expressive countenance! She does not even need to speak to be heard, if you understand me. I had a delightful chat with Lady Minnie, quite twenty minutes of the most salacious reminiscences—on the lady's part, I assure you—and merely for the pleasure of watching its effect on Miss Trevelyan's enchanting visage. I don't believe I have yet come across such expressive eyes. Better than any performance by Kean. I might even consider painting her if she is willing...'

Max reined in on his temper. He knew Wivenhoe was baiting him, but he was uncharacteristically finding it hard to ignore his taunts.

'You must be very desperate to have to resort to teasing country misses for entertainment. Perhaps if you were more generous with your mistresses, as Miss Trevelyan suggested, you wouldn't have to stoop so low,' he said contemptuously and Wivenhoe's pale cheeks flushed a mottled red.

He didn't wait for Wivenhoe's response, just gave his bays their head and the phaeton moved forward. As he pulled out of the square he reminded himself of his resolution to have nothing more to do with the irrepressible Miss Trevelyan and that meant to stay out of her business. It was not his role to warn her about the likes of Wivenhoe. And to be fair, she might be a country miss, but she was no fool. She could take care of herself.

'Your Grace?' his groom asked hesitantly behind him and Max checked his horses, realising he had been about to drive past the Arkwright residence.

'Keep them moving, Greggs,' Max said and strode up to the front door. Another day, another battle.

Less than two hours later Max left the phaeton at the stables and headed up South Audley Street towards home, feeling tired and disheartened, though he knew he had no reason to be. Lady Melissa had given a masterly performance, proving precisely how suited she was to be his Duchess. She clearly understood the rules of the game and had, in all but words, assured him she didn't expect him to profess any emotions he didn't possess and that she would be a tolerant wife if he was a discreet husband. As long as she was allowed to play her role in society to the hilt, she would evidently give him the space he needed. In fact, she was fulfilling every requirement on his list.

It was natural he would be having second thoughts about giving up his freedom, irrespective of his promise to his father, his commitment to his duties and no matter even how perfect the bride. As soon as he was married he would grow accustomed to the new order of things. He had spent five years in the worst possible conditions during the war and, despite these past five years of luxury and indulgence, he was still adaptable. It was just a matter of resolution.

He was just approaching the stairs to his home when he saw Sophie entering the garden with the lumpish pug in tow. He hesitated. Perhaps he should warn her about Wivenhoe after all. He waited for a ponderous coach to pass and headed towards the garden. She was seated once again beneath the chestnut tree, and, as usual, talking to the panting dog with all apparent expectation of being understood.

'I am sorry there are no more birds to chase, but what do you expect? You have frightened them all out of their little bird wits and I really cannot command their presence, you know. You will have to learn to lower expectations, Duke.'

'That would be a pity. Perhaps you should bring some crusts,' Max observed.

'Crusts?' She glanced up swiftly, but there was none of the usual mix of curiosity and expectant amusement in her expression. She seemed to be looking at him from a distance, considering him. He was already on edge, but he went instinctively on alert, though he answered her casually.

'That way you can lure back the birds for another round of exercise.'

'How very Machiavellian. I think I would feel too guilty baiting them only to have Marmaduke chase them away. Your Grace,' she added somewhat ironically and he remembered Wivenhoe had enlightened her about his title. He felt guilty, as if he had hidden it on purpose.

'I understand Lord Wivenhoe paid you a visit,' he said abruptly.

'Yes,' she replied in the same uncharacteristically cool voice. 'Aunt Minnie was shocked when he sent up his card. No one has dared breach the portals of Huntley House other than us pawns, but apparently she has some very…fond memories of his father. Frankly I could have done without having to hear the details of some of them, but she seemed to enjoy herself, which is in my favour, I suppose. They had a wonderful gossip and she invited him to visit again which is nothing short of miraculous.'

'I don't think you should encourage him to do so.'

Her expression did not change, but the same cautionary hauteur he had seen her display towards Wivenhoe at Somerset House entered her eyes.

'I told you there is no need to lecture me, Your Grace. I am well aware he is quite scandalous. He also seems to dislike *you* thoroughly, even beyond the normal degree of antagonism you might naturally excite. He was very amused by the fact that I had reduced you from a duke to a mere commoner and warned Aunt Minerva against the wisdom of allowing me to develop expectations in the direction of the Duke of Harcourt. To make his point he and Aunt Minnie then enjoyed several minutes' gossip, debating which of the various high-born young women you targeted is likely to win the Duchy. From there they went on to discuss someone called Hellgate whose exploits I would have expected to land him gaol had he not mercifully died young. And aside from securing Aunt Minnie's invitation to come visit again soon, that was that. Your Grace.'

'For heaven's sake, stop calling me that!' Max said, annoyed and tense on so many levels he couldn't untangle them. Contrarily his obvious discomfort brought some of her irrepressible humour to her eyes, softening them.

'What should I call you then? Duke? Would you mind sharing the moniker with Marmaduke?'

'As long as you don't call me to heel again,' he replied and she laughed, her shoulders relaxing, and some of the tension seeped out of his body. He felt ridiculous at how tense her unusual show of temper had made him.

'I had forgotten that. Was that why you stopped that day when Marmaduke escaped? How embarrassing. You must have thought me quite mad.'

'You did make a very…distinct first impression.'

'That is a polite way of saying you did, isn't it? I suppose I was going a little bit mad in that house. But never mind. This is a red letter day, do you know? Today I match Arthur's record of two weeks at Aunt Minerva.'

'And how are you celebrating this feat?'

'I wouldn't dare, not yet at least. The day is not over and Aunt Minnie might yet decide to send me packing, literally and figuratively. If I am still here by tomorrow, I shall try to think of something suitable. My options are rather limited though.'

Max sat down on the bench beside her before he even realised what he was doing. Marmaduke ambled over and plopped down at his feet, resting his flabby neck on the tip of Max's boot.

'Marmaduke! That is heresy!' Sophie admonished the pug. 'Don't know you a gentleman's boots are sacred?'

Max smiled and shook his head. He pulled off his gloves and bent to scratch the pug's head and Marmaduke's eyes closed, his mouth opening in a blissful smile.

'They will survive. My valet might give notice, though.'

She laughed.

'He really seems to adore you. It is very strange.'

'Now, how should I take that?' he asked with a smile.

'It was an observation about Marmaduke, not you,' she replied primly. 'I am merely trying to understand him.'

'What's to understand? He's an indolent, contrary pug with occasional shows of good taste. Aren't you, boy? See? He agrees with me.'

'So now *you* understand him?'

'I can be quite bright when it suits me. Like Marmaduke.'

It was foolish, but her tumbling laughter felt like a reward. She didn't answer, though, just watched him pet Marmaduke. The silence was so comfortable he began to feel uncomfortable.

'How did you get that scar on your left hand?'

It was a sign of just how lulled he had become that he almost began answering her question before he realised its peculiarity. She seemed to have surprised herself, too, and she winced, her cheeks turning bright pink.

'Sorry. I didn't mean… Oh, dear.'

She looked so embarrassed he took pity on her and tried to ignore the way every word and gesture of hers just added to his tension. She couldn't know the scar's significance.

'Ancient history. I know it's ugly.'

He started pulling on his gloves again, but she reached out and stopped him.

'Oh, no, it isn't at all, quite the opposite.'

It was an absurd thing to say and he wasn't surprised at the burn of colour that swept up her neck and over her cheeks. He had rarely seen a woman blush quite like her, as wholeheartedly and passionately as she seemed to do everything. He should have felt impatience or been merely touched at this sign of gaucheness, but that wasn't the response it evoked in him. He had no idea what sparked this visceral reaction, but without warning or transition his body woke, demanding he reach out and feel that heat, transform it into the passion he knew was there. There was banked energy in her, waiting, and he wanted it. It would be like watching the sea being transformed from the calm sunniness of summer to the full rage of a storm. The urge to act, to take, was so powerful it bordered on pain and he stood up and took a step away from the bench.

Marmaduke, having lost his pillow, grumbled and transferred his head to Sophie's slipper. She didn't seem to notice anything unusual, but merely glanced up. Her unconsciousness of the storm she had set loose in him made a bitter mockery of it and he turned away, taking in the green and grey of the garden, its sane, familiar expanse.

'I must go now. Good day, Miss Trevelyan.'

He headed off through the garden, as aware of her presence on the bench behind him as he had been of French snipers in the Pyrenees during the war. A kind of stinging, visual alertness to danger. Her informal, light-hearted acceptance of his company only made it worse. He should make it clear to her that her friendly openness could be seriously misconstrued by men. But in a way that would be a lie. She might treat him with unusual candour and amicability, but there was nothing flirtatious about her. It would have been so much easier if there were. He knew how to deal with flirtatious women. He had no idea what to do with Sophie.

He picked up his pace as he crossed the street. Even her name was a taunt, the way his mind enjoyed playing it out. His only rational explanation for such an extreme reaction was that his resolve to marry and put an end to his very comfortable way of life was turning everything on its head.

Some part of him was obviously fighting back against the enormity of the step he was about to take by making a fool of him. The timing of this unwanted desire made it clear this was just a reaction...

If he for a moment contemplated throwing out all his carefully considered criteria for a perfect wife on an urge which in the end was merely a few days in the making, he must be more off balance by the prospect of giving up his freedom than he had thought. Even if she was interested, and she showed no sign of that, she fulfilled almost none of the criteria he had so carefully outlined in his mind for a future wife. He would be making precisely the same impetuous move as he had with Serena and he was still paying the price of that mistake. This pathetic throwback to juvenile sexual excitement just at the presence of a woman would probably fade faster than it took to actually get to the altar. And then where would he be? Tied to a woman he could not control nor really understand and who treated him as she probably treated the many cousins she had mentioned. For all he knew she might even have a suitor back home, some fresh-faced squire's son...

He entered his home and headed directly to

his study. It was a sign of just how low he had sunk that the thought of some hypothetical suitor could spark this burn of jealousy. He had lost all sense of proportion. In a few days she would head back to her corner of Devon and he would realise this had been an embarrassing and aberrant moment of madness. The thing now was to stay out of her way.

Chapter Seven

Sophie angled the easel to catch the light so she could inspect what she had accomplished so far and prepare for Hetty's arrival but she did not yet lay out her paints. She had been very surprised to hear from Lambeth that Lord Wivenhoe had called again and was upstairs with her aunt, ostensibly to deliver a book he had promised her the previous afternoon. Sophie did not remember any such promise and just hoped that this time they would make do without her. She had not admitted it to Max…to the Duke of Harcourt, she corrected herself mentally, but she had felt very uncomfortable yesterday during Lord Wivenhoe's visit. It was not just his taunts, but the intent, calculating look when his dramatic eyes settled on her. And especially his gossip about Max.

She already knew from Hetty that Max was

planning to marry, but it had been painful to sit there listening to them go through the list of the flawless London-bred hothouse flowers lined up for him to choose from who were as different from her as the proverbial chalk from cheese. Not that she was surprised. Max's combination of title, wealth and physical endowments would buy him the very best in the marriage mart. On a more modest scale she had seen the same sordid drama played out numerous times in Ashton Cove and nearby Lynmouth. Until now she had just laughed and shrugged at the game, but somehow her sense of humour failed her in this instance. There was something so disappointing in the thought that he was just like everyone else, which was ridiculous, because of course he was. Why should he be any different? Simply because he had taken pity on a foolish provincial and taken her to see an exhibition…it did not mean a thing other than that he, like his sister, was a basically decent person. Nothing more than that.

Above all he was, as Hetty had said, a man driven by a sense of duty. Whatever she thought she detected behind that cold, controlled surface was likely only the creation of her own overly vivid and wishful imagination. It was just that she was so peculiarly comfortable with him. Whether it existed or not, she felt he took her at face value. She wasn't used to men reacting to her with that mix of curiosity and amusement and she had allowed herself to read too much into it. She wondered whether it was because he had grown up in a predominantly female house that he had acquired the very useful skill of putting women at their ease without even seeming to, without ever giving up that that cool, contained detachment.

And it certainly did not help at all that he was so unfairly male. She almost hated the way her body reacted every time he was near. Or even when he wasn't. It was enough just for a stray thought to enter her head, or the memory of that fleeting, seemingly inconsequential touch of his hand on hers. Really, it was quite pathetic. She was becoming as missish as any seventeen-year-old pining after a story-book hero, just as Hetty had warned her. She felt like cringing when she remembered her comment about his scar. His withdrawal had been painfully obvious. If she had an ounce of sense she would stay well away from him from now on. It would be hard enough to return to Ashton Cove after her time in Grosvenor Square and everything she had seen and done these last few days. Now the thought of going back was as near unbearable as she could imagine. She turned away from the light and closed her eyes. They flew open again as the door opened and Lord Wivenhoe stepped in and closed the door behind him.

'I told your aunt I would show myself out, but really I am quite glad I found you. I was hoping to have a word with you,' he said without ceremony.

Sophie shook her head, too bemused to realise yet the impropriety of his presence alone with her in a closed room.

'A word with me?' she asked, but his attention had been caught by the easel.

'Not bad,' he said absently as he inspected her study of Hetty, before turning to Marmaduke's painting, his cold eyes gleaming with malicious amusement. 'That, however, is abysmal. Not your execution, which is passable, but the subject. I am so very glad I have reached the stage when I can choose my models. At least when this is yours you will be able to paint whatever you like.'

'When this is mine?' she blurted out, startled.

He turned to her, one corner of his mouth pulling up in his version of a smile.

'Of course. Isn't that what this is all about?' He waved a hand at Marmaduke's portrait. 'You have apparently found the surest way to your aunt's meagre heart, though it is the only meagre part of her person. Really, I did not realise one could achieve those proportions and live. No wonder she does not go outside—I doubt she could make it through her doorway. Still, that has its advantages, doesn't it? I think I shall avail myself of her invitation to visit and cultivate her. Together we could do quite well with her, couldn't we?'

Sophie listened to him with rising anger. She supposed he was punishing her for her disdainful treatment of him back at the Exhibition, but there was no reason she had to put up with it.

'No, we couldn't,' she replied bluntly. 'And now, if you don't mind, I am waiting for someone.'

He shook his head mournfully, making no move to leave.

'What a very unworthy excuse. It is clear no one visits this mausoleum, my dear. We are quite alone so why don't you put aside all these modest country airs. I knew at a glance there is more to you than that. You are a very determined young woman, aren't you? If it is the Huntley fortune you are after, it appears you are well on your way. I asked my valet to make some enquiries where it really matters and apparently Mad Minnie finds you much more to her taste than any of the pretenders so far. And she hasn't many more years, does she? If you are just careful and attentive, you might secure a fortune beyond most people's wildest dreams. And I could help you. I think she would look even more favourably on you if she heard you were to become my wife. I think I have come as far as I can painting portraits. I always knew I would have to wed wealth, but I've been postponing the inevitable. And if I have to wed money, I rather like the idea of allying myself to someone who shares my appreciation of art and who is such an original thinker. What do you say? Why, you might even make quite a little splash in the artistic milieu as Lady Wivenhoe.'

Sophie stared at him, trying to assimilate what he was saying.

'Are you actually suggesting I marry you so that we can scheme to get hold of Aunt Minnie's fortune? You would marry me on that long chance? Are you that desperate?'

'You are not being very complimentary to yourself, nor to me, my dear. I find the odds…attractive.'

'Oh, please. After that very honest opening please don't insult my intelligence by trying to convince me you are interested in me for myself, Lord Wivenhoe. You are almost as useless a liar as I am myself.'

His face hardened.

'Don't tell me you are fool enough to have developed any ambitions regarding Harcourt based on his gallantry toward you at the exhibition. He is highly unlikely to choose someone as…pleasantly colourful as you. And don't let that proper façade deceive you. He has an unhealthy impact on young women who are foolish enough to think they can manipulate him. More than unhealthy.'

'The only one contemplating manipulation here is you, Lord Wivenhoe. And now, if you won't leave, then I will.'

She turned and had almost made it when he grabbed her by the waist and pulled her back against him.

'Don't run yet, my sweet,' he said, his mouth so close to her she could feel his breath hot on her cheek. 'You don't know me as well as you think. Shall I convince I can be everything a young woman desires?'

'I don't care if you can. Let me go!' Sophie tugged at his hands, trying to pry them off her, but he was surprisingly strong and her annoyance shifted to the first glimmerings of fear. 'I said let me go! This is ridiculous! I'm not interested!'

'Believe me, you will be. If you will just let me show you what it is all about.' His eyes were bright now, the amber lights in them glowing with an elated look that heightened her fear. She closed her eyes, slackening her body, and he gave a breathy laugh, relaxing his grip enough for her purposes and she shoved him sharply, swivelling away. She had just made it to the door and wrenched it open when he reached her, grabbing her arm.

'Wait, you little spitfire...'

The words died out. They stood facing the butler, his hand outstretched towards the door, and behind him stood Hetty and Max. There was a moment of stunned silence. Sophie was only conscious of Max's gaze, hard and intent, first on her, then on the hand that held her arm, and then up to the man behind her. Then time sped up again, so swiftly she had no clear idea what happened—knew just that suddenly she was free and Max was somehow between her and Wivenhoe, driving him back into the parlour.

And the next moment Wivenhoe had crashed back, landing on the low empire-style table in the middle of the parlour, which promptly cracked and collapsed beneath him. He was only down for a moment and then he scrambled to his feet and launched himself at Max with a feral snarl. This time she saw the blow as Max's fist slammed into Wivenhoe and the artist stumbled back against the wall. She also saw the shocked expressions on Lambeth's and Lady Hetty's faces. Max moved purposely towards Wivenhoe, who stood with his hands braced against the wall, as if ready to spring, and Sophie hurried towards them.

'Enough! Enough!' she said through a throat that felt too tight for speech, placing herself in Max's path as he advanced on Wivenhoe, her hands raised before her. 'Please!'

That final word, between a command and a plea, reached Max and he glanced down at her and stopped just short of her hands, the dangerous look in his face receding.

'Go to Hetty, Sophie,' he said curtly, but she shook her head and turned to Wivenhoe.

'Leave. Now.' Her voice was shaky, but either it or more likely the look on Max's face carried conviction and Wivenhoe straightened, his face resuming its sardonic cast.

'Is that how the wind blows, sweetheart? Much more ambitious that you let on, aren't you? No wonder you scoffed at the Huntley fortune. But you're a fool, girl. That's all right, Harcourt. I'm leaving. I misread the cards, apparently.' The last was directed at Sophie as he passed her and there was a sharp, ugly look in his eyes. No one moved until he passed by the butler. Lambeth, still visibly shaken, recollected himself enough to hurry ahead to hand Wivenhoe his hat and cane and open the front door. Then Hetty gave a little shiver and hurried towards Sophie.

'Sophie! Are you all right? Did he hurt you?'

Sophie realised she was shaking, though she wasn't sure if it was from anger or shock. She just knew she wished she had been the one to do Wivenhoe damage. Then she saw how pale Hetty was and the shaking eased as she felt herself gather back to a stable centre.

'No, he didn't. It is absolutely inconceivable to me how someone so…detestable could be such a good painter! It seems quite unfair.'

Hetty laughed weakly and looked rather helplessly at the crushed table. Behind her Lambeth stood in the doorway, surveying the wreckage as well.

'Perhaps you would like to retire to the Green

Salon, Miss Sophie, while I tidy up here? I shall bring some refreshments, shall I?'

Sophie felt a sudden urge to giggle and was glad when Hetty took command.

'Yes, of course, that is a good idea. I would be glad of a glass of wine.'

Lambeth bowed approvingly.

'This way, please, Lady Swinburne, Your Grace.'

Once in the Green Salon, Hetty sank down next to Sophie on a green-brocade sofa with crocodile's claws for feet, her gaze roaming over the opulent, outdated decor with an absent, wondering kind of awe and Sophie felt her shock ease further. The only remaining tension was the fact that Max, who had stopped just inside the door, had not spoken a word yet. She glanced over at him quickly and then away. He looked cold and distant and detached, and the expression that had shocked her before was gone. The only remnant was in the fact that his hands were still fisted. She thought he wasn't aware of it and wondered if he had hurt himself hitting Wivenhoe.

'Is your hand all right?' she asked, feeling foolish and painfully embarrassed by the whole outrageous interlude. Once again she had managed to put him in an embarrassing and uncomfortable position. And on top of that, Wivenhoe's insinuations were only redeemed from being humiliating by being utterly absurd. She forced herself to meet his gaze as if nothing unusual had happened. For a moment his eyes fixed on hers and though she could not tell what he was thinking, the sense of danger was still there. Then he glanced down at his gloved hand and she noticed the seam had split along his middle knuckle. He calmly drew off the glove and clasped it in his hand, moving into the room.

'Yes. Thank you,' he replied properly. 'What happened in there?'

The question was so calmly spoken it took her a moment to register its meaning. Before she could even think how to respond a discreet knock on the door preceded Lambeth's return with a tray holding a decanter, three glasses and plate of biscuits. None of them moved or spoke until Lambeth poured the wine and bowed himself out. Sophie picked up a glass and sipped carefully at the wine.

'Well?' Max prompted tensely. 'What were you doing alone with Wivenhoe after I expressly warned you about him?'

The bubble of nervous laughter she had been struggling against withered and faded, replaced by a resurgence of the anger she had felt against Wivenhoe. She put down her glass on the tray with a snap and the ruby liquid splashed on to the silver surface.

'I was *doing* nothing with him! He came to see Aunt Minnie and then he came in to the parlour uninvited…how was I to know what he might do? And how *dare* you blame me for whatever that snake—?' She broke off, furious that her voice was shaking. She felt again the alarm as Wivenhoe's arms had closed around her, the shocked fury that she could not dislodge him by force. And now to have this man accuse her that it was somehow *her* fault. That was too much. She surged to her feet.

'How *dare* you?'

Hetty stood up as well.

'My dear, please, Max didn't mean it was your fault—'

'Yes, he did!' Sophie interrupted, trying and failing to keep her voice steady. 'That is precisely what you meant, isn't it? That I had somehow encouraged him to…to maul me and…'

He blinked, as if coming out of a trance, then

frowned at her obvious distress and moved towards her.

'No, of course not,' he said more calmly. 'I'm sorry, I didn't think...here, sit down.' He took her arm gently, but she tugged out of his grasp and he let her go immediately. She stood for a moment, tense and almost afraid, watching him, but he didn't move, just stood there, waiting, and after a moment the tension faded and she sat down again.

'I'm sorry,' she said. 'I shouldn't be angry at you, but at him. I am very grateful you came to my aid. Really. Though I would have preferred to do it myself.'

A flash of a smile flickered in his eyes.

'I am sure you would have.'

'My dear, here, drink your wine, it will help.'

Hetty had wiped her glass and handed it to her and Sophie smiled at her gratefully.

'I am all right now, thank you, really. I don't break so easily.'

'I can see that, but you should go rest. We will continue the portrait tomorrow if you like.'

Sophie wanted to object, but when she placed the glass on the tray, more carefully this time, she was surprised to see her hand was shaking.

'Perhaps you are right. Tomorrow, if you can? I really would like to continue.'

Hetty nodded and stood up.

'Yes, of course, my dear.'

She rang for Lambeth, who appeared almost immediately. Max turned abruptly and she watched as he took Lambeth aside and said something to him she could not catch. Lambeth nodded and bowed and she sighed, guessing he was receiving orders to keep Wivenhoe out. No doubt everyone in the house already knew what had happened. She only hoped this tale wouldn't somehow reach her parents and provide more grist for their mill. Hetty gave her a quick hug and followed her brother and Sophie watched wistfully as they left. Max had not even said goodbye. It seemed he could not get away fast enough.

'Is there anything I can get you, miss?' Lambeth asked, a hint of a worried frown on his usually blank face, and she shook her head.

'No, thank you, Lambeth. I think I shall go rest a little.'

He bowed, but remained standing in the hallway as she trailed upstairs to her room.

Chapter Eight

'I hear congratulations are in order, Max. Lady Melissa is going to look pretty blue; she thought she had you snared,' Bryanston said tipsily as he leaned over Max's shoulder to see his cards. Lord Cranworth, Max's partner at piquet across the card table in the corner of the neoclassical card room at Brooks's, glanced up from his own hand.

'What's that? You finally made your choice, Max?'

'Not that I was aware of, Cranworth,' he replied mildly and discarded an eight of clubs. 'You're blocking my light, Bryanston.'

Bryanston moved, but only to straddle an empty chair by the table.

'Heard it from Wivenhoe at the Royal Cock Pit earlier. The fellow was definitely disguised. He usually carries his drink better than that... Morton was saying he was switching his bet from Lady Penelope to Lady Melissa before the odds shorten further, but Wivenhoe said that would be wasting his blunt because you've been caught by some little country miss he met you with at the Exhibition. Is that the one you introduced to me there—what was her name? Something Cornish. Tremaine? You know, the one with the laughing blue eyes. Is it true?'

Max silently cursed both Wivenhoe and Bryanston, but did not look up from his cards. Two other club members who were idly watching their play straightened attentively, clearly as interested in Bryanston's gossip as in the game.

'I had no idea Wivenhoe was such an authority on my affairs, drunk or sober. Your play, Cranworth.'

Bryanston was never good with hints.

'No, I know that, bad blood between you. Never understood why. Not that I like the fellow, but the name's a good one, even if he dabbles in paints. Still, when I asked him he seemed to know a lot about her. Said he knows her aunt and there's money there. If that's true, it's a damn shame, Max. You don't need an heiress; you've too much blunt already. Should leave some for the rest of us.

No wonder Wivenhoe's grey at the gills. Wouldn't be surprised if he had an eye on her himself which is why he's smarting. He's expensive, Wivenhoe.'

'Quiet, Bry, I'm trying to think,' Cranworth said, frowning at his cards. 'Blast. It all hangs on this.'

'It's all in the odds, Cranworth,' Max prompted, holding on to his temper by a thread. He knew the worst thing would be to show any sign he was bothered by Bry's banter. But any hope he had of a reprieve was banished by Cranworth's next words.

'I know it's in the odds, Max, it's just that I can never keep track of them. So it's all a hum and it's to be the lovely Melissa after all? Tough on the other girl if Wivenhoe goes spreading that rumour about and there's no grounds for it. Money or no money, it won't do her reputation any good...'

'Trevelyan! Sophie Trevelyan!' Bryanston announced, inspired. 'That's it. Just remembered. I'm good with names. Taking little thing, too. Not a beauty like Lady Melissa, but I like her better. Lady Huntley's niece, right? That's what Wivenhoe said. It's coming back to me.'

'What? Lady Huntley?' asked one of the other men standing by them. 'There's definitely money there, Huntley was as rich as a nabob. Lives next to you, doesn't she? So that's the way the wind is blowing? Come on; give us a lead, Harcourt.'

Another man nodded, frowning down at the three cards Cranworth had discarded. 'The odds in the clubs are shortening in favour of Lady Melissa. If there's a dark horse in the running for your Duchess, be a friend and let us know, would you? I could use an inside tip with long odds. What was her name, again, Bryanston?'

'I told you, Sophie Trevelyan. She of the laughing blue eyes. But don't lay the bet near Max, he don't care for that sort of thing. Private. Very private is Max.'

'True,' Cranworth assented mournfully as he frowned over Max's move before recklessly making his own discard. 'Very sad.'

'Not as sad as this. My game,' Max said, wishing he could physically take Bryanston and toss him out of the room.

Cranworth groaned as he inspected the cards in front of him.

'Piqued, blast it. I'm all in. You think after all these years I would have learned not to play piquet with you. At least I have enough sense not to play for more than chicken stakes.'

'Your lady wife won't let you, you mean,' Bryanston interjected. 'You should warn Max not to take the plunge. It's a dog's life.'

Max gathered the cards and shuffled them absently, debating how much more of this he would have to listen to before he could leave. He knew well enough the worst thing to do would be to try and scotch the rumours directly. Until now he had been able to regard gossip about his marital plans as simply an annoying side effect of the process, but this was different. The Lady Pennys and Lady Melissas of the world were protected by their families' reputations and they were not being made the object of Wivenhoe's malicious tongue. After what Sophie had been through that day, the thought that she might come under another attack, and this time on her reputation and because of him, was intolerable.

Every time the memory of that moment surfaced, as it had far too often, he was swamped again with a furious wish he had done Wivenhoe a great deal more damage than he had, coupled with the even more disturbing worry that Sophie was effectively alone in that madhouse, no matter how dependable the butler had appeared when he had agreed with him that Wivenhoe was on no account to be admitted to the house. The thought that Wivenhoe might try something like that again… Even the thought that she didn't have anyone to be with her after such a shock. She had recovered quickly, but even through the mist of his own anger and confusion he had seen how shaken she was. And he had mindlessly added to her pain because he had been too caught up in the past to think clearly. That was probably why he had acted so uncharacteristically and started that ridiculous brawl. There had been no conscious transition. He had felt foolish enough accompanying Hetty to see the portrait after everything he had told himself about staying away from Sophie, then the moment she had wrenched open the door and he had seen the fear on her face and Wivenhoe's hand digging into her arm he had just… lost himself. It wasn't even like going into battle. There he had always been aware of everything, but most of all of himself and what he had to ensure he and his men survived. This had been different. It was as if he had ceased to exist.

'Nonsense, Bry, you're just jealous,' Cranworth said in response to Bryanston's condemnation of the married state, interrupting Max's thoughts. 'I wonder why Wivenhoe's spreading that tale around if there's nothing to it. I'm not fond of him myself, but I have to admit it's not like him to go about gossiping. Unless it's the girl that's set the ball rolling. Trying to force your hand, maybe. It's possible. Wouldn't be the first time a girl got up to tricks angling to become your Duchess. Bad *ton*, though.'

'Don't be ridiculous,' Max said impatiently. 'This has nothing to do with Sophie. Wivenhoe is just being poisonous because she rebuffed him.'

The moment the words were out he knew he should have kept his peace and he certainly shouldn't have slipped up and used her given name. There was a distinct shift of focus around the table. Bryanston was a rattle, but Cranworth and the others were no fools and they loved a good gamble, the longer the odds the better. Cranworth's clear brown eyes settled on Max, widening slightly before looking away and Max barely held back a groan. It was clear new wagers would be made the moment his back was turned and any attempt on his part to prevent it would only make matters worse. He was letting this situation put him off his stride. With any luck a new scandal or piece of juicy gossip would catch the *ton*'s shifting fancy and this would be nothing more than a flash in the pan.

Chapter Nine

'I don't know why I bother going,' Bryanston moaned as he followed Max and Cranworth down the front steps of Harcourt House the next day on their way towards Gentleman Jackson's Boxing Saloon in Bond Street. 'Jackson never lets me get one over his guard. I've been going for years now and I've nothing but memories of a black eye to show for it! I had to spend three weeks rusticating in the country until I was presentable again. Can't we go to Tattersall's or something? I haven't placed a bet in two whole days and I'm feeling lucky.'

'You can. I'm going to Jackson's,' Max replied, pulling on his gloves. 'Come. It will do you good.'

'It probably won't. I'm not sporting mad like you and Cranworth with your horses and fists. I will just be bored while Cranworth batters away with the single stick and you and Jackson spar away like two backstreet brawlers.'

'You've no discrimination, Bryanston.' Cranworth chuckled. 'Jackson himself said Max might have made a living of it if he weren't cursed with a duchy. Run along then if we bore you.'

'It is very lucky he was, then. I can imagine nothing bleaker than having to make one's fortune with one's fists. Here, Max, isn't that your delightful Miss Trevelyan in the gardens? What on earth is she holding? Is that a dog?'

Max turned toward the gardens involuntarily, in time to see Sophie enter with Marmaduke nestled cosily in her arms. He felt Bryanston's and Cranworth's curious eyes on him and was about to resolutely turn and continue when he saw another familiar figure.

'I say, isn't that…?'

Max didn't stay to hear the rest of Bryanston's question. He crossed the road rapidly, reaching Sophie at the same time as Wivenhoe. She had stopped when she noticed Wivenhoe's approach and half-turned back, only to stop again as she saw Max. He could see the relief in her eyes and he held her gaze until he reached her.

'Shall I see you back to your aunt's, Miss Trevelyan?' he asked, taking her arm. Wivenhoe's mocking sneer didn't mask the annoyance in his eyes or voice.

'What, do you hover nearby, waiting to snatch the brand from the fire, Harcourt? I never pegged you in the role of nursemaid. Let the girl have some fun before she must go back to wilds of wherever. Hello, Cranworth, Bryanston. Whither are you all headed?'

'Jackson's,' Cranworth replied, casting a curious glance at Sophie and the somnolent pug.

'Alas.' Bryanston sighed and directed an elegant bow towards Sophie. 'A pleasure to meet you again, Miss Trevelyan. Allow me to introduce Lord Cranworth. Did you enjoy the Exhibition?'

'Lord Cranworth.' She nodded at Cranworth and acknowledged Bryanston's bow with a smile. 'Very much, Lord Bryanston. I might have spent a week in there and not tired of it.'

Max watched as her face relaxed and the light returned to her eyes, sparking a responsive smile on his friends' faces. If he weren't so much on edge about Wivenhoe he might have appreciated the facility with which she put these two jaded men at their ease with no more than a frank and friendly smile.

'Good gracious!' Bryanston laughed. 'A week! It just goes to show that one man's, or woman's, heaven is another man's hell.'

'Language, Bry,' Cranworth said lazily and Sophie laughed.

'I don't think "hell" qualifies as a curse, Lord Cranworth. If it does, my father the vicar is guilty of extreme impropriety. It is one of his favourites.'

Cranworth's eyes widened.

'Your father is a vicar!'

'They do have children, you know,' she replied innocently and Max smiled despite the tension that held him as Wivenhoe remained standing there, the mocking smile on his face and something else in his eyes as they moved over Sophie. The image of a much younger Wivenhoe standing by Serena's portrait with a similar gleam in his eyes came back to him, bridging all the years that had passed.

'In quite the usual way, too, shocking though it might seem,' Wivenhoe interjected provocatively.

'Is that thing alive?' Bryanston asked, smoothing over the uncomfortable silence which followed Wivenhoe's comment, and Sophie laughed, lowering Marmaduke to the ground. Marmaduke opened his eyes, shook himself, sauntered over towards Max's boots and sat down beside them, panting gently.

'It likes you, Max,' Cranworth said maliciously.

'Animals always like Max,' Bryanston said. 'Remember that stray pup you tried to hide from the headmaster our first year up at Eton?'

Max was not in the mood for Bryanston's reminiscences. He just wanted to get Sophie away from Wivenhoe and back to her aunt's house.

'You are a master of inconsequentiality, Bry. Come, Miss Trevelyan, we will see you home.'

'Stray pups, Harcourt? Is that it?' Wivenhoe said softly. 'But there really is no need. I promise to behave. You fellows be on your way to Jackson's and I shall see Miss Trevelyan safely home. I'll even walk the dreaded pug. Here, my dear, give me the leash…'

He reached for the leash Sophie held, but she pulled back her hand abruptly and Marmaduke, with unusual perspicacity, stood up and gave an ominous growl. After a moment's surprise Cranworth and Bryanston burst out laughing.

'So you have two snarling guardians now, my dear,' Wivenhoe said lightly, but his pale cheeks were flushed. 'Your talents clearly extend beyond your sketch pad. And all with that light, innocent touch. Most impressive.'

Max's hold tightened on Sophie's arm and she glanced up at him, her eyes no longer smiling. Cranworth and Bryanston had also stopped laughing, clearly aware of the poisonous atmosphere. Sophie glanced down at Marmaduke.

'Come, Marmaduke. It is time to go home now,' she said calmly but Marmaduke remained sitting, his round eyes fixed balefully on Wivenhoe, not even getting up when his leash was fully extended and Sophie gave it a slight tug to no avail. Wivenhoe laughed.

'What a stubborn little duke you are,' he mocked and extended his cane, giving Marmaduke a nudge. Marmaduke, unaccustomed to such rough usage, fell back with a yelp and Sophie scooped him up with a frown.

'It is a very bad habit to vent ill temper on creatures weaker than you, Lord Wivenhoe!' she scolded and Wivenhoe's expression shifted, his lips pulling back in a strange mirror of Marmaduke's snarl, his hand holding the cane stretched out towards Sophie, and without even thinking Max found himself between them again, his hand hard around Wivenhoe's raised wrist and he squeezed until the cane dropped from Wivenhoe's grasp and clattered to the path.

'My hand!' Wivenhoe panted, his face livid. 'You're breaking it.'

'Stay away from her, Wivenhoe, unless you want to try painting with your left hand,' Max bit out, tightening his hold mercilessly before releasing it.

'She's not your property either, Harcourt!' Wivenhoe spat at him like a curse, cradling his bruised hand.

'No, but she is my betrothed and if I see you near her again or hear that you even mentioned her name I *will* break your hand. With pleasure.'

He turned and took Sophie's arm and guided her firmly out of the gardens, ignoring the interested looks of several onlookers who had stopped to watch the altercation. Cranworth and Bryanston followed in silence and as they reached Huntley House Max realised with a sudden wash of clarity that penetrated his anger precisely what he had just said, and in the presence of Bryanston, one of the *ton*'s most incurable gossips, as well as several residents of the square.

'You two go ahead,' he said, taking Sophie's

arm and leading her up the steps. 'I will join you later.'

'Of course, of course,' Bryanston said hurriedly. 'Don't give it a thought. No hurry at all. Miss Trevelyan, your most obedient servant.'

Cranworth took Bryanston by the arm.

'Off we go, Bry. Miss Trevelyan, I am very glad to have made your acquaintance. My warmest congratulations on your betrothal.'

Max didn't wait for her to respond, but opened the door and guided her inside and led her directly into the green parlour, closing the door behind them and pulling off his gloves. Sophie moved into the middle of the room, looking down at the outrageous claw-footed green-and-gold divan as if she was seeing it for the first time.

'You can put Marmaduke down now,' he said as the silence stretched out and she started and placed the pug on the floor. Once again Marmaduke ambled over towards Max and sat down by his boots and she gave a little gasp of embarrassed laughter and then raised her hands to her cheeks.

'I'm so sorry!'

'It's not your fault,' he said stiffly.

'It is such bad luck that he was there just as I came out. And that you came across us.'

'It wasn't luck. He didn't chance to come across you, he was waiting for you.'

'But that's…what on earth is wrong with him? It makes no sense. He must be mad.'

'That is one explanation. But that's hardly the relevant point at the moment.'

'No, of course not. Thank you for coming to my aid. It was kind of you, to try and scare him off like that, but it really wasn't very prudent. How will you explain it to your friends?'

'Explain what?'

'What you said about being—' She broke off, flushing and spreading her hands out helplessly.

'There is nothing to explain. They are both reasonably intelligent men, they understood me quite clearly.'

'Oh, then they know you were just saying it to warn him off? I was worried they might take you seriously. I don't think Wivenhoe will mention it.'

Max breathed in slowly. This was harder than he would have thought. Could she really be so naïve?

'Sit down, Sophie.'

With a hesitant look she sat down on the divan and he pulled up a chair opposite her.

'You do realise I have just announced that we are engaged in a very public location in front of several members of the *ton*? Of the lot of them you are quite right that Wivenhoe is the least likely to mention it, but Bryanston is probably happily communicating that choice piece of gossip to all and sundry as we speak, while my other friend, Lord Cranworth, is probably on his way to Brooks's to collect on his wager to that effect. And I can only conjecture what the passers-by who were enjoying the spectacle are going to do with their version of that scene. So the only explaining that needs to be done is apparently to you.'

He stopped before the bitterness seeping into his voice became too obvious. It wasn't her fault and the churning frustration wasn't even directed at her. He still couldn't quite believe what had just happened. The whole point of his careful search for a perfect bride had been to avoid being driven by impulse into choosing someone unsuitable and he couldn't find a better description of what had just happened. He had no idea what rankled more—making a fool of himself in public, finding himself tricked by his own temper and the insistent pull she operated on him into announcing a betrothal he had not even considered two seconds previously, or the fact that she was so obviously blind to the implications of what had just happened.

'But, that's ridiculous. One can't just…I mean, no one would expect you to…' She trailed off again and then continued resolutely. 'I mean, you are hardly to blame for what happened. You merely came to my defence.'

'It's my fault you met Wivenhoe in the first place—'

'Nonsense,' she interrupted. 'You aren't responsible for me. And no great harm has been done after all. Soon I will return home and everything will return to the way it was.'

'Is that what you want?' he asked and her eyes rose to his, a deep insistent blue that struck heat through his body, making it clear that part of him at least was very willing to proceed down this path. He continued before she could speak. 'It doesn't matter if it is. Once word of our betrothal spreads, if either of us repudiates it, the damage to your reputation may be much more substantial than you realise. Wivenhoe was already brewing a nice scandal at your expense even before this afternoon and this announcement is falling on fertile ground. But once we formally announce the engagement no one will dare say a word against you. Not even Wivenhoe.'

She considered this.

'So announcing an engagement will be enough? We won't actually have to go through with it?'

'What…? Of course we will have to go through with it! You can't just announce an engagement and do nothing about it!'

'I suppose you couldn't jilt me, but after a while I could jilt you, couldn't I? And then you could…'

'Sophie. Listen to me and listen well. We are trying to prevent damage to your reputation. And mine. If you are bird-witted enough to believe you can do this by getting publicly engaged and then jilting me, let me tell you—'

'Oh, fine,' she interrupted. 'It was just an idea.'

'A hare-brained one.'

Her mouth tightened and once again he saw the bedrock of stubborn temper that underlay her warmth and humour.

'First I was bird-witted and now hare-brained. Are you certain you want to contemplate marriage to a menagerie?'

'Sophie…'

'Miss Trevelyan, please. I don't remember giving you leave to call me by my given name.'

'Miss Trevelyan, then. I want you to listen to me with all the sense I know you possess. Whether you like it or not, your name has been linked to mine ever since I was foolish enough to accompany you to the Exhibition. On top of that every servant in this house probably knows what happened yesterday with Wivenhoe and there is no way they won't be sharing that choice piece of gossip which will tie in nicely to the malicious interest in why Wivenhoe is spreading poison about you. So at the moment speculation is rife about who Miss Sophie Trevelyan is and the odds that I will offer for you or for Lady Melissa. And now all those elements collided in that ridiculous scene which was witnessed not just by us, but by everyone else who happened to be passing by at the moment. Do you really think that you would be immune to this gossip merely by going back home? From what I know of small-town gossip you would likely find yourself in the middle of a much worse scandal than the one that is brewing around us. As a vicar's daughter you should know full well the damage such a blot on your name could have not just for you, but for all of your family. Do you really want to put them through that? The only way I can see to protect both of us from all that is to cut through this Gordian knot. Am I being clear enough?'

He didn't like being so brutal, but she had to understand how serious the situation was. It might be unfair that she had to pay for his mistakes, but right now he couldn't afford to consider that. All that mattered was that she realise there was no choice. He moved to sit by her on the *chaise longue* and clasped her shoulders gently, trying to atone for his severity, and her muscles flinched under his touch, but she didn't move away.

'Perfectly clear,' she replied, her face pale. Clearly the mention of the impact on her family was more convincing than the possible damage to her own reputation.

'Well?' He moved his hands down over the muslin sleeves to her arms. A tremor shook through her and it spread to him, and he had to hold himself hard against the need to do more.

'Very well.' Her voice was low and husky and for a moment he was not certain what question she was responding to.

'Very well what?' he asked carefully.

'Very well, I will marry you.' Her voice had dropped even lower, as if afraid someone outside might overhear.

'You will? I mean…good.'

'What do we do now?' She looked up at him, her eyes wide with anxiety and curiosity, and he realised that nothing would ever be the same again. He watched her expressive face mirror his own tangled emotions. It was done. It could not have taken very long but he felt as he had after a long march during the war, exhausted and relieved to arrive, but already impatient to explore the new location. Her question was so naïve as to be almost absurd. He knew he should answer her purely on a formal level because there was indeed a great deal to do now.

'We seal our bargain,' he said instead as his baser self elbowed its way to the front of the stage. They could get to the details later.

'How do we do that?' she asked seriously and he laughed, more at himself than at her, swamped by relief that it was done, that she had agreed, and that he could now, finally, do what he had been waiting to do since that day in the gardens. Right now marriage seemed a reasonable price to pay to get this woman in his bed and sate this aggravating desire.

'Like this,' he said, raising her chin and bending to brush his lips across hers, very lightly, trying to find the right balance between feeding his hunger and not scaring her, especially after what Wivenhoe had put her through. But the slide of her mouth under his, soft and smooth and warm, wouldn't release him and he carefully placed his hand on her waist as he might in a dance, feeling the soft heat under his palm, the friction of the muslin cloth, just pressing his fingers into the curve of her skin.

He was standing at the very edge of a cliff, carefully balanced and fighting his need to just cast himself off, let gravity and nature take over. Suddenly she gave a small shiver and leaned forward, not breaking contact with his mouth, just angling her head, her lips catching against his, clearly demanding more than he had intended to allow himself.

'Sophie...'

She answered with an impatient, shaky breath, her hands settling tentatively on his coat, then tensing into fists as he slid his tongue gently over the parting of her lips. He stroked her gently, almost idly, his mouth and tongue exploring hers, his hands moving over her back, building a deceptively soothing rhythm. It was agony to hold that leisurely pace and not sink in to her, drag her against him, bare her. He wanted her with him, lulled, pliant, but she was chipping away at his control, her hands shifting against his chest with unconscious impatience, her mouth searching, revealing the passionate nature he both yearned for and feared. He slid his hand over the silky hair at her nape and she pressed her head back against his hand, like an arching feline, her breath a soft sigh against his mouth and he gave up, pulling her to him so he could kiss her thoroughly, the way he had been wanting to for the whole of this hellish, endless week, giving silent thanks that she clearly wanted this, that the passion he had suspected in her was there and open to him.

Her mouth was as warm and generous as she was, opening under the pressure of the kiss, meeting him and sliding against him in a search for something he knew he couldn't give her yet, but that he wanted so much it was scalding him. He held himself at the edge, playing with her lips, tasting the full damp curve he had watched so often lengthen into her amazing smile. He almost begged her to smile so he could feel it, like wanting to touch the sun on a wave. He nipped at her lips, pulling them between his lips and teeth, tasting the hot inner curve, following that moist promise inwards and she half-rose towards him, her thigh against his and her hands rising to twine into his hair, pressing on his nape.

Her need, so raw and unashamed, was demolishing his restraints. It was agony not to follow instinct, to feel the shakiness of her breath against his mouth and tongue and the pressure of her hands and body as she pressed against him. He struggled against the drugging pull of the lust she was unleashing, aware that he was as close to losing himself to passion as he had just lost himself to violence.

That thought, foreign in flavour and intensity, dragged back his awareness of where he was, and with whom, and he grasped her arms and pulled them down as gently as he could, fighting the resistant tension in his body. Her eyes half-opened, warm and languid, almost turquoise, and as much a caress as the friction of her body against his, and the desire sharpened unbearably. It seemed much more sinful to be walking away from that promise than succumbing to it. But he knew that however desperate he was to explore just how far he could take her obvious passion, her unstinting response placed all the burden of prudence on him. He held her there, waiting for the strength to move away.

'That just goes to show you how wrong one can be,' she said dreamily, her voice low and almost humming, and he struggled to make sense of her words.

'About what?'

'About kissing. I always thought it was rather tedious. I never imagined it could be so nice.'

This observation, delivered in the same faraway voice, managed to penetrate his own painfully pleasant fog.

'You *always* thought? How many times have you kissed someone before?'

Her eyes opened further, clearly surprised, and she finally sat back.

'How many? I suppose…five times, if you count Timothy, though that was hardly a kiss…well, I mean, I *am* twenty-four. And I was almost engaged once,' she informed him confidingly.

Max wavered between annoyance and amusement at her practical view of the matter, but decided not to ruin the moment by talking propriety and focused on her final statement.

'Why almost?'

'Because of this. I didn't like the way he kissed. The thought of a whole lifetime of having to… well, I couldn't do it even though Mama and Papa liked him. And John said women weren't meant to enjoy it anyway, which seemed absurd and quite unfair. I could tell even Augusta and Mary didn't mind kissing their husbands and they are as proper as they come. And now I know I was right about women enjoying this. But I dare say you have had a great deal more experience than John.'

Max laughed, caught in a tangle of confused emotions at these artless disclosures.

'It's not just experience. There has to be an attraction, or not all the experience in the world can compensate to make it anything more than tolerable.'

Her eyes, curious and unusually anxious, rose to his.

'And is there? I mean…are you attracted to me at all?'

He could hardly believe that question needed to be asked after the embrace they had shared and the way he felt right now, with the heat swirling inside him, like a furious genie trapped in a bottle, demanding release and threatening havoc. But he just nodded and answered in the same direct coin she employed.

'Yes. Very much. And you?'

'Yes…' she breathed, heat staining her cheeks again. 'That's good, isn't it? If we are to be married?'

'Yes. Very good.'

He took her hands again; the need to touch her was so strong it felt almost foreign, as if there *was* some element of possession here. And there was something pleasantly detached about her great-aunt's outdated mausoleum, a universe set apart from his own world with its rules and norms. He knew this thought was deceptive and that just a few feet from them the real world was waiting, but right now he didn't care.

'Engaged or not, we shouldn't be doing this,' he felt compelled to warn her, even as he slid his hands up her arms, focusing on the soft texture of her skin under his fingers, especially the warm pliant skin of her inner arms. He could feel her pulse there and on impulse he gently raised her arm and pressed his lips to that pulse and she breathed in sharply, her arm quivering in his grasp.

'I won't tell,' she murmured, her eyes dreamy again. 'Besides, I don't understand what is so very wrong about this…if we are engaged.'

At the moment neither could he. He had to

marry her anyway, what difference did it make
if he derived some pleasure meanwhile? He would
obviously not go too far. It was like spirits—one
had to know one's limits. Except that he had a
suspicion that he had already passed his. That he
was in that pleasant and dangerous territory of
thinking himself both rational and omnipotent.
Hetty would clearly disagree that he was still act-
ing responsibly. Any sane person would. The fact
that Sophie didn't was just a sign of her naiveté.

He closed his eyes briefly and let go her arm,
shifting back.

'No.'

Her hand reached out and touched his coat and
he caught it firmly.

'No. This is all very good, but we have to be sensible. There will be plenty of time for this later.'

'Plenty?' she prompted and the amused mischief
in her eyes danced through his body. She moved
back on the *chaise longue* as well and he breathed
in, between relief and regret at her acceptance of
the boundaries he was trying to set.

'Plenty,' he promised and stood up. 'Now I must
go speak to your aunt. Unfortunately there is some
business I have to attend to for a few days in
Southampton that can't be put off, but once I'm

back I'll put the announcement in the papers. So I suggest you write to your family by the afternoon post. I presume someone in your community reads the London papers?'

Sophie grimaced. 'The squire's wife reads every scrap of town gossip and she particularly loves the bits about weddings and obituaries. She won't miss it.'

'Well, then you had best make sure they're prepared for the announcement. Tell them I will write to apply formally—'

'But that's silly, you don't have to,' she interrupted impatiently. 'After all, I'm of age. I make my own decisions.'

'It may be a courtesy, but this is how it is done.'

'I beg pardon,' she apologised meekly and Max sighed at the very unapologetic laughter in her eyes.

'And then we need to decide when we will go to Harcourt Hall so you can meet my family and when we will go to meet yours.'

'Oh, dear. If it didn't defeat the whole purpose of saving face, I would suggest eloping.'

'And if I didn't know there is very little likelihood of it, I would suggest you take this seriously.'

Max said with an edge of exasperation and it was Sophie's turn to sigh.

'You're right. I think it's just that I'm so nervous. I've never done anything like this before.'

'It is not as if I have boundless experience of it either,' he pointed out, but the words grated slightly and he wondered if he should tell her about Serena. Eventually he would tell her, but now didn't seem the right moment for ancient history.

'But you've thought it all out. Like a campaign. It's very impressive,' she said, and though the humour was still evident there was also a clear, assessing look which brought back his exasperation.

'Once the announcement is in papers it will resemble a siege more than a campaign, believe me. And now I should go and deal with the details.'

'Is there anything I can do other than writing to my parents? It seems completely unfair that you have to deal with everything. After all, this is more my fault than yours.'

Max hesitated, touched by her innate accountability. For a moment he tried to imagine what this interview might have been like if he had been facing Lady Melissa instead of this unusual and unsettling young woman. It was so dramatically different a scenario that as mad as it might be, he gave thanks that he had at least not gone down that path. Lady Melissa would no doubt perform perfectly to her cues and there would be no humour. Or passion. He might not know what he was getting into with Sophie, but somehow that seemed slightly better than the very clear future he had mapped out with Lady Melissa. At least in this instance he preferred the murkier outlook.

'There will be plenty for you to do soon enough, more than you will want, believe me. For the moment you are for better or for worse in the position of the reserves. Hetty will come by later and the two of you can work out all the…female details. She's a veteran of all my sisters' weddings so she knows what needs to be done. All right?'

Both her flush and the humour in her eyes deepened as he spoke, but she just nodded. He should leave it at that, but behind the laughing sprite she looked wistful again and his body, tight with the memory of their kiss, heated, demanding another taste. A quick one, he assured himself and strode back to her, cupping her chin to raise her mouth to his. Her hand brushed against his cheek and neck, brief but as searing as a brand and he stepped back. Her eyes opened and she smiled tentatively.

'Siege rations already?'

He could tell she was trying for lightness, but her voice was husky and inviting and he shook his head, more at himself than at her, and headed back to the door.

'I am sorry you find it such poor fare,' he said as he turned back to her, his hand on the door-knob, and the soft laughter disappeared from her face immediately, replaced by concern.

'Oh, no! That isn't what I meant at all! I was just being...I say things I ought not when I am embarrassed...' She stopped suddenly, her eyes searching his. 'Are you laughing at me?'

'That would be quite uncivil of me, wouldn't it?'

She relaxed visibly. '*And* unchivalrous.'

'Very. Now wish me luck with your aunt.'

'Just be careful you don't sit on one of the pugs by mistake and you will be fine,' she said reassuringly and he shook his head again and headed out to find Mad Minnie.

Sophie pressed her hands to her cheeks as the door clicked shut behind him. They felt hot, or perhaps it was her hands that were cold. A snort made her look down and she realised Marmaduke had slept through the whole scene and for a moment she wondered if it were possible that she had imagined the whole afternoon.

Surely this was madness. She could not possibly be engaged to Max. But she could not in her wildest dreams have imagined that kiss and the way it shook her to the core, made her do things she had never dreamed of doing... Or the way he had touched his mouth to her inner arm; she had not realised such a brief touch, to her arm, of all places, could feel so...explosive. She felt shaky and urgent inside, fearful and bubbling and...and also terribly guilty. It was surely absurd to expect him to make such a sacrifice merely for the sin of not being able to prevent her from getting into trouble?

But Hetty had warned her that Max played by the rules. The mistakes might mostly be hers, but he would take his own seriously. Far too seriously, obviously. To pay such a price... She could still feel her shock when he had told Wivenhoe they were betrothed. It had been overshadowed by the general shock of that sudden conflagration between Max and Wivenhoe that she instinctively knew had its roots in something well outside Wivenhoe's pursuit of her. It almost seemed he and Wivenhoe stood in some separate space, away from them all, and she wondered what had happened between them in the past.

And behind all these roiling emotions, like a bank of creamy clouds piled high on the horizon, was a joyful warmth that was more terrifying than anything because she wanted to be with Max more than she had ever wanted anything in her life. And she was certain she would ruin it. Her whole life she had struggled in vain trying to live up to expectations and had mostly failed. She must be mad to willingly try to assume a role where she was bound to disappoint. And such a role! She was nothing like Max's ideal—someone stately, demure, fashionable, content to assume the roles expected of his Duchess. There was no licence for individuality in that role. It wasn't as if he had any love for her that might bridge the gaps between them. She was not fool enough to imagine there was any parallel between the emotions he evoked in her and the attraction he admitted to feeling for her. She would have to come to terms with the gaps between them. Somehow.

But even though it was folly and she might come to regret it with as much force as the passion that urged her forward, she wanted this…she wanted *him* with an intensity she had not known was possible. To walk away would be an even greater madness than to proceed, almost a crime against herself. Something that burned inside her, that set her apart from her family with their rural, predictable lives, was finding an echo in this great unrelenting city and this inexplicable man whose fate had become tangled with hers against his will. She pressed her hands to her cheeks again, torn between anxiety and bubbling excitement as the realisation was beginning to sink in that everything would be different now. Nothing would ever be the same again.

Chapter Ten

Max walked into the upstairs drawing room and tossed his gloves on a table. Hetty looked up from the book she was reading.

'I thought you were going to Jackson's?'

'I was, but we came across Miss Trevelyan in the gardens. Wivenhoe was there. He was waiting for her.'

She straightened, her eyes searching his face.

'Wivenhoe! Waiting for her? What on earth is he doing?'

'It doesn't matter. What matters is that I am engaged.'

'Engaged! To whom?'

Max walked over to the window. The gardens were full now as nannies took advantage of the warm weather to air their charges. It was incomprehensible that they had managed to play out that completely melodramatic scene in such a prosaic setting. Now that he had left the Huntley madhouse the remnants of the desire she dragged out of him were as much a taunt as a pleasure and he felt frustrated and contemptible that he had lost control on more levels that afternoon than he had in almost a decade. And as a result he had changed the course of his life on the strength of a whim. That was what this whole thing amounted to. What did he really know about Sophie? About her family? He turned away from the vista of trees and shrubberies and faced his sister.

'To So…to Miss Trevelyan.'

Her eyes widened.

'Max! Are you serious? That's wonderful!'

Max frowned at her unbridled enthusiasm.

'Is it? I would have thought you would be offended I didn't choose someone from your list.'

'Oh, stuff! I like her. She's different.'

Max gave a short laugh.

'That sums it up nicely.'

Hetty looked at him and put aside her book.

'Come sit down and tell me what happened,' she invited.

Max remained standing, but gave her an expurgated version of the events in the park and an even briefer account of his discussion with Sophie. He just hoped she wouldn't question him too deeply about why he had felt it necessary to tell Wivenhoe Sophie was engaged to him. No one in his family other than his parents knew what had really happened with Serena and he preferred to keep it that way.

'Why do you and Wivenhoe hate each other so?' Hetty asked when he finished his story. 'Does it have to do with Serena? I was sixteen and it was all hushed up, but we knew something terrible had happened and I overheard Mama and Papa say something about Wivenhoe later.'

'That is not what is at issue at the moment.'

'I see,' Hetty said carefully, clearly still curious. 'Well, I know this isn't what you planned, but I must say I'm glad. The more I think about it, the less I think Lady Melissa will do for you.'

'And that madcap will?'

Hetty frowned at the bite of frustrated anger he could not keep out of his voice. He breathed in, calming himself. It was done. There were other things to think about now than this incomprehensible disconnect between his body and his mind.

'It's damnable that I have to go to Southampton just now, but it can't be put off. I'll be back in three days at the most. Everyone will just have to stew for a few days until I publish the formal announcement. Meanwhile, I know you have to go back to Somerset by next week, but I need your help before you do, Hetty.'

'Of course, Max. Shopping and things?'

He nodded. 'And things. Once the announcement is out the sooner we introduce her to people the better.'

'Of course. We should start by introducing her at the Seftons' ball—'

'That's in four days' time!' he interrupted.

'Precisely. We shall take the warehouses and modistes by storm and I can guarantee she will look completely fashionable once we are done.'

'Can you do the same with her manners?'

He could have kicked himself as Hetty's smile was erased and her soft grey eyes hardened, making her look more like their mother.

'I will make allowances for your vexation at being pushed into an engagement that was not part of your well-thought-out plans, Max, but if the best you can do is insult her then I suggest you bite the bullet and call it off now. It would be better.'

He turned away from her.

'I would still have to marry someone.'

'If this is who you mean to be, then Lady Melissa *is* the perfect choice for you after all. When you make up your mind, let me know. I am going to my room.'

'For heaven's sake, Hetty, don't sulk.'

'I am not sulking. You are.'

This incontestable truth deflated his bubble of confusion and anger. He held out his hand.

'You're right. About Lady Melissa as well. I don't know if I could have done it. Maybe it's a blessing not knowing what I am getting myself into. Will you help?'

She grasped his hand.

'Of course I will, Max dear. And don't worry so, everything will be just fine.'

Max refrained from saying aloud just what he thought about this inane attempt at reassurance. He had no clear idea what he had let himself into, but somehow the words 'just fine' did not seem adequate to describe possible future scenarios of his life with Sophie.

Chapter Eleven

'Well! That was delightful!' Hetty announced merrily as Sophie sank wearily into one of the very comfortable dark blue velvet armchairs in the drawing room of Harcourt House. 'Shall I have Gaskell bring up some tea? Shopping always make me hungry.'

Sophie had no idea how Hetty managed to look so cheerful and full of energy. Over the past three days of being swept up in the whirlwind of shopping orchestrated by Hetty she felt as if she had walked from one end of Exmoor to the other. Which was rather close to the odyssey they had undergone. Sophie had not been in the least prepared for the campaign her future sister-in-law had led her on. For three days silk warehouses and milliners were interspersed with gems like a visit to a lovely little market specialising in ribbons and buttons, then there were gloves and sandals and dancing slippers for balls and a charming shop selling fans and reticules and all kinds of bric-a-brac. But the most wearying had been the long sittings at Madame Fanechal's where a small army of seamstresses had surrounded her while Hetty and Madame discussed necklines and waistlines and hues with all the seriousness of field marshals.

At first Sophie tried to protest the expense and then guiltily tried to keep track of the cost of their acquisitions, but Hetty had cleverly countered Sophie's protests with the argument that the money spent was of more use to the shopkeepers and seamstresses than to the coffers of the bank where it sat. And just when Sophie had begun to hope that it was over, Hetty and Madame whisked her into a discreet backroom where she was ordered to strip behind a screen while a very sour-faced old woman brought her an array of the most amazing silk and satin and lace petticoats and nightgowns and robes that seemed far too fragile to even try on, but which Hetty had insisted were an absolute necessity for a bride-to-be.

It was only at this point that the reality of what was happening began to sink in. That if everything Hetty had forced upon her until that point were to make sure she made Max proud in public, here were items that only he would see. That there would come a moment when she would have to stand in front of him dressed in these transparent, floating gowns that were almost more indecent than sheer nudity because of the coy pretension to conceal while leaving very little to the imagination.

Looking at her body in the long mirror in the gently lit room, Sophie had remembered what she had told Max that day at the exhibition. That there was no reason for women to be embarrassed by female nude paintings because it was something they saw every time they undressed and had a decent mirror nearby, but standing in these seductive shifts and with the realisation that Max would see her like this, she felt thoroughly embarrassed and inadequate and as close to terrified as she had been in her life. There was no possible way someone as thoroughly unremarkable as herself might appeal to him, beautiful nightclothes or not. And she wanted to appeal to him in a way that was utterly foreign to her. She had turned, raising her arms and watching as the diaphanous silk floated about her before sinking back, clinging to her like liquid poured over her flesh. His hands would be touching this silk, her skin through it, pulling it off her...

The heat had rushed upwards through her even before she saw the flush stain her cheeks and she had turned away from her image, trying to steady her breathing. She had never known she was so wanton. How was it possible that she had lived twenty-four years without realising her body had a...a life of its own? That it wasn't just a vessel to serve her, but part of what she demanded from life? She felt Max had cast some fairy-tale curse on her, like those princesses forced to dance the night away against their will, enthralled and appalled as body ruled will. No, not will, just what everyone tried to convince her should be her will.

Her body was still tingling when they sat down in the drawing room in Max's house. It was decorated in a strict classical style, its symphony of blues and silver-grey a sharp a contrast to Aunt Minnie's red, green and gold cacophony. Despite the comfort of the armchairs it thoroughly reflected Max's character—tasteful, uncluttered, austere and blatantly wealthy. Sophie thought it looked beautiful, but she felt utterly out of place. All the more so because the room seemed designed as the perfect backdrop for the likes of a Lady Melissa.

She wished Max would return, but she dreaded the moment. The memory of the way he had kissed her in Aunt Minnie's parlour followed her about more closely than her shadow, feeding her yearning and her fear and making it hard for her to fall asleep in her little room. There it seemed to swell and fill the narrow, stuffy space and she would stare into the dark, occasionally squeezing her eyes shut tightly. She needed him to come back so she could escape herself and this conviction that she was being unbearably and foolishly selfish and that she would pay for her greed like one of her father's sermons that she had always secretly scoffed at.

The worst was when she tried to think what might be going through Max's mind during those hours. Whether he, too, was kept awake, only with regret at the rash move he had made. But then the thought of him in a bed, in the dark, brought with it images of slipping between those sheets, seeking the heat of the hard body she had felt beneath her hands, and she would turn over with a groan and shove her face into her lumpy pillow and beg her brain to let her sleep. Something in her had awakened that she had never even guessed existed and it was rapidly taking her over.

The door opened and she straightened, between hope and dismay at the thought that it might be Max. But it was just Gaskell, the butler, who placed the tea tray in front of Hetty.

'Max is always off on some business,' Hetty explained as she poured. 'In that sense he is just as industrious as Papa. Not that Papa would have deigned to go to places like Southampton or the City himself, he was far too proud, but he was never indolent like some gentlemen. It was all about responsibility with him. He was very disappointed he had so many daughters and only one son. As if it was a personal failure. Poor Mama was, too. I think I was the crowning disappointment because after me there was some complication and she could not have any more children which meant there was no chance of another boy. They never said anything, they were much too proper, but we knew. It put a lot of pressure on Max, as you may imagine. Especially since my eldest uncle, who is Max's heir, is quite as shatter-brained as Papa was scrupulous.'

Sophie drank her tea and absorbed Hetty's words. This was not the first time Hetty had fed her little titbits about their life at Harcourt and Max's many responsibilities. It was very clear this wasn't just idle talk. Hetty was preparing her for her new role and to do her credit she was doing it in a very palatable manner.

'Do they get along? Max and his uncle?'

'Oh, goodness, yes. Mortimer is a dear and so is his son, Cousin Barnaby. But neither of them is very dependable except when it comes to horticulture. Max is closer to my other uncle, Charles. I told you about him, didn't I? The painter. He was as much a father to us as Papa ever was and when he wasn't off somewhere in the world or in London, he would be with us at the Hall. I think you will like him. He will certainly like you. He was very much against the idea of Max—' She broke off with a little cough and reached forward to choose a biscuit. 'Well, never mind all that family nonsense. Or, rather, tell me if you have had any news from yours yet?'

Sophie hesitated, wondering what Hetty had been about to say, but there seemed no polite way to ask. She nodded.

'I received a letter from home this morning. It took a little deciphering since not only Papa and Mama, but also two of my sisters and one of my brothers, insisted on adding their opinions, crossing each other's lines like a horde of stampeding ants. Cautious approval on my father's part was mixed with a concern that this development, as he put it, was related to the excessive liveliness he has warned me against and if that was the case then he hoped I would not see this as a sign that such behaviour was being rewarded. My mother was delighted to discover that there were at least some offers I was not too fastidious to discourage and if she had known I was holding out for a duke she would not have bothered introducing me to all the perfectly eligible young men she had gone out of her way to find for me in north Devon, and that if I wished she would come help me choose my bridals, but that it would have to wait until after the Ashton Cove Women's League meeting because if she is not there, Mrs Stinchcombe is sure to rule the roost. I won't bother sharing my sister Augusta's advice on entering matrimony, because it is thoroughly depressing. Mary's suggestion was that letting men think they have won an argument is her best advice for a happy marriage, which is useful, I suppose. George, who is one of my favourite siblings, had the most positive contribution. He informed me that he has heard of

Max and that he is a bang-up whip and as handy with his fives as anyone who frequents Jackson's saloon and he was glad I wasn't going to marry some namby-pamby dandy, but that he was most proud of me for beating Cousin Arthur's record and winning his bet for him and that Arthur and Aunt Seraphina were as blue as a megrim about the whole thing. His last line was that he wanted me to ask Max something about a prize fight that was to take place in a few weeks. And then he ran out of paper.'

Hetty had fallen into a fit of giggles halfway through Sophie's account and Sophie, who had not felt very amused while reading the letter, started laughing as well. Somehow talking to Hetty was putting everything into proportion.

'Oh, dear,' Hetty gasped. 'I'm so sorry...but it is so very absurd... And please forgive me, but your mama sounds just like mine...'

'That's a frightening thought,' Max said from the doorway, surveying them as he entered the drawing room. 'What is so amusing?'

Sophie felt the familiar inner expanding heat that always accompanied his appearance. It reminded her of the mirror opposite of that moment of slipping into the cold waters of the bay—a first slap of physical shock and then the body adapted to the cold water and the tension eased, but never completely.

'Max! Welcome back!' Hetty exclaimed, holding out her hands and Max walked over to her with a smile and bent to kiss her cheek lightly. Sophie put down her teacup carefully.

'Sophie was telling me about the letter she received from her family.' Hetty explained as Max turned towards Sophie. She had forgotten how blank his expression could be. There was no hint in that distant, hooded scrutiny where his thoughts had taken him these past three days. But there was also something unnervingly intimate in the steadiness of his gaze as she approached her and it did nothing to calm the flickering heat that had remained on a low burn since trying on the night-shifts and petticoats at Madame Fanechal's. She could still feel the slide of the silk against her skin and she hoped he attributed her flush to their laughter.

'Hello, Sophie.' He stopped in front of her and she held out her hand automatically and he took it. Even through her gloves she felt its strength and heat, and everything, her confusion and fear and yearning, became edged and present, like a physical threat. His hand tightened slightly as she remained silent and she forced herself to respond.

'Hello, Your... Max. Did you have a good trip?' she asked, feeling infinitely foolish, and even more so as a faint smile touched his mouth.

'Yes, thank you. So, what was so amusing about this letter?' he asked as he turned away and sat down on the sofa, draping his arm over the back. Sophie wished she had chosen to sit on the sofa instead of the armchair. She wondered what they would think if she stood up and went to sit beside him. Lady Melissa certainly wouldn't do anything so obvious and undignified.

'Sophie?' he prompted and she straightened.

'I'm not sure amusing is quite the right word. It was just that they were more occupied with other matters, though my brother is very interested in your knowledge about some upcoming prize fight and in the fact that Cousin Arthur and Aunt Seraphina are blue-devilled about my breaking their record.'

'So your coup with Mad Minnie is more exciting than your upcoming marriage? That's not very encouraging.'

She shrugged and Hetty leaned forward to pour him some tea.

'Sophie's mother seems to regret you are not from north Devon, Max. It reminds me of what Mama said when she heard I wanted to accept Ned's offer. Remember?'

Amusement softened Max's expression.

'But he's only a baronet, dear. And from some wild place up north. Must you really?' he mimicked and Hetty burst into giggles again and Sophie smiled, ignoring the little spurt of jealousy at the easy affection between Max and his sister. The truth was she liked him even more when she saw them together. Something about Hetty's presence softened that hard shell that made her so wary and gave her hope that perhaps with time she could reach that place herself.

He turned to Sophie.

'Hetty's husband Ned is from Somerset, but my parents tended to think the world suffers a severe decline in intelligence once one leaves the South Devon coast and only picks up again in the safety of London.

Sophie smiled.

'I think in my mother's case it is pique rather than prejudice, since she is convinced she personally had a hand in all my elder sibling's marriages. She likes managing things.'

'I'm afraid to ask what your father wrote.'

Sophie tried very hard to keep her mouth prim.

'I'm afraid he is likely to be suspicious of anyone who contemplates marriage with me. Still, he says your father was known to be a very worthy man and that he has heard no ill of you.'

'Fulsome! How will I live up to that? And your siblings? Are they similarly flowery?'

'Mary says I am to let you win arguments.'

'I applaud her advice, but I think Mary clearly doesn't know you very well. Or perhaps she does, which is why she is giving you this advice. Does it get better?'

'Indeed it does. Augusta warns me to keep my expectations low and promises to send me a volume of sermons she finds very improving for brides-to-be.'

'So it *does* get better. You should probably skip the sermons. Was that the lot? Remind me, how many siblings do you have?'

'Eight. But most know better than to add to a letter Papa will likely read before it is sent. Except George because he doesn't care. He is most interested in your knowledge of prize fights and winning his bet with Cousin Arthur. That was it.'

'And how is your aunt adjusting? She assured

me you could stay with her until we went to Harcourt, but from the brief exchange we had when I spoke to her three days ago I wasn't quite certain if she approved either.'

'So I gathered, but that was because she admitted she had been contemplating asking me to stay on with her as a companion to Marmaduke. Still, she cheered up when she realised that I would be living next door at least part of the year and so I could continue to take Marmaduke for walks.'

'Generosity does run in your family, doesn't it? I suppose you didn't point out to her you would have other concerns once you were married?'

'No. I said thank you nicely and took Marmaduke for a walk.'

Hetty chuckled and stood up, giving her skirts a little shake.

'I think I will go and have a little rest now. I am quite pleasantly exhausted from all that shopping. Max, could you please see Sophie back to her aunt's when you are done with tea?'

She came over and gave Sophie a quick hug.

'I had a lovely time, today, my dear. I will come by tomorrow evening then to take you to the Seftons'. Madame Fanechal promised she will have the first gown delivered by the afternoon.'

Sophie resisted the urge to beg her not to leave her alone with Max. She had missed him so much she was certain she would do something foolish and confirm all his suspicions about her unsuitability to be the future Duchess of Harcourt. Instead she returned the hug and thanked her. There was a moment of silence as the door closed behind Hetty and Sophie forced herself to turn to face Max. He was watching her and she wished she knew what he was thinking.

'Are you upset? About the letter?' he asked abruptly.

'Upset? Why?'

'Usually parents are rather more excited than yours appear to be about one of their children getting married.'

'You can add especially when they have come close to despairing over ever getting rid of that child. Mama told me only a few months ago I had better not discourage my next offer because she and Papa were hopeful that when my two younger sisters married they would be able to move into the smaller rectory. It is less draughty than our current home.'

'Then I am surprised they didn't applaud your filial duty more enthusiastically. Have you turned down many offers, then?' he asked politely and she held her mouth as primly as possible.

'It would be most indelicate for a gently reared young woman to discuss such matters, Your Grace.'

'Is that an evasive way of saying "none"?'

She knew full well he was baiting her and wished she could make more of her meagre court-ships, but honesty overcame pride.

'Well, "turned down" might be stretching the truth. More precisely Mama said she has never seen anyone with my skill for discouraging per-fectly eligible young men from actually propos-ing.'

'Did she? I think Hetty is right, your mother does sound like mine. Not a very motherly thing to say. May I ask if you wanted to marry any of those perfectly eligible young men?'

'Not at all. But she was right; it was my fault each time. It is only fair that you know that.'

He shifted slightly on the sofa.

'That is very honest. May I ask how precisely how you discouraged them?'

'Well, there was the bad kisser who I stayed away from after that. And there was Robert, who saw me swimming with George, my brother, in the next bay and he, or rather his mama, was rather shocked. And then there was Gerry. He made fun of Will Trevithick who is a little clumsy and I might have been just a bit a too disapproving. And of course Bertie. He told me he expected I wouldn't continue to dabble with painting after we wed.'

She had been right, somehow his eyes managed to fill with laughter without him moving a facial muscle. She had expected to shock and disgust him, not amuse him. The warmth in his eyes made him look much more human and some of her tension faded.

'I'm afraid to ask what your response was to that expectation,' he said.

'Well, I was quite young at the time so I hadn't yet learned to curb my tongue. I think I said something along the lines that I expected he would continue to be a poltroon after *he* wed, but that luckily it wouldn't be to me. Unfortunately both his mama and mine were listening at the keyhole from the next room. I was sent for a month to my cousins in Cornwall as punishment. Unfortunately for Mama I had a lovely time there. Though for Mama and Papa's sake I did try to be a little less blunt after that.'

'I see. So, five kisses and several almost offers. Anything else I should know?'

She shook her head, resisting the urge to turn the question back on him. Even if he was willing to share anything of his amorous history with her, she preferred not to know too much. Her imagination and Wivenhoe's gossip provided sufficient material.

He stood up and moved towards her and the heat licked at her insides.

'I am glad at least one of your family approves of me, even if it is only for my knowledge about prize fights.'

'And horses,' she murmured, tilting her head back as he drew her to her feet and then reached out, tracing the side of her throat.

'I have other skills, you know,' he said.

She nodded, focused on the soft slide of his fingers on her skin, holding herself still against the need to move towards him. His fingers drew a line along her collarbone to the edge of her gown and stopped.

'I should see you home,' he continued, his voice gentle and almost impersonal.

'Already?' she asked before she could stop herself and his fingers trailed downwards along the neckline until they reached the dip between her breasts and stopped again.

'Probably. You really shouldn't be alone here with me.'

'Why? What might happen?' her voice barely formed the words, everything in her focused on the soft press of his fingers.

'This,' he said softly as his fingers gently moved up, easing the shoulder of her gown from her shoulder. A hot tingling radiated out from his touch, tightening her skin, waking it up. She could feel places she rarely felt, the arch of her lower back, the inside of her thighs. Every part of her was stirring, asking to be touched. She closed her eyes so nothing could interfere with these amazing sensations. The pull of the fabric over her skin as he eased the shoulder of her dress down an inch became a thudding ache deep inside her and without thinking she moved towards him, sliding her hands up over his chest. Her hands had never felt so powerful. She could feel everything, she could almost see with them through the crisp cotton of his shirt to the heat of his skin, the hard muscles beneath. When he clasped her wrists she still tried to pull away, but he held them firmly and took a step back.

'That's enough for now.'

The amused tolerance in his voice struck her like a slap and heat transformed into a flush of shame. Frustration quivered through her at the unfairness of being taken like this to the brink of something unknown and powerful and then set aside like a mindless doll. She turned and headed towards the door.

'I should go.'

He nodded and walked to open the door for her, following her out. They didn't speak until they had reached her aunt's house and Lambeth opened the door. Max hesitated and then stood back.

'The announcement will appear in the papers tomorrow and Hetty and I will be by in the evening to take you to the Seftons.'

'Very well, Your Grace,' she replied properly and went inside, proud of the veneer of calm she was learning to draw over the roiling feelings he evoked in her. Soon she would be as proper as any of those London misses who had vied for his attention.

Max closed the door to his study and went to sit down at his desk. Even in three days a lot of business had accumulated and once the engagement was announced there would be a hundred distractions he would have to deal with. He had better get to work right away. He picked up the first piece of correspondence that his secretary had left for his attention and laid it before him, smoothing it out.

It didn't help that he was developing a very bad habit of letting his mind wander. And at the most inappropriate moments. Another negative impact of this engagement. The owner of the shipping company he had gone to finalise an agreement with had had to recall his attention twice during their meetings. Max cringed in remembered embarrassment at these lapses. That kind of behaviour was unforgivable. It was natural to feel apprehensive about the move he was about to make; he could deal with that. But it was harder to excuse his mind's newfound tendency to revisit his encounters with Sophie, playing them out with disconcerting vividness.

On the way back to London, he had told himself he was going to handle the situation differently from now on. Establish some distance until the wedding and focus on helping Sophie fit into his world as smoothly as possible. And he had almost failed in that resolve within the first half-hour of his return. He had had enough strength of mind not to follow through on her seductively innocent invitation, but not enough to keep his hands off her in the first place. And the fact that the need to touch her had been plaguing him from the moment he had walked out of her aunt's parlour three days ago was no excuse. It was just that she had looked so vulnerable, trying to shrug off her disappointment at her family's response to the news.

He felt a flash of resentment that they so obviously took her for granted. It was amazing that she was so full of empathy when she seemed to receive so little from her family, but perhaps he was being unfair to them. He should reserve judgement and not let himself be swayed by this…protective urge. She would have to deal with a great deal in the next few weeks and months and her family's self-involvement was the least of it. He couldn't start leaping to her defence, mentally or otherwise, every time he detected that bruised look she tried to mask with a smile. Fundamentally she was a strong, intelligent girl and she would cope.

At least he hoped she could. She could certainly assume an air of dignity when it suited her, but he doubted it would ever completely overcome the impulsive, passionate force that drove her, or her peculiar, humorous approach to the world. That much had been obvious in her deceptively light retelling of her failed courtships. He might find it amusing now, but weren't these precisely the kind of characteristics that had led to such disastrous results with Serena? Impulsiveness, inability to conform, a sensuality that she clearly had very little ability or will to restrain...

There were differences as well, of course. He couldn't imagine Serena talking with a dog or protecting a clumsy boy, or caring one iota about anyone but herself and her needs, but the problematic behaviours weren't that dissimilar. Not that he had any choice in the matter any more, but he could still do his best to help Sophie adapt her behaviour to her new station in life. And that meant he shouldn't encourage her by giving in to temptation every time she...

He frowned at the letter and put it down with a curse. This was pointless. He was always tense when he returned from a business trip. He should go expend some energy at Jackson's and then he might be in better shape to get some work done.

Chapter Twelve

'Lady Sefton will be nice, so you needn't worry about her. And Countess Lieven will be cutting, so you needn't worry about her either except to be as meek as possible until she moves on to other prey. We will do our best to avoid Mrs Drummond Burrell until we absolutely cannot and as for Lady Jersey she is very fond of Max, but she is out of town so we unfortunately can't count on her tonight...'

Max watched the interplay of amusement and dismay on Sophie's face as Hetty laid before her the social structure of the London *ton* that she was about to face. He wished there was some way they could circumvent this trial by fire. Under normal circumstances a young woman from the countryside could expect to be mostly ignored by the leading lights of London society unless she possessed fabulous wealth or beauty. But with the announcement of their engagement having appeared in the morning papers she was going to be anything but ignored. There was no way he and Hetty could completely shield her from the curiosity and even the malice that was awaiting her. He hoped that the inner strength she seemed to possess would help her weather this better than most women might.

She didn't look overly nervous, aside from the fact that she was avoiding looking at him. But in light of the fantasies that his mind and body were constructing around the sight of her in that very seductive gown he was half-glad he didn't have to meet her expressive eyes. It was his fault for having indulged his need to touch her. Adding reality to the fantasy was fanning his desire and he was having a hard time reminding himself he did not yet have the right to explore these urges. Like the urge to peel off that very fashionable dress which was too low cut for his peace of mind. Surely she had never worn something like that in Ashton Cove.

'Is that a new gown?'

Sophie and Hetty turned at the abrupt question.

'Yes,' Sophie answered a bit stiffly. 'It arrived today.'

'It's lovely, isn't it?' Hetty said. 'I was a bit worried about the colour, but Madame Fanechal was absolutely right that Sophie can carry off that combination of blush and old gold. And she was right, wasn't she, Max?'

Max nodded. The colours did suit her beautifully, but that wasn't what concerned him. It was the deep sweep of the bodice which dragged back the memory of his fingers tracing that line, the heat of her skin...the thought of Bryanston, of anyone, thinking anything close to what he was thinking now...

'It's a bit low cut, though,' he said curtly.

'Oh, pooh! Nonsense. Sophie isn't some silly schoolroom miss to dress in white with round necklines and silly frills. This is the latest Paris design. I think you look lovely, Sophie.' Hetty shot him a frowning look and he could have kicked himself for his stupidity as he saw how Sophie's mouth tightened at his words. He was making it harder for her for no reason whatsoever. Or for the worst reasons.

'That's the problem,' he said, trying for humour. 'I was hoping for a quiet evening and an early night, now it is clear there is no chance of that. We are going to be besieged.'

Hetty's frown relaxed, but Max was focused on Sophie and though she didn't speak or meet his eyes, he could see the flush spread across her cheekbones. It should have relaxed him, but it just pushed the possessive heat up another notch. His mood wasn't helped by the fact that they arrived at the same time as Bryanston who hailed them cheerfully and bowed very deeply over Sophie's hand. The look on his face as his eyes scanned Sophie from head to toe was unmistakable.

'What did that Byron fellow write? She walks in beauty like the night, though these certainly aren't cloudless climes. You know, Max, if you weren't a friend of mine and more importantly a devilish good shot, I'd call you out. It's dashed unfair that you snatched up such a lovely lady before anyone had a chance to try their luck with her.'

'I'm happy to oblige, Bry. At least something might finally stop that loose tongue of yours.'

'I said "if". You know I'm never awake before noon and who heard of a midday duel?' He turned back to Sophie. 'May I dance with you, oh, vision?'

'Here?' Sophie asked, her eyes glinting with

mirth as she looked around at the press of people making their way up the wide stairs to the ballroom.

'Here, anywhere. I could dance with you on the head of a pin for surely you must be an angel come to earth.'

'For heaven's sake, Bry,' Max said, between disgust and amusement.

'You may have the cotillion and a country dance, Lord Bryanston,' Hetty ruled and Bryanston sighed.

'My kingdom for a waltz?' he countered hopefully.

'You haven't got one. Unless your aunt expires,' Max said.

'Besides,' Hetty added more kindly, 'Miss Trevelyan cannot waltz until she has been approved by a patroness of Almack's. Which reminds me, we must procure a voucher for Almack's. Oh, dear, I wish I didn't have to go back to Somerset in two days. There is so much to be done! And don't look at me like that, Max, I know you loathe the place, but Sophie should make at least one appearance there before you go to Harcourt, for form's sake.'

'I'll escort you, Miss Trevelyan,' Lord Bryanston said with a malevolent grin towards Max.

Without thinking Max reached out and took Sophie's hand.

'Going with you is the only thing that might make it bearable.'

Bryanston chuckled. 'Max being gallant! What on earth will happen next?'

'Keep moving, Bry. You're holding up the line.'

Since they had reached Lord and Lady Sefton at the head of the receiving line they were taken over by Lady Sefton's very friendly greetings and congratulations. Despite his annoyance with his friend's flirtatious nonsense, Max was glad Bryanston had attached himself to them. From the moment they entered the ballroom they unintentionally became the focal point of another receiving line as friends and acquaintances kept coming up to congratulate them on the engagement and to ferret out whatever information they could about his unknown intended. Most people were polite, but there was an avid and not always generous curiosity that buzzed around them and Max could tell Sophie was well aware of it. He and Hetty did their best to soften and counter some of the less subtle comments or questions, but as the introductions progressed he felt Sophie struggle to hold on to her society manner.

He was just about to call a halt to the introductions and lead her on to the dance floor when he saw Hetty stiffen and look at him with something approaching panic and he turned in time to see Lady Arkwright and her daughter heading in their direction, accompanied by the Dowager Lady Pennistone. He must have tightened his hold on Sophie's arm because she glanced up at him with a slight frown, but it was already too late.

'My dear Lady Swinburne!' Lady Arkwright exclaimed brightly. 'And Your Grace! Do please accept our heartfelt congratulations on your betrothal.'

Max gritted his teeth and made the introductions. Lady Melissa stood as cool and calm as ice, with the faintest of smiles as she surveyed Sophie from her superior height. By the colour that flooded Sophie's cheeks it was obvious she recognised the young woman's name and her murmured greeting and thanks were barely audible. It lasted no more than a moment before the Arkwrights moved on, making way for Lady Pennistone, looking alarmingly hawk-like, with her timid granddaughter in tow. The Dowager surveyed Sophie from head to toe and Sophie straightened, the colour ebbing from her cheeks and a distinctly martial look erasing the confusion of the previous moment, reminding Max of those rare moments when her temper had flared. He met Hetty's eyes. It was clearly time to call a halt to the introductions for the night.

'Minerva's great-niece, is she?' Lady Pennistone enquired of no one in particular, her tones anything but approving. 'Doesn't take after her, at least, but she can't hold a candle to Lady Melissa or that other one,' she added with a sniff.

'Grandmama!' her granddaughter said in a pained whisper.

'You are quite correct, Lady Pennistone,' Sophie answered before Max could think of anything to say. 'And yet here I am, enjoying the pleasure of being introduced to you. Wondrous are the ways of the Lord, don't you think?'

Bryanston gave a snort of quickly stifled laughter and Lady Pennistone huffed and marched off, her granddaughter glancing back apologetically at Sophie as she was dragged in her wake.

'I think that's enough introductions for the moment,' Max said, taking Sophie by the arm and leading her towards the dance floor.

'About time,' Bryanston announced as he followed them. 'Unspoken rule is that you have the first dance with your betrothed and if you don't do it soon, I'll never get my two dances, so go and dance, you two.'

'An excellent idea, Bry. Come, Sophie.'

'I'm sorry. I shouldn't have said that.' Sophie said as they took their places. 'I think it was just one too many, especially after... Are you angry?'

'Not at you. I'm sorry you had to be put through that. Not just that harridan, but some of the other as well.' He shied away from mentioning Lady Melissa. Some things were better just ignored.

'You needn't be, it is hardly your fault that some people believe being well born gives them the right to be shockingly vulgar and impertinent. In that sense London is no different from what I am used to. I am usually less sensitive to such non-sense. Maybe it is because I am used to being on my home ground and...well, whatever. I will be better prepared next time.'

She sounded so determined he smiled.

'Hopefully that was the worst of it. And after this dance I'm going to take Hetty's advice and ask Sally to let you dance the waltz. I'm damned if I will be forced to dance nothing but country dances and quadrilles while we are in town. Do you waltz?'

'I do indeed. Papa disapproves, but Mama and the other ladies of the Lynmouth Society which manages the Assembly Rooms will have no one say we are behind the times. They are very proud of their progressive views. There are even card parties!'

Max smiled at her tone. 'Armageddon looms! So your mother defies the vicar? That's not the image you painted.'

'It's not defiance because Papa knows better than to argue with Mama on social matters. There she reigns supreme. Or rather she and Mrs Stinchcombe and Lady Margaret, the squire's wife. Papa merely says he hopes the increasing laxity of morals in Ashton Cove will not lead us all to regret we were not more forward in our efforts to instil caution and proper mores in today's youth, but that he will defer to her judgement in the hope that her principles counsel her correctly.'

'Good lord, he doesn't really talk like that, does he?'

'That is an expurgated version. He was master of debate at Oriel, but I think he only used to win because he talked everyone else to a standstill. You think it's funny now, but only wait until you meet him!' she scolded as Max burst out laughing, but her eyes were sparkling and he could even feel how the tension had vanished from her hand as the dance progressed.

They were separated for a moment by the dance and when she came towards him again he felt a peculiar surge of pride in how well she was taking this rather outrageous situation. When the dance ended he guided her towards a relatively quiet corner, handing her a glass of iced champagne from a tray held by a liveried footman.

'Now that I think of it,' she said, tilting her head to one side, 'those introductions really weren't so bad, under the circumstances. I expected it to be much worse. But I think people are a little scared of you.'

'Scared? Nonsense.'

'Well, wary, then. Even when they spoke with me they were watching you out of the corner of their eye the way people do around a dog who is currently calm, but which they know might bite. Definitely wary.'

'I'm not sure what to think about being likened to a canine. A capricious one at that. Hetty will tell you I am boringly predictable.'

'Are you?'

She looked up at him with clear curiosity, as if

trying to reconcile what he said with some other, private, thought, and for a moment he had the strange sensation of losing track of himself. As if answering her called into question his ability to judge.

'Yes. I am,' he stated and her curious look was overtaken by the return of amusement.

'You know best,' she assented, clasping her hands in front of her.

'Do you know you are a very poor liar?'

'I know…it is very sad.'

'Not at all. You father should be happy about that at least.'

'I think he would be happy if I didn't try at all, not that I don't succeed. That quite a different thing, you see.'

Once again his amusement overcame some inner barrier of reluctance.

'I think you are more like your father than you might like to admit. You would do very well in a debate yourself.'

Her eyes widened in surprise.

'Oh, no, what a thought! I assure you I am not in the least like Papa!'

'Of course. You know best,' he countered meekly and she burst out laughing, but before she could answer Bryanston strode up to them, followed by Cranworth and a very pretty petite brunette with large dark eyes.

'Here you are! I say, it's dashed unchivalrous of you, Max! They are halfway through what was supposed to be my dance. Cranworth, you'll be my second if I call Max out, won't you?'

'You know, some day someone will take you up on the offer of a duel, Bry,' Cranworth said. 'Good evening, Miss Trevelyan. Allow me to introduce my wife, Lady Cranworth.'

Sophie smiled back at the brunette, who came forward impetuously and clasped her hands in hers.

'I'm so happy to meet you! What a lovely gown! It is absolutely Parisian and I am quite, quite envious. Do come with me and I will make you known to some particular friends of mine...'

Without waiting for agreement she pulled Sophie in her wake.

'Here! That was my dance!' Bryanston called after them, but they were already lost in the crowd.

'Don't worry, Max, you know Sylvie, she'll take good care of her.' Cranworth smiled.

'But what about my dance?' Bryanston objected, outraged. 'This is a conspiracy!'

'Go ask Miss Pennistone, she was eyeing you back there,' Max suggested.

'Good lord, no, her grandmama will have my head on a platter. Next to your Sophie's. I don't think anyone has ever given her such a set down in years. Good for the gal. I'll go find Hetty instead. At least she won't have to worry about her wanting me to marry her for the price of a dance.'

Max shook his head as Bryanston wandered off.

'Remind me why we put up with that conceited pinkest of pinks of the *ton*, Max?' Cranworth asked languidly and Max smiled absently, wondering if he should go and see how Sophie was faring.

'Because he's a good friend and would do anything for you as long as it didn't involve waking up too early.'

'True. Stop looking for Your Sophie, as Bry calls her. I have a feeling she can take care of herself, country miss or no. I've never seen you this anxious, not even when we ended up behind the French lines outside Toulouse. Between that and actually looking as if you were enjoying that country dance, you're doing damage to your dour Duke image, you know.'

'My what?'

Cranworth grinned. 'That's better. Now come and help me talk Meecham into selling me his long-tailed bays. Graham is after them as well, but Meech is a little scared of you and I could use the added pressure. You can go soft again once we're done.'

'You're as bad as Bry sometimes, Rob.'

'That's right, hold that frown and we'll be done before you know it.'

Max sighed, but followed Cranworth towards the card room. Cranworth was right—at least that it was ludicrous to be standing there waiting for Sophie to show up again like an anxious chaperon or a jealous lover. It was even more ridiculous that he felt like that. He told himself it was only be-cause she was out of her element. If it had been Lady Melissa he probably wouldn't have spared a thought about her welfare in such a setting. But he knew he could trust Sylvie Cranworth to take good care of her. Cranworth was just finalising his transaction when Sylvie and Sophie entered the room and Max scanned her face. She looked relaxed and happy and Max felt slightly foolish at how much tension left his body.

'Are you all right?' he asked under cover of the noise around them.

'Surprisingly, yes. Lady Cranworth has been very nice. I like your friends. You are very lucky.'

'I suppose I am. Though I could happily strangle Bry sometimes.'

'Oh, no. He's adorable.'

'You sound like you are talking about Marmaduke. Just as long as you don't take his flirting seriously.'

'He's not flirting and so there is nothing to take seriously. He is merely being kind in his way and it is clear it is out of affection for you, not out of any interest in me. He's a good person.'

Max took her arm, leading her slightly further away from the rumble of people, aware he was simply seeking an excuse to touch her.

'Is this a habit of yours? To see the good in whomever you meet?'

'Most certainly it isn't,' she replied primly. 'There aren't that many people I really like, but those I do, I do.'

'Summarily put. And you like Bry.'

'And Hetty, and Sylvie, and Cranworth, I suppose, and you. That's not such a very long list. Well, there are others back in Ashton Cove as well.'

He didn't know whether to be flattered or offended to be tacked on to a list.

'And Marmaduke,' he pointed out and she smiled up at him and he wished he could pull her into one of the embrasures that lined the ballroom and pull down the velvet curtains on all this noise and nonsense and sink in to her. He turned her so that she stood half in the shadow of a pillar while he blocked out the view of the rest of the room, creating an illusion of separateness.

'There is a scale of preferences, though. I like you better than Marmaduke, for example,' she said, her voice husky, inviting. The urge to touch her overcame prudence and he reached out and brushed his fingers over her lips. They parted, her indrawn breath cool against his skin.

'I'm glad I rank higher than a pug.'

'Just don't tell him. He's sensitive,' she murmured, her eyes softening. He was beginning to recognise her expressions, and this one, languid, halfway to surrender, was devastating. His pulse surged ahead, setting a painful rhythm that wouldn't relent until he made her match it. He almost reached out to pull her to him, but he leaned his hand on the wall beside her instead, drawing on the calming influence of its cool surface.

'I won't boast. Come, we should get back to the others before we are discovered in the corner.'

'We aren't doing anything wrong, though,' she pointed out wistfully.

'If we don't leave now, we will be. And, no, that is not an invitation,' he added as her eyes widened hopefully and she laughed and let him lead her back towards the main ballroom.

'Very well. Besides, they are striking up the quadrille and I don't want to be uncivil to Lord Bryanston.'

Max watched as Bry headed towards them purposefully and resisted the urge to tighten his hold on her arm. He had to remember his resolution to lead this relationship at his pace, not hers. In a few weeks he would have every right in the world to do something about this grating desire and he was perfectly capable of keeping his hands to himself until then. It was the laughter in her eyes that was worst. He couldn't remember the last time humour had been part of his relationships, at least not with women, and he certainly had never realised its aphrodisiac qualities. Perhaps Cranworth was right, Serena and the war had fixed him into his…what had Cranworth called it…? His dour Duke image. And Sophie's laughter was having the same lightening effect on him as the sight of the sea near Harcourt, the same call to throw off shackles, clothes, everything, and cast himself into its freedom. But it was deceptive, this freedom, because eventually he would have to return to his reality. He had to remember that.

Chapter Thirteen

'I'm so dreadfully sorry about Grandmama's behaviour yesterday!'

Sophie looked into Miss Pennistone's anxious eyes. She hadn't been sure what to expect when the young woman had approached her as she was seated by Hetty on the sofa in Mrs Bannerman's drawing room. Hetty, with a quick glance at Sophie, stood up and went to join their hostess across the room, while Miss Pennistone, after a moment's hesitation, sat down beside her and blurted out her apology.

'Please don't,' Sophie said impulsively. 'I'm afraid I was a bit nervous or I wouldn't have answered as I did.'

'Oh, I'm glad you did,' Miss Pennistone answered, surprising Sophie. 'No one ever naysays her. I wish I dared.'

'Well, I certainly don't intend to be quite so blunt again. It might feel good at the moment, but it has been sitting on my conscience since.'

Miss Pennistone giggled.

'You are very droll. And I love your dress. I wish Grandmama would let me wear something so dashing. After all I *am* turned twenty, you know. Perhaps I might take better if I could wear something other than these plain round frocks.'

'I think you look very pretty in them, but I must admit it is very enjoyable to wear these lovely dresses. I am not at all used to them either, but they do make me feel quite dashing.'

'Well, I think you *are* dashing. Oh, dear, here comes Grandmama which means we must go now. I do hope we can speak again.'

She stood up and hurried over to the beckoning matron and Sophie smiled at the absurdity and being taken for an authority on anything fashionable. She scanned the room for Hetty just in time to see her step into the adjoining room with another fashionably dressed woman. Sophie sighed and resigned herself to some moments of social discomfort, trying to look unconcerned, when she suddenly saw Lady Melissa entering the room. Sophie, mentally beckoning Hetty back to the drawing room, tried to look fascinated by an advertisement for Denmark Lotion in the ladies' magazine spread out on the low table in front of her.

'May I?'

Sophie looked up in dismay to meet Lady Melissa's very cool blue eyes.

'May you what?'

'Join you.' Lady Melissa clarified sweetly.

Sophie indicated the sofa, fully aware of the subtle change in the tone of conversation in the room around them.

'Please do,' she said, hoping her smile looked natural.

Lady Melissa at down, arranging her skirts with unconscious ease. She looked so lovely and assured Sophie felt her confidence sag. She could think of no way to deny the aggrieved beauty this attack, for that was clearly what it was, but she had no intention of serving as a spineless scratching post. She had found that the best way to deal with situations where she was out of her depth was to adopt the persona of her supremely placid sister Mary. Somehow Mary never appeared to be upset by anything, not even when a whole tray of ices had landed in her lap while attending a dance at the Lynmouth Assembly Hall.

'So, Miss Trevelyan, are you enjoying London?'

'Very much, Lady Melissa,' Sophie replied. 'Such lovely weather we are having.'

Lady Melissa blinked at the inanity of her reply.

'Indeed. Well. It cannot be easy knowing how to conduct oneself when one is clearly unaccustomed to town life. I trust everyone is being kind?'

Sophie kept her face politely blank, thinking hard of Mary.

'Oh, most kind. It is so very good of you to be interested.'

Lady Melissa's smile did not waver, but Sophie could feel her annoyance heat up.

'Not at all. I believe I overheard Lady Swinburne say you are doing a portrait of her?'

Sophie straightened at the disdainful amusement in the question.

'So I am. You are more than welcome to come see it if you wish.'

This was a little too much for Lady Melissa and her eyes flashed for a moment before she had herself in hand again.

'Why, how kind of you. It is quite nice that you and Lady Swinburne deal well together. I believe my mama told me she was not very fond of Harcourt's previous fiancée, but that was a long time ago. Perhaps it was just a touch of jealousy. After all, Lady Serena was a legendary beauty. A diamond of the first water, Mama said. What a sad, sad tragedy.'

Sophie struggled to understand what Lady Melissa was saying. Amidst the confusion of thoughts and emotions she held firm to the image of Mary calmly removing the bowls of ice from her lap.

'Very sad,' she managed. 'Did you know her?'

'Dear me, no. I was still in the schoolroom. But Mama said she was quite the most beautiful and vivacious girl she had ever seen. It was to be the event of the Season, their marriage. And then she fell ill and died quite suddenly and mysteriously. Harcourt was clearly heartbroken for he joined up and went to serve with the Duke of Wellington in Spain. Quite a touching story, don't you think?'

It took every ounce of control Sophie possessed to keep her face blank throughout this little speech. Everything seemed to have slowed down, moved away from her. Even Lady Melissa's complacent vindictiveness was diminished to near insignificance next to this revelation. And under the shock and pain was a stab of anger that Max had not thought it right to tell her something so significant. That she had to find out like this, from this spiteful young woman who was obviously relishing her confusion and embarrassment. The silence stretched, but Sophie could find nothing to say and finally Lady Melissa stood up unhurriedly, her perfect rosebud mouth curving in a pleasant smile.

'Good day, Miss Trevelyan. Good luck.'

'Good day, Lady Melissa,' Sophie forced out.

When Hetty returned a moment later she didn't question Sophie's request that they return home.

Just as they pulled up in Grosvenor Square, Sophie turned to her.

'Hetty, I would like to speak with Max for a moment. There is something… Could you please ask him to call on me…when he can?'

The smile in Hetty's eyes dimmed. 'Is everything all right, Sophie?'

'Of course. There is just something I wish to ask him.'

Hetty reached over and placed her hand on Sophie's tightly clasped hands.

'I know it isn't easy just yet, but you will be

fine, believe me. Don't let anyone upset you. It just takes time.'

Sophie's eyes burned with misery.

'It's not that. But thank you. For everything, Hetty.'

'It is my pleasure. Oh, I wish I didn't have to return to Somerset tomorrow but I have been away quite too long already. Lady Cranworth said she will be delighted to act as my replacement chaperon for the next week until you leave for Harcourt and then of course we will join you there in a couple of weeks to prepare for the wedding and to let you meet my band of mischief makers.'

'I would love to meet them,' Sophie said truthfully, wishing she could beg Hetty to stay. 'Have a good trip home, Hetty. And thank you again for everything.'

'It has been my absolute pleasure. Really and truly. And I will tell Max to call on you as soon as he can.'

Sophie returned Hetty's warm embrace and let the footman hand her out of the carriage. For once the thought of seeing Max left her empty and cold.

Sophie looked up from book she had been trying to read. For a household unaccustomed to visitors, the servants were very prompt in answering the door and it was not more than a couple of minutes after the knocker sounded that she heard Lambeth welcome Max. She laid down her book and stood up, too nervous to remain seated.

'His Grace, the Duke of Harcourt,' Lambeth announced grandly as he opened the door.

'Thank you, Lambeth. You may show him in.'

Max entered, smiling faintly, but there was also a questioning look in his eyes and she wondered what Hetty had told him. Sophie took a deep breath, trying to gather her resolution about her. Max stopped, his eyes narrowing, and the smile faded.

'What's wrong?'

'Nothing. No, that's not true. There is something I wish to ask you.'

His expression didn't change but he seemed to have moved away from her.

'Very well. What is it?'

She turned towards the window. Perhaps if she didn't have to see him it would be easier.

'Lady Melissa spoke to me at Mrs Bannerman's this afternoon. She took great pleasure in informing me about your previous engagement and had a fine time with my confusion. But that isn't the point. The point is that I would have thought you might have…prepared me. You should have known someone would mention it.'

The silence stretched out behind her, but she didn't turn. Finally he spoke.

'I am sorry you were…embarrassed. And you are right that I should have mentioned it. It was a long time ago.'

She forced herself to turn. He had become statue-like again. There was no anger there, there was nothing. He might be looking at a stranger or at a shop window. She wondered what he would do if she put her head back and screamed. If any-thing could shake him when he shut down like that. His very lack of passion about the topic only increased her burning jealousy of the lively beauty Lady Melissa had described. She knew him well enough by now to know when he was closing down on something that mattered to him. Clearly this Lady Serena had mattered to him. She walked over to the sofa and sat down, arranging her skirts in unconscious imitation of Lady Melissa. When she realised what she was doing she stopped and looked up at him.

'I would like you to tell me whatever you think is necessary for me to know so I do not have to fear being ambushed by your…your friends or your enemies.' She put up her chin, proud of the calm, reasonable statement she had managed to produce despite the rumble of hurt inside her.

He breathed in deeply and moved to stand behind the brocade Louis XVI chair opposite the sofa, placing his hand on it. She wanted to tell him to sit down and not loom over her like that, but she kept silent, waiting.

'Very well. I was engaged to Lady Serena Morecombe some ten years ago. She was the only child of my father's close friend, Lord Morecombe. She was very…high spirited. A month before we were to be married she killed herself. That piece of information is not widely known so I would appreciate it if you kept that to yourself. It was put about that she died of a fever and, though I don't know if it was fully believed, it was accepted as the official version. That is all.'

Sophie's pain was displaced by shock and a surge of pity. Somehow the cold, passionless delivery of something which must have been devastating for him made it almost unbearable. Even her jealous hurt was out of place here.

'Oh, Max, I'm so sorry,' she whispered, holding out her hand. He didn't move, but something hot and stormy broke through his almost blank gaze, then it was gone again.

'It was a long time ago,' he repeated and she shook her head, dropping her hand. There was no point in saying that it was still present even if Lady Serena wasn't. She had never felt so distant from him. She wanted so much to reach and ease that core of pain she knew was there and she had never felt so inadequate or out of her depth.

'I didn't mean to pry. And I am sorry to bring up something that pains you. That wasn't my intention. I just...'

Max kept his breathing steady, resisting the urge to take the offered hand and accept the solace of that invitation and the absolution it offered. She was right—it was ridiculous to have kept it from her and he had no idea why he had. No, that wasn't true. He didn't want her, or anyone, knowing the truth about him and Serena.

As he had told Sophie the barest facts about Serena he had expected shock, or revulsion... He hadn't been prepared for empathy, for the warm invitation in her eyes and voice and that outstretched hand. But he couldn't claim what he didn't deserve. He might even have been more comfortable with the kind of responses he had come to expect from Serena, for whom compassion had been as foreign as restraint. He had never understood the fury of Serena's jealous rages when all the time she had been the one engaged in an illicit affair while he had battled both the desire she had had no compunction about fanning and the need to find satisfaction elsewhere, clinging like a fool to notions of fidelity.

She had taken him in royally and instead of guilt all she had felt was resentment that he had refused to dance to her tune. In the end he had just sought any excuse to go back to Harcourt on business just to escape her. And himself. He had never hated himself as much as when he had been with Serena that final month. The thought of sharing any of this with Sophie…that would never happen. He didn't want her or anyone to see that side of him. She could never understand or forgive the pitch of hate and frustration he had reached. It would be foolish to accept her unconsciously seductive offer of sympathy.

Still, when she lowered her hand and headed towards the door he moved after her without knowing quite why.

'Where are you going?'

'I…upstairs. I think I would like to rest before the ball.'

He reached the door before her. He should let her go, but he didn't want to, not yet. He searched for something to say, something that would bring back that embracing warmth. She might offer just as much to a dog, but right now he didn't care, he needed it. She had dragged back not just the memories but the emotions he dreaded and he didn't want to be left alone with them. He turned the key in the lock, leaning his hand on the door.

'You can leave in a moment,' he said as she looked up at him in surprise. 'You're right. I should have told you. That was poorly done of me. But I'm not used to…sharing information about myself.'

To his astonishment she picked up his free hand and just held it. His breath hitched, changed rhythm. It was the heat of her fingers on his palm, the way the curve of her thumb fit against his. She might hold a child's hand just so, but it didn't feel like that. It felt…inescapable. An invitation more seductively posed than any of Serena's carefully calculated postures. And then she did something worse. She raised his hand and touched it to her cheek.

'I'm sorry, Max,' she whispered and let go of his hand, except that he didn't release hers.

Sophie was unprepared for the kiss this time. There was nothing gentle or teasing in the way he drew her to him, his mouth covering hers. It was urgent and demanding, sending heat coursing through her, and her body surged against his, seeking relief from all the confusion and yearning that had been building up since she had met him.

The world outside the boundaries of their need faded and all that mattered was that he wasn't pushing her away, that his hands were sliding down her back, curving over her behind, pressing her against him as the kiss deepened and darkened. The drugging, plundering motion of his mouth and lips and tongue on hers was so intoxicating she shut out the hurt and fear that had preceded it, sliding her arms around his neck and arcing her body against him, trying inexpertly to mirror the still-foreign intensity of his kiss, utterly unlike anything she had experienced before and utterly unlike anything she might have expected from him.

She felt she was stepping out of a tight cave, blinded by light but suddenly able to move. This was freedom. And Max was with her. For the first time she felt he was really with her. She had somehow breached his shell and she could *feel* him, and there was such need there that she was swamped with love and the need to embrace him whole. She wanted to be closer, more. She wanted to give him everything, parts of her she hardly knew existed, with a confidence that was as unfamiliar as it was exhilarating. Most amazing was that these were the parts of her everyone condemned and he wanted them, he wanted *her*. For the first time she felt stronger than him, surer that this was the right thing to do, that he belonged with her. That he needed what she could give him, whether he knew it or not.

The thoughts swirled through while her body rushed ahead, trying to show what she would never dare say aloud. She rose on tiptoe, pressing against him with all her weight, sliding her fingers deep into his hair, and he groaned, his whole body sinking against her, pressing her between his body and the door without for a second abandoning the assault on her mouth. She loved the feel of his body pressed against her breasts which were suddenly so sensitive she felt every rasp of the silk shift pulling against her flesh as he moved against her. Even the pressure of the unyielding surface behind her became part of this maelstrom of sensations, an imprisonment that accentuated the urgent, seeking centre that was taking over, a contrast to the firm silkiness of his lips and the drag of his tongue on hers. She was drowning in sensations, in his taste and feel and scent, and she knew this was only the beginning. If anything, the force was gathering, focusing. They had been carried past the first barrier, like a ship carried by a swell over a reef, and now she felt completely separated from safety, from everything.

His mouth abandoned hers suddenly, his breath uneven, and through her lashes she met his eyes, a fierce stormy grey that should have scared her but didn't. She had no idea desire could be so beautiful, a threat and a promise.

'Max, I want you...' She didn't even realise she had spoken the words, but they seemed to strike him physically. His eyes closed and his hands curved under her thighs, raising her, and she instinctively locked her legs about his waist, even as his body surged back against hers, crushing her, and the pressure just where she needed him most sent a swirl of pleasure through her. His mouth moved with devastating force and precision to the soft, sensitive flesh of her neck, teasing it, drawing it into his mouth, the onslaught of his tongue and teeth exciting and frustrating her, making her twist against him. She felt like a battleground, a hundred forces clashing and erupting in her, and there was nothing she could do but somehow survive it. And at the edge was the need to act, to do as much beautiful damage to him as he was doing to her, to make him suffer and churn like this. To feel him and taste him. And see him. God, she wanted to see him, all of him. It wasn't right to have all these layers between them.

She dragged one arm from his shoulders and managed to get her hand under his coat, tugging his shirt out of his pantaloons. His skin was so hot under her hand, hot and smooth, and it burned all the way up her shoulder, adding to the urgent ache she was becoming. She slid her fingers over the muscles of his back as far as she could reach and images danced through her brain of paintings she had seen, images superimposed on the fantasies about him that had come in the dark in her little room. But it wasn't enough, she wanted to see *him*, to see him utterly bared, to explore every inch of him with every sense she possessed. This was no statue, she could feel his muscles flinch and tighten under her fingers, his breathing as harsh and unsteady as hers, and when a whimper came out of her that she hardly recognised as her own she felt the a tremor run through his whole body and felt a surge of power that elated her. She might not reach him any other way, but here he couldn't keeping her at bay.

'I want to *see* you,' she moaned, digging one hand into his hair and dragging his mouth back to hers and another shudder coursed through his body, but she wished she had kept silent because he pulled back, his eyes burning and intent, but already she could see the withdrawal. He let go her legs and they slid down.

'We have to stop...' His voice was torn and scratchy, but the resolution underneath was unmistakable.

'No!' she said angrily, too frustrated and off balance to be cautious. 'You started this. You can't keep starting this and then sending me on my way. It's not fair!'

'Fair...' He gave a broken laugh, brushing the hair back from her face as if he found it hard to stop touching her. 'Sophie, you're right. I shouldn't have started this. But we need to be sensible.'

He pulled her against him, her cheek pressed

against his chest, and she could feel his heartbeat, hard and fast, echoing against her and inside
her, feeding the throbbing pulse that refused to
calm. She gave a little sob, trying to draw on the
strength of the body encompassing hers to counter the chaos she had become. She hardly realised
her fingers continued to moving gently against
his back. The need to touch him was a compul-
sion, the tips of her fingers so sensitive she could
feel the pulse of blood under his skin, the way his
muscles tensed as she glided over them, the agonised drag of his breath as he fought to regain
control.

'Sophie, stop… We can't do this. Not yet…'

But his words, deep and tortured, were in complete contrast with his actions. The arms that had
pinned her slid down her back, urging her against
him, and she instinctively parted her legs to bring
him closer, only the resistance of her skirts holding back the need to encompass him. Caught in
her own daze she saw the struggle behind the heat
in his eyes and the capitulation. He cursed almost
inaudibly, a low rough sound that was as much a
caress as a profanity, and his hands released her
only to drag up her skirts, his fingers grazing her
bare skin above her stockings. She felt unbear-

ably soft against his hands, as if she could feel herself through him. His gaze held hers as his hands curved over her thighs, moulding them, tracing lines on them, shifting them further apart as the hampering skirts rose, dragging his palms up their softness and down again until her whole body contracted. She had no idea what to do other than cling to him and wait out this incomprehensible, unbearable need that wouldn't relent.

She knew something was going to happen, she was certain of it, that she no longer had to fight him for it. She could just let go and feel. Follow his fingers as they gentled and slowed, just tracing down to the line of her garter before moving up, easing her legs apart slightly with his knee so he could reach the sensitive skin of her inner thighs, higher. She bit her lip to curb the moan that built up, but it pushed through, carried on the waves of unrelenting heat his hands were setting loose, concentrating on the pulsing, demanding fire between her legs. He caught the sound against his mouth, teasing her teeth from her lip, his own replacing them, nipping at her sensitised flesh and the edge of pain released something in her and she finally moved, digging her hands into his hair, pulling herself against him, opening her mouth under his and he gave in and deepened the caress into the hungry kiss that had been held back, taunting.

She could feel everything, his muscle against her even through their clothes, the slide of his tongue against her lips, her own tongue tangling with his with a daring she didn't even know she had possessed. She locked her arms around his neck, moving against his hand as she tried to ease the need, knowing something had to happen, soon, because this was unbearable. She was high on some brutal wave that would crash, she knew it had to crash.

Max held on to her elemental, beautiful body, fully aware he was taking her places she had never been, places no one would ever take her but him. And that he wasn't in control. He was going to give her at least a taste of the pleasure she so obviously demanded, but in every other respect he was following. Not just the entrancing desire she showed so freely, as generous as her compassion, but his own chaotic needs. He shouldn't have stayed, he shouldn't have touched her, he should stop. He had no intention of stopping. He would give her this and take the glory of watching her, more beautiful in her joy than any woman he had ever seen. He wanted the moment she realised where her yearning had been leading to. Then he would tell her this was only the beginning. If he survived that far. Because he wanted her so much, to fit himself into her, feel her skin, hot and damp, against him. To see her as naked as those paintings, waiting for him with the heat in her eyes. His fingers slid against the throbbing heat of her arousal and she rose against him with a gasp and he closed his eyes, gritting his teeth. This was madness, he would never make it out of here alive.

'Oh, God, Max… Max…' Her voice ripped at him, every muscle in his body squirming against his restraints, and he answered by sliding the sleeve of her dress and chemise from her shoulder, tugging at the light stays to release her breast, tracing its soft curve, a groan building up as he felt her skin contract under his fingers, her nipple tightening under the silk, and he bent to kiss it through the fabric, teasing it, dampening it, drawing it between his lips as her fingers tortured themselves in his hair and her hips shifted faster against his fingers, but in a jerking uncertain rhythm that revealed her inexperience and was shredding away at his control. Part of him wanted to get this over with while he was still sane and another part of him wanted it never to end, to keep her just at that pitch of desire and confusion, needing him, utterly lost to the world and under his control. Needing him… He gave in and groaned against the soft curve of her neck, his breath mixing with her distinctive scent, honeysuckle, sweet and clear, and he couldn't bear it much longer. He wanted to be inside her more than he wanted to live.

'Sophie, enough…we have to stop.'

'I can't. Please don't make me, Max…I want you. Please…'

Perhaps it was that one plaintive word that cracked his control. He stopped thinking, his fingers working swiftly on the hooks, fastenings, and laces that stood between him and his need to feel her, truly feel her. His coat followed her dress and stays and drawers in a crumpled heap on the carpet, but he laid her down more carefully on the thick red and gold plush and she let him, which should have shocked him but didn't. She just waited, her hand clenched on the linen of his shirt, her eyes on his, a deep flaming blue. He tugged off his shirt as well and it stayed in her hand as he lay down beside her, half on top of her, his hand touching, sliding, his mouth capturing hers again. As she arched against him he parted her legs wider with his knee, continuing the circling, drawing, plunging of his fingers against the throbbing centre of her heat. She arched her head back, moving with and against his hand. He had her so close. She was completely his. No one had ever seen her like this, or ever would. She was his.

And it wasn't enough to just brand her with pleasure. He would make her his unequivocally. He had never bedded a virgin and he realised he had no idea how to really prepare her for what he was about to do. The thought was almost enough to convince him to stop, but not quite. He raised himself slightly and her eyes half-opened, misty and lost, and his possessive ache deepened.

'Sophie, we stop or we go forward, do you understand? I don't want to hurt you, but it probably will. If you want me to stop, tell me now.'

'You can't stop.' Her voice was dreamy but very clear.

That was so close to the truth he almost groaned.

'I don't want to, but I will if you tell me. Do you understand? There's no going back once we...'

'I don't want to go back. Ever.' She rose on her

elbow, her other arm sliding around his neck and she pressed her mouth to his. 'You can't stop.'

'Sophie…' Her name came out on a groan of relief and need and he kissed her with a thankful greed he had to fight back. He would do everything to make certain she didn't regret giving herself to him. He would take her to the edge of desire before he gave in to it.

His fingers slipped back to the damp silkiness of her arousal and the immediate shudder that ran through her told him she so close, waiting…

Sophie gave in gratefully to the tantalising bursts of pleasure his fingers were teasing out of her, taking her back to that amazing place she had never imagined existed. She was so lost in her own sensations she was almost surprised by the weight of his body as he moved between her legs and the burning heat that replaced his skilled fingers, pressing against the barrier of her body. The sharp snap of pain was so out of place in the swirl of pleasure that she gave a shocked gasp, but he caught her mouth with his and its drugging pull and his hand sliding gently, rhythmically over her breast, dragged her focus away from the invasion and back to the much more insistent ache at her centre. It was all mixed up together, but she was too close to breaking to care about anything but release. She tried to move under his weight, but his hand closed on her hip, stilling her.

'I don't want to hurt you...' His voice sounded choked and ragged through the roaring in her ears.

'I don't care! Just do something!' she gasped against his mouth and he laughed, a deep husky sound that roared through her like the surf and he shifted slightly to one side without releasing her, drawing her leg up slightly, and then his fingers slid between them to the burning heat that locked them together, each circling slide of his fingers calling to her, raising her, sliding him in more deeply, and even the pain became a distraction to be shoved out of the way, because she wanted something beyond it, that promise... And then when it was becoming unbearable his touch finally found the secret lock and she unravelled and fell in a burst of joy and warmth and release. She heard him call out her name against her throat and felt the pain as he moved inside her and then he tensed, his body and breath shuddering until he, too, seemed to break and he sank against her and a little voice, detached from all of this upheaval, said 'There now!' quite distinctly in her head.

They stayed like that for a while, his body half on hers as their breathing evened out, waves settling back into rhythm after a storm. His body was heavy, even with his arm braced against the floor, but it was wonderful to feel him stretched on her. She only wished he had taken off his pantaloons as well so she could feel his leg anchoring hers. She felt infinitely heavy, too, and the pain was much more apparent now, but she still felt wonderful, like a warrior queen fresh from a successful battle, wounds and all. She almost laughed at the absurdity of the bloodthirsty thought.

Then he drew in a deep breath against her and she knew it was over. And that she would have to face him now without the distracting barrier that the urgent heat had provided. With the obscuring desire fading, its place was being taken up by a deep embarrassment that she had acted more wantonly than she had believed possible. Lust was indeed a form of madness and now that she had experienced it she could see why it was such a topic for literature and art. Never in her life would she have imagined that she would seduce a man into bedding her…it wasn't even bedding, since they were on the floor, her lovely new dress a bunched pile of fabric just under the Louis XIV chair, her stays peeping out below and his coat dangling from the sofa.

She wanted to groan her shame out loud, but she held back and closed her eyes. Hopefully he would be able to deal with the aftermath better than she. He moved off her carefully and as the adhesive contact of their skin was broken she felt its absence like a loss. She tried not to look at him as he helped her up very gently, as if aware of the stinging pain between her legs. She took her shift from him and fumbled with it nervously, searching for the opening. Without a word he took it from her, gathering it into folds and slipping it over her head. He did the same with her stays and dress and then turned her around to secure the laces and hooks. Finally she felt his fingers straighten the folds of her sleeve and brush the tangle of hair from her shoulders and she dragged up enough courage to look up at him.

There was an absent but relaxed look on his face as he focused on his task and his mouth had lost some of its tension and it amazed her that this beautiful man had just made love to her...no, that wasn't the right word. It was best not to lie to herself. This had been pure carnality. Wonderful and earth shattering, but it wasn't love. He glanced up and met her eyes and there was a strange mix of lazy heat and sated pleasure there that reached deep inside and twisted a raw, unprotected part of her.

'I'm sorry,' he said finally. 'That wasn't how your first time should have been. I can't believe I…on the floor…'

There was such disarming embarrassment and exasperation in his voice that her own embarrassment dimmed. She should have known he would be a great deal more disappointed in himself and his lapse of control than in her. She had a powerful urge to reassure him.

'Two of my sisters said their first times were horrible after all the fear and anticipation that preceded them, so maybe it is better like this.'

He laughed and tucked her loosened hair back behind her ear and his hand lingered, gently moving against the soft skin just below her ear, soothing and warm, and she wished she could lean into his caress like a cat. He seemed to realise what he was doing and he moved his hands to her shoulders, as if debating where to put her, the line between his brows deepening.

'I'm glad it wasn't horrible. But I still should have had enough self-control to resist. I'm supposed to be protecting you, not taking advantage of you. This was unforgivable.'

She felt a bubble of laughter rise up at the inappropriate return of the Stone Duke. She was still too happy and physically content to be hurt by his predictable withdrawal. If anything she felt peculiarly protective towards him with so many burdens of responsibility weighing on him relentlessly.

'I won't tell anyone,' she said demurely and some of his stiffness faded. He ran his hands through her tangled hair, tilting her head back, his eyes softening again with reluctant amusement overlaying the concern that drew his brows together.

'If anyone sees you like this they won't need telling. You should probably go upstairs before Lambeth appears... And you should ask them to send a hot bath up, it will help with... Hell, this should never have happened—' He broke off, shaking his head at himself.

Even with the remains of the stinging ache between her legs reminding her of the intimacies they had just shared, somehow his mentioning a bath made her cheeks heat painfully again, but also her need to relieve his disappointment in himself. It tugged at her and she stepped forward, seeking an excuse to prolong contact with him.

'I don't think Lambeth should see you either. You are not precisely neat as a pin yourself at the moment, either, Your Grace. Here, I'll see if I can rescue your cravat.'

He stood silently as she did her best with the folds of his cravat. There was a lingering intensity in his eyes and she felt the echo of the pleasure he had given her, or the beginning of that need again and she forced herself to stand back.

'No, it's hopeless. You should definitely try and avoid Lambeth.'

He smiled, an uncharacteristically boyish grin that went well with his dishevelled hair, and walked over to the door, unlocking it.

'Point taken. I'll make a run for it.' He hesitated. 'Will you be all right? Did I hurt you badly?'

She shook her head, her throat closing at the concern in his voice, holding back the words she knew he would not want to hear from her.

He hesitated, then nodded and left.

Max made it safely home without coming across any acquaintance in the short distance between the two houses. Up in his room a glance in the mirror was enough to assure him it would not have taken a great deal of perspicacity to guess what had happened in that room. Despite her attempts, his cravat was crushed and his short dark hair looked like he had done his best to emulate the windblown *coup au vent* style Byron had made fashionable.

He shook his head. Now that she was not there the madness of it all struck him full force. It had been his fault from beginning to end, but he was finding it very hard to drag up any real regret. She had been tying him into knots for days now and that encounter had been wonderfully satisfying. He had known she was passionate, but he had been amazed and disarmed by that mixture of abandon and determination. He could tell himself as much as he wanted that she had been a virgin and he should have done a better job of resisting, but the truth was that he hadn't wanted to. There had been enough moments he could have chosen to step back. He had even told himself he would do nothing more than give her the pleasure she so obviously craved. That watching her abandonment was pleasure enough. But at some point his rationality had gone up in a puff of smoke.

He tugged off his cravat, caught between remorse, embarrassment and guilty pleasure. It hardly made sense that he had deflowered his betrothed on the floor of her aunt's house. But she had been utterly amazing. What on earth was he going to do with her? Right now he and his body were very delighted with her refusal to play by the rules, but that innocent insistence on proceeding down whatever path she thought right at the moment would not always lead to such...pleasant results. In fact, so far it had led them into a forced engagement and even now she might already be with child because for the first time in his adult life he had not taken any precautions.

He looked back at his reflection. It was impossible to chase away that thought so he might as well face it head on. He had never thought of her in terms of children except in the theoretical consideration of heirs, but now the possibility of their child forced its way to the front of a parade of confusing images and emotions. He had so many nieces and nephews already he was used to being surrounded by babies and children, but somehow the thought of her holding his child was unsettling. It made him want to reach through the mental image to a future reality and test it. It was like staring into someone else's window, into their life,

and wanting to step into it. Whatever her peculiarities, she would probably be a loving parent. If
she could lavish so much affection on that unap-
pealing pug, she no doubt would have plenty for
her own children. More than he had. The more
he thought about it, as difficult as it might be to
deal with her unconventional attitudes, at least it
would be good for their children to have one parent capable of real affection. He and Lady Melissa
together would have been too much of a facsimile of his own parents. Correct and attentive, but
not really warm. He just had to make sure she
understood the weight of the responsibilities that
would be on his heir's shoulders. The sooner he
took her to Harcourt so she could see precisely
what he, and now she, were responsible for, the
better. There was nothing like hard proof.

And at Harcourt there were many more places
where he could take her where they could be private. Because even as satisfying as it had been,
now that the genie was out of the bottle he really
didn't feel like waiting until the wedding to bed
her again. And this time there *would* be a bed because he had every intention of taking his time.
She wanted to see him? Fine, he wanted to see her,
too—stretched out on his bed and at his mercy

so he could explore just how far her passionate nature extended. If she could respond like that without any experience and in the unconducive setting of her aunt's parlour, he couldn't imagine what she might be capable of once he had her to himself in the privacy of their bedroom. And he very much wanted to find out.

Heat began uncoiling again at the thought of her naked, waiting for him with that dreamy look and that urgency, those soft whimpers that were almost as potent as her eager, seeking hands… He turned away from the mirror. There was no reason they had to wait too long to get married. At the time it had seemed reasonable to draw out his freedom a little, but that was a lesser consideration now. He could get a special licence and in a few days they could go to Harcourt and have her father marry them. That should satisfy even the most exacting critics. And then he could send everyone to the devil so they could be alone.

Chapter Fourteen

'It was well worth the wait!' Bryanston announced as he led Sophie off the Montagues' dance floor towards where Max was standing in a group of people, one of whom Sophie recognised as the very fashionable and yet scandalous Lady Jersey. In this setting Max looked quite intimidating and aloof and it was hard to reconcile this handsome, imposing man with the passionate lover who had initiated her into physical pleasure in Aunt Minnie's parlour and then faced her with such touching contrition. She didn't know quite which one of these men Max was, or how they all managed to cohabit together. All she knew was that everything she found out about him just peeled back another layer in her, and that the initial, elemental attraction that had drawn her to him was just the first step along a journey that had already changed her in ways she wasn't sure she understood. As she moved towards him, his grey eyes unfathomable but sparking far too much in her, she felt the heat prick at her cheeks and hoped they ascribed her flush to the dance.

'Sally, is it you I must thank for allowing Miss Trevelyan to dance the waltz?' Bryanston grasped Lady Jersey's hand and raised it reverently to his lips. 'If so, I offer you my profound gratitude. She waltzes divinely. Like a nymph or a zephyr or whatever it was that turned into a spray of water. I can never remember their names; it's all Greek to me. Do you know, Miss Trevelyan?'

'I am sorry, I don't, but in any case it doesn't sound very enjoyable for either the nymph or her dance partner,' she replied, feeling her flush deepen as she felt everyone watching her and waiting for her to slip up. She had no idea what Max was thinking and she really didn't want to embarrass him again. At least Lady Pennistone was nowhere in sight.

'Quite right!' Bryanston agreed, struck. 'Who wants to embrace a spray of water? What's wrong with the fellow who wrote that? Sounds like a dashed damping experience, if you pardon my indelicacy, Miss Trevelyan.'

She couldn't help laughing at his comical expression. Somehow his nonsense made her feel less nervous.

'I don't think it was meant so literally, Lord Bryanston, but it is annoying the way poets are forever transforming women into and out of things. If it isn't a water nymph it's a swan or a statue. I suspect they don't know what to do with us as we are.'

Lady Jersey burst into a trill of her distinctive laughter.

'How very true. Then you are quite lucky that Max here has no poetic leanings. And he knows precisely what do with us. As we are.'

'Manners, Sally.' Max said easily. 'Are you trying to scare off Miss Trevelyan?'

Lady Jersey's humorous eyes met Sophie's.

'I don't believe I can. Certainly not like that. Could I, Miss Trevelyan?'

'Certainly not like that, Lady Jersey,' Sophie agreed demurely.

'Oh, marvellous.' Lady Jersey laughed again. 'I *do* like your betrothed, Max. I am quite surprised you showed so much sense in the end. Come, Bryanston, you may dance with me and pay me outrageous compliments as well.'

She led Bryanston off and Max took Sophie's hand and drew her away from the group. Even through her glove she felt the heat of his hand, and it flowed up her arm, reminding her vividly of the amazing interlude of the afternoon. She could feel the colour stain her cheeks like the sting of warmth after being out in a frost. She had thought Max was leading her out on to the dance floor but he drew her down a corridor. She glanced up at him, but he merely gave her a gentle shove round the corner and then let the curtain fall back behind them and she realised they were in another, narrower corridor. There was still enough light behind them, but in the gloom Max suddenly seemed even larger than usual and for a moment Sophie did feel a spurt of alarm, not at what he might do, but at the swiftness with which her body switched into expectation. She took a step back and came up against the wall and they stood for a moment in silence.

'I haven't had the chance to ask you if you are feeling well…after what happened.'

He sounded both distant and contrite and though she was touched, she felt a stab of disappointment. Clearly this was not a seduction.

'I am quite all right, thank you,' she replied and he nodded.

'Come.' He took her hand again and drew her along the corridor, thoroughly confusing her. At the end he opened a door into a room lit by a candelabrum on the mantelpiece which provided enough light to bring to life the painting on the other side of the room. It was an old man seated at a table, looking at her. With a sense of shock she moved towards it, unconsciously still holding on to Max's hand.

'Who painted it?' she whispered.

'A Spanish painter called Velazquez. I have one of his paintings at Harcourt Hall. This is almost two hundred years old. Amazing, isn't it?'

She nodded mutely, hardly even noticing as Max moved to stand behind her until his arms pulled her back against him, enveloping her in heat.

'I wanted to surprise you. I thought you would like it,' he murmured as he bent to touch his mouth to her half-bared shoulder.

'I do…' She tried to focus on the astounding painting, but her eyelids sank and it became hard to breathe with the way his mouth was moving over her shoulder and neck. And then he found a point just below her ear that made her gasp and twist against him. His arms tightened and one hand slid down over her abdomen, sending coils of heat and need through her and her body wakened in anticipation.

'Max...'

'Don't worry, I won't go too far...unfortunately...' he murmured as his other hand slipped inside the bodice of her gown, closing on her breast, his thumb brushing over her nipple. She bit her lip against the cry that gathered in her throat and leaned her head back against his chest, baring her neck again to his mouth. She had still enough sanity to know that if she said anything, anything at all, he would stop. The flickering orange light of the candles seeped through her closed eyelids and she felt like liquid fire from without and within and the whole room seemed to be shaking, vibrating, and she was losing the ability to distinguish between her body and his. The urgent, needy ache between her legs was back, layered over the remnants of the pain from their coupling, and she felt the same bubbling internal confusion, the need to act without knowing what to do. She reached back, her hand moving between them without even realising what she was doing, until her palm slid over his erection and even as a shudder ran through her in anticipation he caught her wrist and she realised it was over. For a second she thought of resisting, but she remained motionless, willing herself back to sanity. Finally he pressed a light kiss to her shoulder and let her go.

'I told myself I would just bring you here to see the painting, nothing else,' he said ruefully after a moment, but there was sufficient amusement in his voice to relax her. 'We should get back. But we need to arrange your dress first...'

She was just about to answer when she heard voices and laughter outside.

'Hell,' Max cursed under his breath and propelled her towards the back door. 'Fix your dress and go back to the ballroom, I'll head off whoever it is.'

The door barely closed behind her when she heard a man call Max's name merrily.

She adjusted her bodice hurriedly when suddenly the curtain at the other end of the corridor swung back and she raised her arm against the glare that hit her eyes.

'Well, well. Providence indeed.'

Sophie dropped her hand. He was still only a

dark shape against the light, but she did not have to see him to recognise Wivenhoe.

'Have you just been to see the Velazquez, my dear? Quite exquisite technique, don't you think? Even if his subjects are less than exceptional. I admire what he does with such a limited palette. I once tried to paint one in his style and I think I did a rather good job. If you care to visit me one day, I will show you.'

Sophie had no idea how he could be so urbane after what had happened between them. Perhaps it really had been an aberration and she was making too much of it. Still, that did not mean she wanted to be alone with him and the suggestion of actually visiting him was ludicrous.

'I don't think that is a good idea, Lord Wivenhoe. Excuse me.'

She started moving around him, but he shifted his weight and, though he did not quite block the narrow passage, he effectively was forcing her to brush by him if she wished to get by.

'Where is your ever faithful watchdog?' he asked as she hesitated. 'If you were mine I would certainly take better care not to let you wander darkened corridors on your own. Has his interest waned now that you have secured him? Never fear, as I know only too well his overly rigid sense of duty won't allow him to go back on his word, no matter how wrong he might be. You can rest easy in your conquest.'

'He isn't a conquest,' she flashed, and his hands rose as if to grasp her arms, but fell back.

'Do you know,' he said slowly. 'I would love to paint you. You are very different from what I usually appreciate, but I find I am quite fascinated by your many layers. You appear so open and yet I would wager there is much more bubbling beneath that charming lid. Yes, I would really like to paint you.'

'Thank you, Lord Wivenhoe, but I don't aspire to that honour.'

His lips curled and she could sense the anger rising above his suave surface. But contrarily it relaxed her slightly. At least this was a human emotion, not the manipulative veneer he favoured.

'Don't try those society airs with me. I know that isn't what you are.'

'And what am I, then?'

'I am not quite sure. A study in contradictions. I wonder what might have happened had I not met you in Harcourt's company at the outset. He brings out the worst in me. And you seem to have awakened the beast in him which is no small feat, believe me.'

'Why do you hate him so?'

There was an expression in his eyes she didn't understand.

'I have good reason. Ask him. You might learn a thing or two about your future husband.'

'I'm asking you.'

'He took everything from me.'

The words were so quiet and banal, but they had a force that caught her breath. Before she could respond the door behind her opened and she turned. She did not know whether to be relieved or dismayed that it was Max and that he was alone. She half-raised her hands as if to stop him, but for a moment he didn't move, then he came forward, his eyes on Wivenhoe and his face a mask.

When he reached them he glanced down at Sophie.

'Are you having difficulties finding the ballroom, Sophie?'

'Yes. Would you mind taking me there?' she replied and the stony look dimmed slightly. He held out his arm.

'With pleasure. Excuse us, Wivenhoe.' He moved forward, not waiting to see if Wivenhoe would step aside, and Sophie almost expected him to walk straight through the man when Wivenhoe bowed and moved aside, his mouth twisting.

When they were safely back in the ballroom she glanced up at him and he turned and looked down at her, the distant look she disliked fading further.

'I really can't let you out of my sight, can I?' he said, and though his eyes remained cold there was a teasing note in his voice and her shoulders relaxed slightly.

'That was sheer bad luck. But he didn't do anything, really,' she assured him, telling herself it wasn't really a lie. He didn't answer and then Lord Cranworth appeared to claim a dance with her and she was relieved to give herself up to harmless banter after the intensity of the past hour. She had always wanted to live a more exciting life than the one she had led in Ashton Cove, and it seemed fate was answering her prayers, in spades.

Max watched as Cranworth led her on to the dance floor, just catching the edge of her smiling face raised towards his friend before she was blocked from view by other dancers. He turned away, resisting the urge to either take her back to the privacy of her parlour or to go in search of

Wivenhoe and make it abundantly clear that Sophie was out of bounds. And he should have kept his hands off her in the first place. It was just that he couldn't get his mind off the events of the afternoon, every sense of his seemed to have been completely subverted by memories of their encounter, playing with images of her, her soft, urgent cries, the sight of her lips parting, her head arched back and eyes dark with pleasure... It was a constant, unrelenting assault that was far more powerful than the guilt and self-disgust that also kept circling him like aggravating gnats. Even her sweet, laughing embarrassment during the conversation with Bryanston and Lady Sally Jersey had pulled at him in ways that were new to him. He had held himself ready to shield her if anyone had dared say anything to make her uncomfortable, but somehow even those, like Sally, who would usually enjoy making mincemeat of someone as unusual as Sophie were disarmed. She had a way of making people comfortable with her that had nothing to do with breeding and everything to do with empathy. It might be unfashionable, but it was undeniably effective.

Still, he wished she had more of a shell to help her draw a firmer line about her. It was precisely that warmth that laid her open to manipulation and hurt. She had not seemed to welcome Wivenhoe's presence just now, but neither had she apparently been able to make it clear to him they had nothing to say to each other. Someone more skilled in society would have had no problem drawing that line in the sand and Sophie would have to learn how to do just that.

He wondered what Wivenhoe was really after with Sophie. When Max had returned to England, his experiences during the wars had made his past with Serena and Wivenhoe appear distant. His fury had faded, leaving behind just wary contempt. Until now. Still, even with his newly discovered jealousy, he could detect no overt sign that she favoured Wivenhoe. Perhaps the man was just doing it to provoke him, but there was something excessive in his persistence. Beyond Max's natural inclination to do Wivenhoe damage, he couldn't help being uneasy. Right now, with the memory of those moments in front of the Velasquez still sharp and hot, that inclination had an extra bite. It had taken every ounce of his self-control not to react when he had opened the door and seen her silhouette and beyond her Wivenhoe looking down at her with an intent look that

Max would have very much enjoyed erasing. He would have to keep a much closer eye on him in future. He might have begun this whole farce because of the past, but he was damned if he was going to repeat it.

Chapter Fifteen

Sophie leaned closer to inspect both blues where Mr Reeves had spread them on the wooden palette. He was right, there was a very, very faint difference, a slightly smoky feel to one that would do very well for the sky in Marmaduke's portrait and for the highlight in Hetty's dress.

'How do you manage that?' she asked, jealous of his ability to mix such amazing colours. He grinned down at his achievement, his bony face shining with pride.

'It takes years, miss. That and almost every compound known to man. One day when I'm not rushed I'll take you to the back where we do our grinding and mixing.'

'Oh, I would love that! I think I will take both after all.'

'Very good, miss.'

As he wrapped them for her she turned idly towards a couple who stood at the other end of the counter talking to a sales clerk. The woman, dressed in a bottle-green dress with *coquelicot* ribbons and a very high poke bonnet pushed back slightly to reveal rumpled black curls, was leaning against a cupboard, looking bored. Sophie stared at her in surprise, recognising her as the woman in Wivenhoe's painting that she had seen at the Exhibition. The woman, or maybe she was just a very well-developed girl, it was hard to tell with her sullen expression and gaudy clothes, noticed Sophie's stare and raised her brows insolently. Strangely, Sophie wasn't offended, but she smiled and some confusion entered the young woman's eyes and she flushed, looking down at the tips of her scuffed red slippers which peeped out from under her skirts.

Sophie thanked Reeves, took her package and walked over to the young woman.

'I'm sorry I stared,' she apologised. 'It is just I think I recognise you from a painting at the Exhibition. Though you looked very…sad in it.'

She snorted. 'Maybe because it were of me and it weren't,' she said sullenly and her companion at the counter turned to them with a frown.

'Here, Liz, go wait outside if you mean to chatter!'

The girl shrugged and headed towards the door and Sophie followed.

'Go away. I'm working and you'll get me in trouble.'

'I'm sorry, I don't mean to. You're an artist's model, aren't you?'

'I am. What's it to you? You one of them female artists?'

'I suppose I am.'

'What, don't you know?' she mocked.

'Sometimes I do, sometimes I don't.' Sophie smiled, unoffended. There was something touching about the stubborn girl and the more she looked at her, the younger she appeared. She might be no more than sixteen or seventeen. The girl tried to sneer at Sophie's answer, but her mouth pulled down and she looked merely tired.

'What did you mean before?' Sophie asked and the girl's dark eyes shot to hers.

'I didn't mean nothing. I do what I'm told. You want me to pose like someone, you ask, I pose. I told him I ain't no actress and I sure as hell don't do tragic. It ain't my fault I look like some dead woman.'

'Like who?' Sophie asked, trying to make sense of what the girl was saying, but her generous mouth tightened as the door opened and her companion stepped out.

'Come on, Liz, let's go catch the light.'

The girl lowered her head and hurried after him and Sophie watched her disappear around the corner.

'Now that is a strange coupling,' a voice said behind her and Sophie froze in shock and turned slowly to face Lord Wivenhoe.

'Buying paints, my dear? And no watchdog today? Of either kind?'

'James, my aunt's footman, is waiting for me in the carriage.'

'You needn't worry. I won't pounce. What were you and the lovely Liz discussing? Harcourt would disapprove of your consorting with fallen women, you know.'

'Did she fall? I recognised her from your portrait and was curious.'

'Curious. About what?'

'The experience of being an artist's model. And why she looked so sad in your painting.'

His clear blue eyes darkened, his pupils expanding visibly.

'What did she answer?'

'She didn't. She had to go.'

His lips pulled back slightly and her sense of danger deepened.

'She is very lovely, isn't she? Lush. Men like that dark, voluptuous look. She looks remarkably like Max's previous betrothed, Lady Serena. Have you heard yet of Serena, Miss Trevelyan?'

Sophie was suddenly very grateful to Lady Melissa for having introduced Serena before Wivenhoe sprang the news on her.

'Of course, Max told me all about her.'

'Did he indeed? All? Somehow that surprises me. I wouldn't think Harcourt liked discussing his failures, even with his lovely new bride-to-be. So he told you that his beloved betrothed was my mistress and that she died by poison? It was never discovered who provided it. Her oh-so-indulgent fool of a father put it out she died of a fever, but the doctor believed she died trying to rid herself of the unborn child she conceived out of wedlock. It happens, you know. Not that it is easy for a gently reared girl to find those kinds of potions. But we men tend to know how to source them when there is a need. You might want to ask Harcourt where they can be obtained if the need arises... or perhaps that would not be wise.'

Sophie had been prepared for some vindictiveness, but not for this. She had to physically hold herself immobile and expressionless. She thought of Max and the few short sentences he had shared with her and the vulnerability and passion that had followed and she wished she could hurt Wivenhoe.

'There is a slight gap in versions between the two of you about Lady Serena,' she replied with a contemptuous lightness she tried very hard not to show was forced. 'Somehow I place my faith in Max.'

'Really? What confidence! Do you know she died in the very bed she used to meet me in? Her cousins were out of town those last few weeks and we used to meet in their empty house and she would moan about your dear old Max. Not that he was old then, just a young arrogant pup who was quite unsuited for such a vibrant, pleasure-seeking creature like Serena. If he hadn't been so wealthy and the heir to a dukedom she never would have even considered him, but their parents wanted it and Harcourt wanted it and she thought she could do what she wanted with him. But he's stubborn, as you will learn. Too stubborn to set her free even when he knew...he *knew* he was wrong for her. She was the most beautiful woman I... She loved being watched, adulated. She was so alive...' He was breathing hard, his eyes molten amber. 'If you were clever, you'd run right back home, my dear. This is an unhealthy environment for women who think they can live as they see fit and for those who care for them. Ask poor old Lord Morecombe, holed up in his dilapidated house in Manchester Square and only coming out at night like some village freak. Sounds rather like your aunt except that at least he has cause for his histrionics. To have one's only child killed...'

The viciousness gathered again, his eyes boring into hers.

'You're nowhere near as beautiful as she was, but do you honestly think someone as cold as Harcourt will do for you, Sophie Trevelyan?'

Sophie listened to this jumbled, vitriolic rush without a word, between shock and a cold fear, her mind tumbling over itself in its need to stop this, to defend Max and to defend herself against the implications of his words. Finally she found the strength to turn away towards Aunt Minnie's carriage. Inside she sank back against the squabs and closed her eyes, letting the shaking take over. As they drew away all that remained was the image of a dark, beautiful woman whom Max had loved and lost so horribly.

Chapter Sixteen

'His Grace is waiting for you in the parlour, miss,' Lambeth informed her as she entered. 'Allow me to assist you,' he added with the flattening of his lips that was as close as he came to a smile.

She allowed him to take the packages from her, feeling rather foolish at how relieved she was that Max was there. Just knowing he was close gathered her together, like a group of scattered ducklings coaxed back into a row. Whatever Wivenhoe had said about Max, and however difficult he might be, she knew him. Perhaps not fully, but at some level she knew what he was and wasn't capable of. Even if what Wivenhoe said was true, and she was far from convinced that it was, it couldn't have been more than a tragic accident. She hurried into the parlour with more haste than grace. Max was standing looking absently at her painting of Hetty but he looked up when she entered and moved towards her.

'Where were you? I've been waiting half an hour.'

She stopped at his abrupt tone.

'I went to Reeves. We didn't arrange to meet, did we?'

'Why didn't you tell Lambeth where you were going?

'Why should I? I took a footman with me...'

He stood stiffly for a moment.

'Next time you go out tell Lambeth where you are going.'

'No,' she replied calmly and his eyes narrowed.

'No?'

'No. I have no intention of reporting to Lambeth about my whereabouts. I am willing to take James with me when I go out, though I am not happy about it, but that is the extent of it. Does Hetty report to your butler every time she steps out of the house?'

'That's different!'

'How? Because she's married? Or is it because she is not some silly miss from the countryside?'

'Because she does not have someone like

Wivenhoe fixated on her!' His voice had risen and he held himself back with obvious effort and Sophie stared at him in shock.

'Do you understand me?' he asked, more calmly.

'I do, but—' She broke off. For once she should try to think before she leaped. Sharing Wivenhoe's words was certain to exacerbate the enmity between the two men and she did not want to cause any more trouble for Max. He had been through enough.

'But what?'

'Nothing. Nothing at all,' she replied, trying to look at him casually. It was clearly a mistake. His eyes narrowed and he moved towards her with the swiftness of a predatory animal.

'But what?' he repeated. 'What happened? Did you see Wivenhoe? Look at me!' he commanded as she looked down at the faded carpet and she found enough anger in her to meet his eyes squarely.

'Stop snapping at me! Nothing happened.'

'I think I told you before that you are a very poor liar,' he said. His voice had calmed, but he sounded more frightening than before. 'Now tell me what happened.'

'Nothing. I came across him at Reeves. He was his usual unpleasant self. That is all.'

'No,' he said slowly, watching her. 'That's not all, is it?'

For a moment she wondered if she could somehow brazen it out after all, but the pressure of his slate-grey eyes and of her own confused emotions gave her no stable point of resistance and she moved towards the canvas. She wished she didn't like painting at all. It was nothing but trouble.

'He told me about…his relationship with Serena. Another detail you forgot to tell me. Perhaps I should ask what else I should know before someone else decides to enlighten me? As you pointed out, I am a very poor liar and my powers of dissembling are being stretched to their limit. At least now I understand why he has "fixated" on me, as you said. I knew something had happened between the two of you. You should have told me!'

'That is not the nature of our relationship.'

His words hit her with all the power of a physical blow and she leaned her hand on the edge of the easel, pressing into the cool varnished wood. He, too, seemed to realise what he had said and he took a step forward, but she raised her hand, halting him. The silence stretched.

'I am sorry. That was uncalled for,' he said finally.

'It's the truth, though,' she answered with equal coolness. 'But I think it is best you tell me if there is anything else I should be prepared to deal with.'

'I think you have the gist of it now. After Serena…died, he and I met and fought it out. Then I joined up. We haven't come much in each other's way since then. Until now.'

'There was a duel?'

'Nothing so romantic. More like a backstreet brawl. We were both drunk and I don't remember much of it, but he left me with this—' he indicated the scar along the edge of his left hand '—and I broke his arm. His left arm, unfortunately.'

The image of that moment in Grosvenor Square gardens, with Max's unrelenting grasp on Wivenhoe's hand and Wivenhoe's white, pain-suffused face, flashed before her. Everything made sense to her suddenly. The foolishness of her dream. And the pointlessness of caring.

'If it had not been for Serena, you never would have said what you did to Wivenhoe. About being betrothed. You weren't talking about me at all.'

She heard her voice, calm and reasonable and very distant. There was no pain there, or anger, or anything of the misery burning inside her. She was learning to at least emulate his cold manner and she wished she could make it go more than skin deep.

'Serena has nothing to do with us.'

She spread her hands out, but then clasped them together.

'You may be a better liar than I, Max, but that is going too far, even for you,' she said quietly and left the room. She was glad he didn't try to stop her. Even kindness would be unbearable now. She felt like a savage, wounded animal; all she wanted was to be alone. Halfway up to her room she heard the front door open and close.

Chapter Seventeen

'His Grace, Miss Sophie,' Lambeth said gently and Sophie started and dropped the brush that she had been holding. Since it had completely dried while she stared vacantly at Marmaduke's painted grin, it didn't leave a stain on the rug, but she still scuffed at the rug with her kid slipper, keeping her head down to hide her flush. For a moment she debated having Lambeth send him away. A day might have passed since their confrontation, but she was still raw. She had never thought herself prone to melancholy, but she was learning fast. She laid down her brush carefully and nodded to Lambeth. Putting off seeing him again wasn't in her character. And she missed him, fool that she was.

He walked in and stood just inside the door as

Lambeth closed it behind him. When she didn't speak he took another step inside.

'I came…I wanted to invite you to go to Richmond Park. You can bring your sketch pad.' The stony coldness of yesterday was gone and he looked merely uncomfortable, and whatever pretensions she might have had to firmness began crumbling.

'I'm not dressed for the park,' she replied, hanging on to her cool manner, and a glimmer of a smile appeared in his eyes.

'I have five sisters. If there is one thing I have learned, it is how to wait for them to change.'

She looked down at the floor, amazed she was so willing to succumb to that smile. She had never thought herself so weak. She shrugged.

'Ten minutes, then.'

The smile reached the edges of his mouth.

'Twenty.'

Sophie didn't bother responding, but she left the room determined to somehow look her best without being a minute above ten.

She didn't quite make it. Now that her engagement was public, Aunt Minnie had insisted on assigning her one of the parlourmaids to be her personal maid and Susan, delighted with her promotion, was waiting to pounce on her when she entered her room. Having been trained by Aunt Minnie's own woman, a terrifying battleaxe, she was quick and precise and had Sophie into Madame Fanechal's lavender promenade dress with its mulberry and silver pelisse and the new straw bonnet with matching lavender ribbons that Hetty had chosen for her. Sophie spared a quick look at the mirror before hurrying downstairs. At least she looked the part now. Now she had only to act like it. She stopped before the door and drew a deep breath before stepping in with dignity. Max looked over from the paintings and moved towards her, holding out his arm politely with the hint of a smile just tightening the corners of his mouth.

'Well?' she prompted as she picked up the cloth bag with her sketch pad.

'Well, what? Oh, your dress. You look lovely. You have definitely found your style.'

She flushed at the appreciative warmth in his eyes as they moved over her. 'That is not what I meant. I wasn't fishing for compliments! How long was I?'

The smile flickered again.

'I wasn't counting.'

'I told you I wouldn't be above ten minutes,' she said confidently.

'Twelve.'

'You weren't counting.'

'I know better. And even if I was, twelve is already an impressive feat on its own. The fact that you could achieve such charming results in so little time is nothing short of wondrous. But you don't have to hurry. I don't mind waiting for you.'

Sophie looked at him suspiciously as they stepped into the hallway. This switch to humorous gallantry from the bitterness of the day before was disorienting, but she was grateful he was making an effort to bring them back to normality. As painful as it was for her, he had been right in pointing out that their relationship was not one of emotional intimacy and it was best to keep their exchanges light and impersonal. It wasn't his fault she naïvely allowed those amazing physical experiences to convince her something significant was growing between them. He had never once attempted to deceive her about the 'nature of their relationship' as he put it. She should have the courage and strength to respect that and not start indulging in romantic and dramatic fits. At twenty-four years of age, and after almost as many of tucking herself back in, she should be able to manage some restraint. She might be foolish enough to live in hope that something else might evolve with time, but for the moment she would follow his lead.

'I am taking Miss Trevelyan driving, Lambeth. We will be back in a few hours,' Max informed the butler as they moved towards the front door.

'Will you be needing the leash for the dog, Your Grace?' Lambeth enquired politely.

'The what...?' Max's question died out as Marmaduke interposed himself between them and the front door.

'No, you may not!' Max told Marmaduke. 'Go back to your room!'

Marmaduke flattened at Max's stern tones, paws outstretched.

'Poor Marmaduke,' Sophie said before she could stop herself.

'Sophie, you can't mean to take this undergrown canine with us to Richmond!'

Sophie laughed, the tension leaving her body at the absurdity of the moment.

'I don't mean anything. He is clearly enamoured of you. Go back to the parlour, Marmaduke!'

Marmaduke shuffled towards Max's boots,

looking up at him, his pink tongue out and panting gently.

'You heard her. To the parlour!'

Marmaduke lay down again, looking like a furry prostrate Buddha except for the eyes gazing mournfully up at his idol.

'Oh, for heaven's sake…and you standing there laughing isn't helping, Sophie!'

'I can't help it. Oh, very well, I'll take him back to the parlour.'

She scooped him up and started towards the parlour, but Marmaduke squirmed and leaped out of her arms, scurrying to stand between Max and the door where Lambeth still stood waiting to open it for them, his face carefully neutral as he stared at the wall.

Max frowned down at the pug.

'Fine. Just take his leash with you. Or maybe not—with any luck he'll run away in Richmond.'

'Max!' She laughed and went to take Marmaduke's leash from the side table by the front door. 'Come, Marmaduke. You are going to discover a whole new world of fowl today. I hope you like curricles.'

'If he barks at my horses, I'm leaving him on

the side of the road,' Max said as they went outside towards the awaiting curricle.

'So far the only one barking is you, Max. Up you go, Marmaduke. There, see? He's a natural. As long as he has your boots to cuddle up to, he's as merry as a grig.'

'Just keep your eye on him. I don't trust him an inch. And keep him down there. If anyone sees me driving a pug around, I'll never live it down.'

'Hear that, Marmaduke? On your best behaviour, now. Otherwise we might not get invited again.'

Max sighed and guided his team west, and Sophie held herself in readiness to grab Marmaduke, but he just sat panting happily at their feet as they drove towards Kingston Road. She resisted the urge to give the dog a hug for having so effectively defused the tension between her and Max. And for having reminded her that despite the walls Max set up so effectively, there was a kindness to him she wasn't certain he was aware of himself. It gave her hope that he could at least find companionship with her, if not return her love. She raised her face to the sun as it burst out from behind a cloud like an actor rushed late on to the stage. She would have to find Marmaduke an extra-special treat.

'Oh, beautiful!' Sophie breathed, her hand half-outstretched as if the view of the park and the city beyond it from King Henry's Mound were a painting she could explore with her fingers. And it *was* beautiful, Max had to admit. They had spent so long exploring the park that it was already late afternoon and the sun was low behind them and St Paul's dome in the distance had lost its grey cast and looked rosy and gilded, rising from the paler mass of the city and framed by the vivid new green of the park.

He had been to this park more times than he could count over the years, but somehow it was different today. Like at the Exhibition, he noticed things that he had never paid much attention to, the shading of the sun on Pen Ponds, the silence that fell when they caught sight of a stag and doe standing haunch to haunch in the forest just three yards from them. The way Sophie had grasped his hand in an unconscious sharing of her wonder, her eyes glinted up at him in happiness.

It had taken a great deal of willpower not to pull her to him and try to capture that joy in a more physical way, but it had felt almost sacrilegious. He was well aware of the fragility of the peace they had reclaimed after yesterday's clash. He had been wondering how to mend some of the damage he had inflicted but he had not imagined his olive branch of a trip to Richmond would be so successful. It was just that her enjoyment was contagious, even of things as foolish and mundane as the efforts of a line of ducklings that trailed after their mother with fierce determination, scattering and reforming around obstacles until they made it safely to the ponds while he kept a firm hold on Marmaduke's leash and hunting instincts. And his own.

It didn't help that the park seemed to have emptied of its afternoon wanderers and they now stood alone on the hill, having left the curricle, groom and the exhausted and slumbering dog on the path below. The trees and shrubs surrounded them in a green cocoon which was only broken by the gap open to the vision of the shimmering city.

'I wish I could paint that light...' she said wistfully.

'Can't you?'

'No. It wouldn't come out right. Your Mr Turner

could, I think. Like the sea. I keep trying to paint the sea off the cove and it's never right.'

'Maybe it's the inadequate north Devon light. You can try your hand in the bay at Harcourt. I think we should travel there this week. I could get a special licence and as soon as your family arrives your father can marry us at the Harcourt chapel. That should satisfy even the most exacting critics.'

'So soon?' Her eyes widened and she wet her lips nervously and he moved towards her.

'Since we've already anticipated a crucial aspect of the ceremony, I don't see any point in waiting, do you? And once it's done we can get rid of everybody and go out on the Shepstons' boat to Old Grumble—there's a beautiful view from there and you could even take your easel out there.'

She seemed slightly dazed at the barrage of information, her hands clasped tightly in front of her like an obedient schoolgirl.

'Old Grumble?'

'A tiny island near Port Jacob. We…the fishermen use it sometimes. It's named after the sound the waves make on the rocks.'

That caught her attention.

'You fish?' She cocked her head to one side, her

embarrassment fading, and the curiosity in her eyes tempted him forward.

'That's all I wanted to do when I was a boy. I used to go out with old Mr Shepston and his sons since I was seven or eight whenever I was home from school. Sometimes I spent more time with them than at the Hall.'

'I'm impressed your parents allowed you. Papa never liked it when George went out fishing with the villagers.'

He shrugged. 'They didn't allow it, they just didn't know about it. We didn't spend much time together when I was home at the Hall. They found out by chance when I was thirteen and my father happened to be in Port Jacob one day and he saw me coming into port with the Shepstons.'

'Was he angry?'

'Not angry, disappointed. He wasn't a man of strong emotions and he was very conscious of the Duke's role. He always told me it was important to know each and every one of our tenants and their families and show the proper amount of attention. He just felt I had carried this dictum too far and that there was nothing to be gained by becoming over-familiar with people who were dependent on us for their livelihood. I pointed out that the fishermen were dependent on the sea, not on us. I was still too young to understand economic logic and social distinctions. As far as I was concerned, the fishermen were royalty. My father delivered a very enlightening lesson on the local economic structure and our role in it. After that he made sure I was fully occupied learning about estate affairs and understanding that lesson down to its finest detail.'

'Isn't thirteen a little young to be inculcated into crop rotations and irrigation and the like?'

He smiled at the subtle bristling in her manner, as if preparing to mount a defence of that long-gone boy. It was touching, but misplaced.

'Not really. The fishermen took their children with them so they could learn the trade. It was no different with me. It was just that at that age I preferred their trade to mine. But my father was right…about that at least. I can't turn my back on my responsibilities. Too many people depend on our doing our job right. That's all it is.'

'But if you enjoyed it so much… Didn't you go fishing with them again after that?'

He almost bent the truth just to draw out the concern in her gaze.

'Of course I did. Not as often, though. My father was cold, not a fool, and he knew interdictions were ineffective. I think what bothered him most was that none of his people, as he called them, had told him about my activities during all those years. I think he was insulted, which is ridiculous.'

'I don't know. After all, if his life was about his duty towards these people, it might have felt like a betrayal if they withheld something they knew was important to him. It would hurt.'

Max turned away, riding out the sudden, feverish heat that coursed through him, mute and shocked by its power. He would never have credited empathy with any more aphrodisiac effects than humour but he would have been wrong on both counts. It had been a mistake to leave Marmaduke in the curricle. He could use a chaperon right now, even a canine one.

'Is there no one you won't champion?' he asked lightly after a moment.

'That doesn't mean I would have chosen him over you,' she said seriously. 'It is just that I think I can understand why it might have hurt. That's all.'

'I think you overestimate my father's capacity for being hurt. It doesn't matter. I don't know why I told you any of this. Come, let's find a good place to sit so you can sketch.'

'Oh, there's no need, you probably wish to return.'

'No. Do you?'

She hesitated, her eyes searching his face, and then her shoulders sagged.

'My fingers are burning to try. I'm sorry, I won't take long.'

'You shouldn't apologise if you've done nothing wrong. It's a bad habit.'

'I'm not...well, a little. I know you would prefer me without all the nonsense about the painting.'

'I don't know what you would be like without the painting. It's not just something you do, it's how you see the world.'

Her eyes widened.

'No one has ever said that to me before.'

'Is that good or bad?'

'I...good, I think. It's like those dreams where you are going about and suddenly realise you are only in your petticoats, you know?'

Max threw back his head and laughed.

'No, I don't. Not petticoats.'

'Well, not petticoats, but you *know* what I mean. Finding yourself exposed.'

'That doesn't sound very enjoyable, then, and that is not what I meant to do. It was just a thought. Why did you think it was good, then?'

'Because it means you see me.'

His smile faded slightly as he looked at her, but he kept his voice light.

'Right in front of me. Hard to miss.'

'You know what I mean.'

'Yes. It's not always a good thing, though. To be seen. I thought you said it made your life harder at home.'

'Well, I should perhaps have said seen and…understood. Someone seeing past the obvious faults to what is behind them. But that is probably not what you meant anyway.'

'It is what I meant. But they aren't faults. They might not be easy to deal with, but they aren't faults.'

She turned towards the view, but he grasped her arm lightly and turned her back to him and was surprised to see her eyes had reddened with tears.

'What have I done now?' he asked and she touched her fingers to her eyelids.

'You're being nice.'

'A cardinal sin. And very out of character, I know.' Max took her hand and drew her towards the shade of a broad-leafed tree. 'There's a clear view from here. Wake me when you're done.'

She sat down and pulled out her sketch pad and Max sat as well, leaning against the tree trunk and watching her through half-closed eyes. The remains of the summer sun sparkled through the leaves shifting in the breeze, shimmering over her like golden medallions, and the fading warmth and quiet lulled him into a sensation of lazy comfort he remembered from those times on the fishing boats when nothing was happening and he was utterly relaxed. He could almost feel the shifting of the water, soothing and caressing. But underneath he was anything but relaxed. He knew she was totally unaware of the invitation of her alternating laughter and empathy, which only made it more potent. She looked so intent as her hand moved lightly over the sketch pad. But he wasn't watching the drawing. She had a lovely profile, he realised, more defined than he had thought, or maybe it was because she was looking so serious now, her mouth tense. He wanted to trace that line, linger on her lips until they softened and lifted in the smile that somehow always managed to crumble his defences, then slide over her de-

termined chin and down the sweep of her neck...
lower...

As he watched she bit down on her lip in concentration and then let it go with a soft sigh and it
slid out, damp and just touched with light. It was
such a tiny inconsequential movement, it made no
sense that it should drag him out of his lazy contemplation and into a maelstrom of hungry desire
that clenched his body and was as out of place in
this sylvan setting as her irreverent and unconventional nature was in his carefully controlled
life. He almost wished someone would break into
their solitude, but aside from the birds and the
faint buzzing of bees from the honeysuckle bushes
there was no sound. The scent carried, reminding him of her scent and taste when he had been
buried in her, sweet and warm and edged with
something exotic and elusive that kept him wondering, searching. It brought with it the memory
of her body, tense and tightening as he brought
her to release, her heat and abandon and the urgent
cries she had tried to stifle. He wanted to take that
sketch pad from her hands, press her back against
the grass, strip her and cover her naked body with
his, this faint breeze cool on their damp, flushed

skin, her breasts bared to the fading light, to his hands and mouth...

He raised one knee to ease the tension and leaned his head back on the tree trunk, looking out over the park. His hands were burning and he tugged off his gloves as if that might relieve the heat and, though the cooler air was soothing, it just heightened his need to reach for her and pull her to him. He almost smiled at the triteness of the scene and of his response to her. He would have thought that turning thirty would have brought wisdom and prudence. Instead he was sitting here, an inch away from making an utter fool of himself because he was hot to bed his future wife. He kept his eyes on the view, breathing slowly. Finally he heard her shift and looked over. She closed her sketch pad and she looked over at him and smiled.

'Thank you for being so patient.'

'Wrong word,' he said with more bite than he had intended and her smile wavered.

'I'm sorry if I kept you...'

'No, that's not what I meant. Forget it. Come.'

He stood up and held out his hand to help her up, cursing his clumsiness. It wasn't her fault his self-control was so tenuous. She gave him her hand, but the open, laughing ease of the past hours was gone and the rosy flush on her cheeks had nothing to do with pleasure. She turned back towards the path, pulling her hand from his, but he tightened his hold. It had been a lovely afternoon and he didn't want the whole of if tainted by his stupidity. He searched for some way to retrieve his mistake.

'I enjoyed myself very much this afternoon,' he said, aware he sounded stiff and formal. His fingers were just touching the base of her wrist and he could feel her heartbeat, fast and sharp, or perhaps that was his own pulse, he couldn't tell. But the tiny surges of flesh against his were hammer blows on his defences and the heat that had stung and caught him as he had watched her sketch was back with an immediacy and force that shocked him.

'Look at me!' There was something of the desperation he felt in his voice and she did look up, her eyes almost teal coloured, bruised and wary, and the wariness cracked his resolve. He didn't want her wary of him. He wanted…he *needed* that smile he had chased away.

'The only impatience I felt was with myself.

This is neither the time nor place for what I was considering.'

Under his fingers the pulse hitched and picked up speed and her flush deepened, but at least the distant coolness in her eyes faded.

'It still isn't,' he said, more to himself than to her, and the laughing smile filled her eyes like sun settling on water. The relief that flooded him was almost as infuriating as the urgent desire that had gripped him. He shouldn't let her moods drive him like this. But her voice, raspy and breathless, took the sting out of his own weakness.

'Perhaps if you tell me what you were considering I might be able to suggest a better time and place?'

'I would rather show you,' he said, touching the soft pucker of her lower lip and her mouth parted and he caught her lip very gently between finger and thumb, gliding over the silky damp inside, bending towards her. 'I never knew watching someone sketch could be so…inspiring.'

'It doesn't sound very inspiring,' she said breathlessly as he released her lip, his hand sliding over her nape, her hair warm and silky against his palm.

'And yet it is. I kept thinking of doing this…' He captured her lip between his, tasting it with his tongue, following the gilded line he had watched, loving the way it softened when damp, revelling in her taste, so unique and enticing his whole body was recognising it and what it signalled, a promise in itself. He wished he had some creative talent so he could express one iota of the sensations she sparked in him. But the only way he knew was this, with his body, giving itself to exploring her, arousing her. As much as it scared him, he loved the way she responded to his touch and kisses, urgent and demanding and languorous all at once. It seemed the most natural thing in the world to be doing this here, in the middle of the park; it made no difference that any moment now someone might appear. He was already digging his fingers into her skirts to draw them up when Sophie suddenly pressed her hands against his chest and pushed back, her body stiffening. It took him a moment to hear the burst of sharp barking rising up from the path below and he cursed under his breath. The blasted pug. Sophie shivered slightly, but then laughed.

'Marmaduke has awakened. Your poor groom.'

Max straightened as well. It was probably for the best. 'We should get back.'

'Yes. Thank you, Max, I had a lovely afternoon, too.'

Her words were formal and correct, but her smile had the same confiding warmth as before and the ache expanded, pushing at him from inside. He gave in to the urge for one last contact, just touching her cheek, and she leaned her cheek briefly against his hand. For a moment he stayed there, caught. That tiny movement of trust, and tenderness, was so foreign it stood out like a diamond flashing in a coal scuttle. He felt a powerful urge to step into it and an equally powerful urge to reject it, move away from this ache that was dragging him further and further into her territory. It was all well and good to explore, but at the end of the day one went home. The warmth and ease of the afternoon had lulled him into accepting this countryside idyll as an optional reality, where everything flowed and looks were as telling as words. It was as maudlin as any third-rate poetry. Life was hard work and a great deal of conflict and this afternoon had been the exception, not the rule. He dropped his hand and stepped back.

She was still smiling, but the warmth in her eyes was clearing, like water settling. He knew she had read his change in mood and was moving back as well and he didn't know whether to resent being read so easily or to be grateful she was beginning to learn to respect his limits. He should be grateful.

'Come. We should go reassure Marmaduke I haven't carried through on my threat to abandon him in the park.'

Chapter Eighteen

Marmaduke sniffed suspiciously at the out-stretched and very grubby hand. Then his pink tongue flicked out and tested one of the sticky spots and the boy snatched back his hand, but squealed in delight.

'See? He likes you,' Sophie said and the boy grinned.

'May I try again, please?'

'Of course, just as you did before, that was perfect.'

Marmaduke closed his eyes and suffered himself to be petted.

'Master Peter!'

Sophie and the boy looked up at the hurried approach of a slight man in a sombre coat.

'My tutor,' the boy grimaced. 'I must go. May I pet him again another day?'

'Marmaduke will be delighted, won't you, dear? See, he's smiling.'

The boy's grin widened and he jumped up and ran off across the garden to his beckoning tutor, his black curls bouncing, and Sophie gave Marmaduke a last scratch before picking him up and heading towards the gate. The boy must be about ten, close to her youngest brother's age. She stopped abruptly as it occurred to her that if Serena hadn't died, if the child had been born, it would have been about this age and to all intents and purposes Max would have been its father, legitimate or not. They would have been living right here in this square...

If Max hadn't been involved, she might have felt a little sorry for a woman so incapable of appreciating what she had that it had ended up destroying her and scarring the people who cared for her. For the life of her Sophie couldn't understand anyone preferring Wivenhoe to Max, no matter how stupid they were. But then for better or for worse she couldn't imagine Max talking about anyone with the fevered intensity Wivenhoe had spewed at her outside Reeves's. Serena must have loved that kind of adulation. Sophie felt a very uncharitable surge of contempt for people who indulged in such high dramatics.

'Why the scowl? Did Marmaduke misbehave?'

Sophie looked up and stopped abruptly, which was a good thing because otherwise she might have ploughed directly into Max, who stood on the first step of Huntley House. She hadn't expected to see him until the evening, but she was immediately filled with happiness at the sight of him. And then a little guilt about her less-than-kind thoughts about Serena.

'Is something wrong?' he asked, a line forming between his brows and she shook her head.

'Marmaduke behaved exemplarily. Nothing is wrong. I was just thinking...'

'Ah, I see the problem. Come in and rest, then.'

He tapped the knocker and the door opened before she could respond.

'Very amusing,' she muttered as she put Marmaduke down in the hall and Max smiled at her and took her hand, leading her to her parlour. Once inside he leaned back against the door and the look in his eyes was so uncharacteristically warm she felt answering heat creep up her neck and into her cheeks. It wasn't the desire, but the hint of affection in the quirk of his mouth that did it and she actually took a step towards him before stopping. Too soon, silly, she told herself and sat down on the divan.

'Would you care to join me?' she asked properly, but somehow the words sounded off to her. Apparently they did to him too because his smile deepened, but he didn't answer and the prickling heat surged and she gritted her teeth. If there was one thing she wished she could fix in herself it was this horrible tendency to blush.

He sat down on the divan.

'That's unfair, you know,' he said. 'That blush is more potent than my resolution.'

That just made it worse.

'I hate blushing.'

'I…this will probably sound wrong, but I think it's adorable.'

Slightly better.

'It sounds frilly and fluffy and I'm not.'

'No, you're not that. I'm still working on what you are.'

'Now, *that* sounds suspicious.'

'It's a compliment. A poor one, but sincere.'

'Then I will take it as such. And stop while I'm ahead.'

'Clever girl. Now tell me what was bothering you before.'

Oh, please don't ruin it. And the worst was that no matter what she said now, he would know she was avoiding something and in the end he would get it out of her. It was better to just make a clean breast of it while he was in such a mellow mood.

'I was thinking about Serena,' she said in a rush. 'And before you poker up, remember that *you* asked and that it is only natural that I will think about her. That much is unavoidable. If you don't wish to talk about her, I understand as well, but then I suggest we come to some agreement about your expectations of honesty from me.'

The warmth did disappear from his face, with spectacular swiftness.

'You are telling me to ask you to lie?'

'No, I'm telling that if you wish me to respect your boundaries, you must learn to respect mine. Lying…at least lying convincingly is not an option for me. And not thinking about the past is not an option for me either. I will respect your wish not to discuss it, but I won't lie.'

He looked as if he might get up, but he remained seated, staring at the carpet.

'What were you thinking?' he asked almost sullenly and her hands curled into fists. Dangerous ground.

'Do you want to talk about it?'

'I would rather not talk about it ever again in my life, but if you are thinking about it, which I suppose *is* unavoidable, then that wish is moot. So, yes, I want to know what you were thinking.'

Her mother always said better out than in. Hopefully she was right. She rushed ahead.

'Very well, you said she killed herself, but Wivenhoe said she took a potion to rid herself of a child, so I was thinking it might just as easily have been an accident. She just doesn't sound like someone who would commit suicide.'

There. And he wasn't jumping up in anger.

'Wivenhoe said? When?' His voice was flat, carefully controlled, and though her heart jumped, she managed to answer calmly.

'Outside Reeves's. It came to mind today because there was this little boy, maybe ten years old, in the park and it made me think…well, never mind. That's what I was thinking.'

Max stared at the faded fleur-de-lis pattern on the carpet. He wished his past would fade as well, but it kept seeping in through the cracks in his life, inexorable, inescapable. He knew he should leave this conversation until he had himself under better control. He was wavering at the edge of a landscape he preferred not to enter and his mind at least was telling him to get some distance before he proceeded. But he remained.

'I said she killed herself, but I don't think it was suicide either. She probably hoped to pass the child off as mine, but we had to put back the wedding date because my uncle died. And when she didn't manage to seduce me as a means to cover for her…slip, she sought other means of solving the problem. I don't think she realised the dangers of those remedies. Or of anything. She had a presumption that the world would fall into line for her.'

'Would she know how to find such a remedy?'

He glanced up at her.

'Would you?'

'No, Wi…' She hesitated for a moment, clearly uncomfortable. 'Wivenhoe said men knew how. I would have thought he was the one who gave it to her, but it didn't sound like that when he spoke to me.'

He unclenched his jaw. She wasn't Serena. Maybe if he said it enough times, it might sink in.

'What did it sound like…when he spoke to you?'

She frowned at his tone, but continued.

'It sounded like he cared for her and mourned her.'

'Unlike me.'

There, it was out. She didn't answer.

'No insightful comment, sweetheart? Did you imagine Wivenhoe and me as two lovelorn suitors enslaved by the siren Serena? You want honesty? Well, by the time she died whatever juvenile attraction I had for her was crushed under her dainty heel and I was so sick of the sight and sound of her that my first feeling when I saw her lifeless body in the bed where she used to meet her lover was relief that by some miracle I had been spared the purgatory of spending the rest of my life with her. Not a very nice thought for a twenty-year-old to have standing by the death-bed of a beautiful young woman while her father crouched on the floor wailing loud enough to bring the neighbours' servants in on us. I don't need you with your soft heart to tell me that I am despicable. Despicable enough to feel relief even today, even knowing that fool Wivenhoe did care for her, even knowing her death destroyed her father's life. I went away to war to escape the realisation that I was so glad to win my freedom I couldn't even regret the price. Every time I see Wivenhoe I remember what I am. I didn't care for her and I don't mourn her, and I wish to hell I never had to think about her or about what she brought out of me for as long as I live, so forgive me if I prefer to avoid the topic. Is that honest enough, Sophie?'

She was pale and looked much more stern than he had thought possible. He had never told anyone any of this. At least Spain and the brutal reality of war had put Serena and Wivenhoe and even his own guilt in some perspective. There had been very little room for such emotional self-indulgence in the raw push and pull of battle. And that perspective had held even on his return to his former life and duties. Until now. Until Sophie had come and turned his life on its head almost more dramatically than Serena had. And now she knew. He waited, readying himself.

'Very,' she replied. 'And I'm sorry I and this engagement brought it back, but you will never be able to avoid the topic. And nothing you told me makes you despicable.'

'Don't you dare presume to forgive me!' he flashed.

'I don't forgive you. I just don't blame you. She sounds like a thoroughly selfish and manipulative young woman and I'm impressed you had the good sense not to adore her. '

He stood up abruptly.

'And don't make light of it!'

She raised her hands.

'I'm not. Really.'

He stalked over to the window. Nothing good would come of this. Was she really so naïve not to see that if it weren't for his cowardice and stubbornness a young woman would be alive? Serena might have been selfish and manipulative, but she didn't deserve to die. He might not be solely to blame for what happened, but he held his share of guilt. He never should have insisted Sophie tell him what she was thinking. He knew it was trouble. She was trouble. And now she knew the truth and it would always be between them. She might be in her compassionate mood right now, but it was inevitable this would colour her perception of him, an inescapable taint. He should have had the sense never to embark on this discussion; instead he had goaded her on even though he had known it was heading in the wrong direction. What was wrong with him?

He turned back to Sophie. She was so easy to read sometimes. Her teal-blue eyes were filled with regret, as if she wished she could take it all back and somehow shield him from what he had revealed. And just as it had that day he had first told her about Serena, her warm, generous empathy was like a searing brand, unsettling and unwelcome. She had no right to keep dragging into the open events that were firmly in the past and then expect him to succumb to that inviting warmth. He could feel that pull all too strongly, a crescendo of heat had clung to him since he had met her, like a persistent low-grade fever, flaring at the most inconvenient moments and making him do things that he would have scorned to believe himself capable of just a week or two ago. He didn't even know if there was anything personal behind her empathy. Aside from the obvious passion he had tapped into with her, she might feel just that degree of concern towards her siblings or even Marmaduke. All he knew was that she kept throwing his whole well-ordered existence into unwelcome upheaval and he was fast losing his patience with her and with himself.

'Whatever happened, it happened years ago and it doesn't concern you. I think I will accept your offer to respect boundaries on this issue. And from now on if you need to go to Reeves I will come with you. If it is your intention to push me or Wivenhoe to the point where we have no choice but to resort to violence, you are doing a very good job of it'

The empathy vanished and she stared at him in shock.

'That is *not* my intention. Do you really think that is what I want?'

'I don't know what you want!' he exploded. 'What *do* you want?'

'I'll tell you what I want…'

A howl, loud and pitiful, penetrated the closed door, followed by a tentative knock. Max threw up his hands and marched back to the window and Sophie breathed in deeply.

'Enter.'

The door opened and Marmaduke rushed in.

'I beg pardon, Your Grace…miss,' Lambeth said, looking off into space. 'But he insisted. Apparently he, like Lady Huntley, is not fond of loud voices. I will leave him with you, miss, if I may.'

Sophie nodded as Lambeth closed the door once more and pressed her hands to her blazing cheeks. Marmaduke meanwhile shuffled over to Max and lay down, yawning widely. They both looked at Marmaduke for a moment, but he just gave a little snort and closed his eyes, clearly settling in for a nap.

'If you laugh, Sophie, I swear...'

She shook her head and looked down and his resentment and fear drained away, leaving a tight ache in his chest at the pain she was so obviously trying to hide. What did *he* want? He went to sit down by her and picked up her hand. Why couldn't they just stay in that sylvan idyll they had found in the park?

'I'll tell you what I want.' She looked up abruptly, the ferocity in her eyes startling him. 'I won't get it, but I want you to admit that she was a spoilt brat who would have driven any sane man to the end of his tether. That you were a silly boy who took himself far too seriously and was too full of pride to admit he was in over his head. That your parents and hers were fools for not seeing you were completely unsuited and helping both of you out of that disastrous situation which is what reasonable and loving parents should have done. If any of the lot of you had had the sense to call a halt to the situation you would have suffered from nothing more than a little humiliation and Serena and Wivenhoe would probably be married and miserable as they deserve. But life doesn't work that way and this is what happened and now it's over and it doesn't make you a bad person. What on earth did you expect of yourself? Just what do you think you are? You're just Max! And I am so tired of unreal expectations and… I'm just tired and I'm going to rest!'

She tugged her hand out of his, but he caught it again, too shocked to respond, but not enough to let her go.

'It's still morning,' he protested.

'It feels late. I wonder why. Let go.'

He let go of her hand, but only to pull her on to his lap.

'Not yet. Please.'

She froze, one hand braced against his shoulder.

'You can rest here,' he added.

'This isn't restful.'

The anger had gone out of her voice, but it was still abrupt. He took the hand pressed against his shoulder and gently shifted it to his neck, turning her towards him. Her eyes rose to his. They were fierce, but not just with anger, and he breathed in, welcoming the burn of desire that coursed through him. Definitely not restful. He didn't want restful.

He wanted her. To hell with sylvan. He needed something hotter, wilder.

'Actually, you can rest in a minute,' he corrected, smoothing his hand up her back and down again, his other hand moving up her arm, and when he reached the edge of her sleeve, he slid his fingers under the gathered seam. He loved the liquid feel of that skin just there, the pale part of her inner arm he had kissed the day they had become engaged. He could remember how it felt against his lips. Soft, exquisite...a subtle, irresistible invitation. He turned over her arm and touched his mouth to it... Her hand jerked against his neck and she said something he couldn't make out, but she didn't stop him when he tucked his hand into the hair at her nape and drew her mouth towards his.

'Sophie...'

Max's voice was uncharacteristically hoarse and Sophie detached her gaze from his lips and looked up. She had seen passion in his eyes before, but never so unveiled. The Stone Duke was utterly gone. His eyes were dark and filled with a heat that swept her thoughts and fears away like an unrelenting flood. Nothing mattered but the thudding urgency of the desire emanating from them. It was utterly foreign and the most natural thing in the world. It made no sense that this feeling hadn't been with her always, because for the first time she felt herself fully, as she ought to be. And what she needed was to feel him, to see him, to give herself fully to this new reality.

Her lips parted under his as he kissed her, deep and drugging and desperate. Some faraway voice said *this is what it is like to be drunk on love* and it was wonderful. The heat was rising and gathering between her legs and the lost, empty sensation was being replaced by something impatient, demanding.

'Max.' She breathed against his mouth, her hands pulling at the fabric of his shirt, trying to get under it to feel him. It was no longer acceptable to have clothing between them, anything between them. She wanted *him*.

'Max!' she moaned impatiently and he gave in with a curse and shrugged off his coat and she pulled at him, trying to get closer to him, but hampered by her skirts. She gave them a tug so she could rise on her knee, pressing against him, and his hands grabbed her skirt, shoving it up and urging her the rest of the way and she found herself straddling him, her hands on his shoulders, his thighs as rigid as stone between her legs and the unmistakable heat of his erection, hot and hard, pressed just inches below where that scalding, aggravating tension was building, filling her with a choking drumbeat. It was hard to breathe and a wave of confusion almost woke her to the wantonness of what she was doing, but Max was already on another plane, his hands urgent and impatient as he unhooked and unlaced her, tossing her dress and stays to the floor. The scrape and pull of fabrics left every nerve-end tingling and urgent, adding to the fire raging at her centre.

Max's gaze moved over her and that and the cool air made her aware of how closely her filmy silk shift clung to her damp skin. She sobered, suddenly scared that she was teetering on the edge of an abyss, about to willingly abandon control to a man she didn't know if she could fully trust. But then his eyes rose to meet hers, holding her, and time slowed and stretched out. He reached out, gently tracing the skin above her chemise, shaping the swell of her breast, his fingers slipping between them, lingering reverently as if he was drawing her, forming her out of elemental sensations. She came into being under his hands, alive and yearning...she grew under every stroke, unfurling and filling up with sensations and emotions she had never imagined. She locked her eyes on his face, the dip of his lashes over those amazing cheekbones, the contradiction of passion and ruthlessness in his mouth that she wanted on her. Dragged along by the tide determined by the movement of his hands on her skin, rising and falling, now sliding down the centre of her abdomen. Then he slid a hand under her bottom, raising her a couple of inches as his fingers slid very lightly, almost unbearably lightly, between her legs.

The sheer fabric dragged over her sensitised flesh and the sensation was so powerful she arched against him, an uncontrollable shudder running through her. Max breathed in sharply as she shifted convulsively, but though his other hand tightened on her bottom, his fingers kept the rhythm of the gentle caresses. Her eyes kept drifting closed, but she tried to keep them open, to take in everything. His mouth, sharp cut and firm, looked softer and, without thinking, she reached out to trace it with her fingers. His erection surged under her and a lightning bolt of need wrested her from her sensuous passivity. She dragged his shirt up impatiently and he let her go long enough to pull it off, doing the same to her chemise before pulling her towards him, bending to kiss her neck, his mouth hot and urgent on her skin, his hands on her breasts, rough and soft and maddening, and everywhere they touched she felt seared and alive. She moved against him without thinking, searching and finding. She wanted it over and she wanted it never to end.

'Sophie, damn it, I promised myself the next time would be in a bed,' he groaned.

'Fine…' She gasped as his teeth closed gently on the lobe of her ear, spilling molten ecstasy through her body. 'Next time, then…'

She felt his laugh against the sensitive skin of her ear, followed by his tongue, dipping, testing, finding more sensation in that small space than she could have believed possible.

'I want to take my time…touch you everywhere…taste you…'

'Next time…' she repeated, squirming against him in search of relief. She felt his fingers against the fastenings of his pantaloons and then his arousal against her thighs, hot and silky. She pressed against him, she didn't care if it hurt again, she wanted to possess him, to force him to give himself to her. She might not be able to reach him on any other level, but here she felt almost equal, she wouldn't let him keep her at bay.

He didn't argue any more, answering her urging by guiding her down over him very slowly. She had expected the pain again, but it was different, a stretching ache as he filled her, hot and hard, and now that she could feel it more fully she was overcome by how strange and frightening and exciting it was to be entered like that, to possess him inside her. She wrapped her arms around him, burying her head against his neck, breathing him, tasting him as his hands moved over her back.

'Sophie…' he called out her name as she sank down on him, his voice deep and tortured. 'Sophie, don't move, just let me feel you,' he whispered, easing her back without breaking the bond of their bodies so that she half-leaned against the side of the *chaise longue*, and his fingers glided over her body, mapping her with feather soft touches before sliding down again to the urgent thudding between her legs where she was pressed against him, coaxing her, swinging her between joy and frustration. Each time the shudders of pleasure climbed, intensified, until she just couldn't hold still any longer, her body moving against his, drawing him in deeper and deeper. She couldn't separate between the shifting of his body under hers and what his fingers were doing to her. They became more rhythmic, insistent, dragging wave after wave of bittersweet agony out of her, and she twisted against them, trying to meet the waves or break them, anything to gain release. She sank her teeth into her lower lip, trying not to cry out her need and his body shuddered under her and then he pulled her against him with a broken groan, fusing their bodies together, kissing her, his hands moving over her back, her waist, her hips, grasping them as he moved inside her and she lost herself in the frenzy until the world cracked and he caught her cry with his mouth, holding her there as he stiffened under her and for a moment she ceased to feel anything but the flow and ebb of warmth and it was beautiful.

When she opened her eyes she was stretched out on him, her cheek on his shoulder, and they were both balanced rather precariously on the *chaise longue*. The line of his collarbone was glistening with perspiration and she was just reaching up to touch it when he straightened abruptly and slid her off him with a groan.

'Hell! The door, I didn't lock it...'

He strode over towards the parlour door, adjusting his pantaloons as he went. She laughed and turned over, lying stomach down on the *chaise*, too exhausted to contemplate moving and slightly annoyed that he could snap so quickly back into reality after that amazing experience.

'That is definitely locking the stable door after the horse has bolted,' she remarked dreamily and he turned with a mocking gleam in his eyes and surveyed her. She surveyed him back, wishing she could demand he stay where he was while she brought her sketch pad. Even without the rosy haze of urgent desire he was the most beautiful thing she had ever seen. She should have done a better job of undressing him. It was quite unfair that he had managed to keep his pants and boots on, mostly. She wished she could have him to herself, naked for a week. No, for ever. She knew she ought to be embarrassed or ashamed, but she still felt too wonderful and fuzzy and light and those unpleasant emotions were still wholly academic.

He came back to the *chaise* and sat down beside her and ran his hand very gently down her back, from her nape to the curve of her backside. She sighed. His hand was warm and it felt so good.

'Could you do that again? That's nice…' she purred.

He laughed, a low, warm sound she loved, as caressing as his hand on her back. She began to drift pleasantly under the slow, soothing motion of his palm.

'I feel like I'm floating in the ocean,' she murmured. 'Except it's warm…lovely…'

His hand stuttered on her back and then regained its rhythm.

'I'll take you swimming,' he promised, bending to kiss her shoulder and she smiled without opening her eyes.

'That sounds very improper,' she murmured.

'Very. And cold.'

'Thus, the ever-practical Duke. I'll keep you warm.'

His hand stilled again and she heard his indrawn breath and then he stood up and she knew it was over. She never knew when she would cross a line, but somehow she always managed to go too far. She sighed again and closed her eyes, holding on to the sensations, securing them in her mind like a miser hoarding his coins.

'Come, heads up, time to dress.'

She sighed again and sat up. As he lowered the

slip over her she wondered what on earth had happened to her embarrassment. She knew it would come back soon, but for the moment she just revelled in the fleeting touch of his hands as he helped her dress and this freedom to look at him.

'Cravats are very impractical. Someone should conceive of something that is easier to re-tie,' she said and his eyes met hers, lightening again with laughter.

'They aren't usually supposed to be subject to such abuse, you know.'

'Still—' She broke off at a low growl and they both turned with surprise. Marmaduke was still asleep on the floor, but growling faintly, his stubby legs scrabbling in pursuit of some imagined prey.

Max burst out laughing. 'I forgot the blasted dog was here. Thank God he can't talk.'

'He wouldn't tattle on you even if he could. You're his idol.'

'And you're a menace. I told myself I wouldn't—' He broke off, shaking his head ruefully as he headed towards the door.

'Wouldn't what? Nothing at all happened here,' she said demurely, moving towards the easel. 'Good day, Your Grace. It was kind of you to call.'

Max stopped at the door. His face was serious

again and the pleasant heat that enveloped her began to dissipate.

'Sophie, we can't keep…it is too risky on too many levels. Believe me, I'm glad you enjoy this, but we have to be more prudent until the wedding.' He hesitated and came back to her, raising her chin. 'Do you understand?'

His voice was gentle and she tried not to let him see it stung.

'Of course.'

For a moment he remained where he was, looking down at her, and then he took a deliberate step back and with a nod he turned and left. Sophie remained standing long after she heard the click of the front door closing.

Max stood by the window of his study, watching the clouds gather over the houses beyond the gardens. The wind was rising and whipping at the treetops. He shifted restlessly. He was getting no work done, his mind shifting back with annoying insistence to the morning's events.

He was still struggling with the way she had dealt with his guilt. The more her words sank in, the harder it was to recapture the stench of self-disgust that had plagued him all these years. Not that he wanted to recapture it, but that he could so easily be divested of it simply because she read him a lecture on practicality and hubris seemed… weak. He might be 'just Max', but she was just Sophie and he should not depend on her, or anyone to be the arbiters of his conscience. He never had and it was ridiculous to start now just because she kept him at such a pitch of desire and confusion that made him lose track of himself and act completely out of character.

And when he did try to get back to himself he just felt like a fool. His attempt to impose some sense of decorum after his latest transgression had been more pathetic than convincing and had only upset her. She had been so wonderfully relaxed and appealing and he had had to go ruin it by talking propriety and discretion. He had seen the withdrawal in her eyes, but he hadn't been strong enough to face it head on. To admit he no longer had any idea what he was doing or why. Or to admit that her open, honest warmth was becoming as necessary to him as…he couldn't even think of anything at the moment that could finish the thought, which was a form of madness in itself. He had a childish urge to head back to her just so he could coax a smile out of her, light the amusement in her eyes. He wished they were by the sea right now, so they could slide into the licking waves, the heat of her skin against him and the cool water carrying them. It was fitting that she could swim, she was as elemental as the sea and he was as drawn to her and threatened and fascinated by her as a man as he had ever been by the ocean as a boy.

As if his thoughts had conjured her up, he saw her hooded figure hurry across the road to the park, Marmaduke in tow. Instinctively he turned to head downstairs, but stopped and went back to the window. She was just taking the dog for a walk, for heaven's sake. He should have sufficient self-respect to manage a few hours without seeking out her company, no matter how unsettled he felt. The wind grabbed at her cloak, tossing back the hood from her hair and the rush of nature around her echoed through him. He was right, there was something elemental about her, vibrant and real. And foreign to him. And necessary.

It took him a moment to even notice the man striding after her into the garden. And by the time he had realised it was Wivenhoe, the bastard had raised her hand to his lips and moved away.

He stayed by the window, his hand on the curtain, watching her as she stood for a moment longer before heading back out of the gardens.

'Miss Trevelyan.'

Sophie froze and then tightened her hold on Marmaduke's leash and the dog abandoned his attempt to snap at a little swirl of leaves the wind had kicked up.

'I won't do anything. Please wait a moment.'

Surprised by the entreating note in Wivenhoe's voice, she stopped. He didn't come any closer, but he reached out towards her and she saw he was holding a sealed letter. Marmaduke came to stand by her legs, but other than eyeing Wivenhoe warily, he didn't react.

'I will do this quickly before your other guardian appears. I was about to deliver this letter at your house, but I saw you crossing the road and I thought perhaps I should be man enough to apologise in person. I would very much like to blame Harcourt for my abysmal conduct, but since blaming him has become something of a theme in my life, I should probably make an effort to get out of that comfortable rut. Somehow that bastard always manages to come out without a stain on his impeccable armour while I am mired in mud. But what I wanted to say is that I shouldn't have taken out this…resentment on you. You're a decent sort. Too decent for someone like Harcourt. Surprisingly I wouldn't like to see you hurt.'

Sophie considered him. He looked different without that cynical gleam, but she could not tell if this was a new ploy or had they actually reached a bedrock of sincerity.

'I appreciate your sincerity, Lord Wivenhoe, and I would like to take you up on this gesture of goodwill, if that is what it is. Let's just forget everything that happened since that day at the Exhibition, if possible.'

'I don't think I can quite go as far as forgetting it. Regrets and grudges cling to me. But I would be glad if *you* could. I wish you happiness. I suspect you deserve it.'

He tucked the letter back in his coat and held out his hand and Sophie instinctively held out hers and he bowed over it, raising it to his lips in a manner long out of fashion. As he walked off Sophie remained immobile. She was still suspicious, but she could not help that side of her that wanted to believe everyone had redeeming features. And mostly she wanted to end the enmity between him and Max. If that meant being civil to Wivenhoe, then so be it. She tightened her hold on the leash and headed back to Aunt Minnie's, thankful the wind had emptied the gardens of strollers and there was no one to witness her meeting with Wivenhoe.

Chapter Nineteen

Sophie's heart thudded as she stepped out on to the pavement, excited to see Max again after the dramatic start to the day. He stood by the carriage and in the dark he looked even more intimidating than usual. She clasped her thin satin cloak about her against a tug of wind. She was wearing a very daring pale yellow crêpe gown with delicate gold lace sleeves and she hoped Max would disapprove again for all the right reasons. It wasn't until he helped her into the carriage that she realised he was angry. She didn't know how she knew, except that he had withdrawn behind his stony façade, watchful and unemotional. What on earth had she done now? Her anticipation dimmed and she felt a kick of resentment that she was letting this man's incalculable moods dictate her own.

'This cloak is thinner than paper. I should have

worn a warm pelisse. It's chilly in here,' she said defiantly after a moment of silence.

'One doesn't wear a pelisse to the theatre or to a ball, no matter what the weather,' Max stated without even bothering to turn from his contemplation of the passing streets and she felt her hackles rise at his bored tones.

'I see. Are goose bumps in fashion, then?'

'Don't be flippant. Well-bred young women don't admit to suffering from something so mundane.'

'What else has been bred out of them? They don't perspire, so extreme heat is clearly no enemy either. And naturally they don't suffer from excessive emotion, despite possessing exquisite sensibilities. In fact, they are strangers to all emotional or physical extremes. If we could only produce enough of them we could end all wars and most human suffering. Of course, the world might be a trifle boring, but that is surely a reasonable price to pay for universal equanimity. What a pity I am such a sad specimen of the breed.'

Max finally turned to look at her, his eyes inscrutable.

'Is there a point to this?'

She debated answering in kind, but she didn't

really want to. She wanted the other Max back. He might be as stony as he liked but she knew he was still there.

'Yes, Your Grace. I am getting all my social solecisms out of the way before we arrive. I used to make my brother George run three times around the village before guests arrived and then he would be as good as gold.'

A fugitive smile appeared in his eyes, but then it faded and his mouth tightened and he turned to face her more fully.

'Would you mind telling me why you met Wivenhoe in the gardens this afternoon? Why he was holding your hand? And why you haven't said a word about this so far?'

She froze. She hadn't been prepared and for one second she debated denying it, which was sheer foolishness.

'He came to deliver a letter of apology for his behaviour. That's all. I didn't mention it because… I knew it would make you angry and I didn't want to ruin…tonight. And that's it. There wasn't really anything to tell, so…'

'He gave you a letter?'

'No…I mean, he brought one, but he decided to apologise in person when he saw me walking with Marmaduke, so he didn't actually give it to me in the end.'

Stop talking, she moaned internally. She had done nothing wrong—why did she feel so guilty? It wasn't as if he was even saying anything, just looking at her with the same cool disinterest as always. She would have preferred his anger. She could react to that.

'You really don't trust me, do you?' she blurted out.

A charged silence descended on the carriage and Sophie pressed her lips firmly together, wishing she had done so before she had spoken. Everything she said and did was just heaping proof upon proof of her unsuitability. She turned towards the window, but he caught her chin in his hand and turned her back to him. She wasn't prepared for the simmering heat in his eyes and in a second she was breathless and lost.

'You're wrong,' he said quietly. 'I trust you to always try to do what you think is right. It's just that sometimes our versions of what is right aren't aligned.'

'Must they be?'

'No. But I wouldn't mind other aspects being aligned at the moment...'

* * *

Even in the dark Max could see the flush of colour rush over her cheeks and he relaxed further, sliding his fingers lightly along her jawline, into the hollow below her ear, resting there to feel the flutter of her pulse. He had no idea how she did it, but he had entered that carriage tense with confusion and jealousy and now he was subject to a completely different and a much more pleasurable tension and Wivenhoe had been relegated to more a nuisance than a threat.

Her guilt had been so palpable it had contrarily kicked some sense into him. He kept seeing her through the prism formed by Serena's betrayal, but she was nothing like Serena. He might not like that she had so obviously forgiven Wivenhoe, but that was his problem, not hers. The fact that she couldn't hold a grudge was a blessing.

Her pulse beat against his fingers and he was so tempted to replace them with his mouth, pull off the satin cloak, take her back to her little parlour and this time he would lock the door before undressing her. The memory of her stretched out on her stomach, arching slightly under the slide of his hand over her backside, was annoyingly persistent. As was the thought of exploring every inch of those slopes and dips with every inch of his body. He was getting tired of snatching these embraces with her and feeling guilty before and after about breaking the rules. It was sacrilege to sully these moments of sheer glorious lust with something as negative as guilt. He wished they were married already so he could have her naked, in his bed, without barriers and without rules, and with no other person within a mile of them. For a week. At least. He wanted her to himself and away from everyone and everything that weighed them down. They would have to come back to the world eventually, but not before he did something about this unrelenting, aching need that had gone well beyond the physical.

The carriage pulled up outside the theatre in Drury Lane and for a brief moment as he helped Sophie alight he couldn't resist moving in front of her, forcing her to look up, her eyes locking with his, and he didn't move until he saw the flush rise once more over her cheeks. It was childish to need to feel that he could do that to her, make her respond, but it was undeniable.

'You're holding up the whole street, Harcourt!' Cranworth said as he and Sylvie stepped down from another carriage and Max waved the driver to move on.

'Sophie's cloak was tangled in the door.' Max said blandly and Sophie gave a quickly choked laugh.

'That wouldn't happen with a pelisse,' she muttered under her breath and Max pressed her hand and drew her forward.

Sophie glanced around the throng of women entering and exiting the ladies' retiring rooms during the intermission. She was waiting for Sylvie, but she was beginning to wonder if she had missed her in this chaotic and colourful press of silks and satins. She turned and caught the critical eye of Lady Pennistone and with a quick nod she hurried out before she was pinned. It was ridiculous to be so cowardly, but she still felt out of place and too fragile at the moment for an encounter with someone like Lady Pennistone. Besides, why should she have to deal with anyone she didn't wish to? After all, she was not merely Miss Trevelyan of Ashton Cove any more, but would soon be the Duchess of Harcourt. She raised her chin. If she wasn't careful she *would* end up like Miss Pennistone and she wasn't like

that, not inside. Come to think of it, neither was
Miss Pennistone herself, but that was precisely
the point. She liked people, but she had never bent
over backwards to ensure they accepted her and
she had no intention of starting just when she was
about to embark on her new life.

And where was she, anyway? She paused in the
middle of a corridor, trying to remember if they
had come down that way. There was no one else
there and that probably meant she was heading
in the wrong direction, so she turned and halted
as a man appeared behind her.

'Are you lost?' he asked.

He was tall and very thin and for a moment she
wondered if he was one of the actors. He looked
vaguely familiar, but it was an elusive sensation.

'I think I am. I had no idea this was such a big
place. I am trying to find my way back to the
boxes.'

'Come, I will show you the way to the foyer.
This way.'

She turned and followed him gratefully as he
took her down a set of stairs to a passage at the
end through which she could see the distinctive
burgundy-and-royal-blue carpets of the foyer. At

the end of the passage she turned to thank him, but he spoke before her.

'I am Lord Morecombe, by the way. Serena's father. You are Miss Trevelyan, yes? I saw you that night with Harcourt outside the Seftons.'

She almost stumbled in surprise and he stopped, grasping her arm solicitously.

'I apologise. I startled you. I did not mean to, but I have been looking for an opportunity to speak to you since I read of the engagement.'

She stared up at him, caught between shock and guilt.

'Lord Morecombe. I…I am so sorry…'

'Why, my dear? You have nothing to be sorry for. You were not part of our tragedy and have no part in our guilt. I rarely leave my home any more, but I admit I was very curious to see who Harcourt had chosen. And a little surprised. You are so very different from my daughter.'

'I heard she was very beautiful. And lively.' She cringed at her choice of words, but he didn't seem to notice, a soft smile suffusing his thin face.

'She is. Even as a baby I knew she was…extraordinary. A queen.'

His tone was reverent and Sophie's heart squeezed. *'I rarely leave my home any more'.* This wasn't like Aunt Minnie's self-indulgent seclusion, but the kind of implosion of will that happened sometimes to people after a devastating loss. Like a widow she knew in Ashton Cove who had lost all three of her sons to the sea. Sometimes the woman would drag herself into the village and try to smile and be interested in people, then she would retreat again and no one would see her for weeks.

'She does sound like an extraordinary person. You must miss her terribly.'

She almost regretted her words when his eyes filled with tears and he pulled out a handkerchief and pressed it to his eyes with his fingertips before returning it to his pocket.

'Every day. I think…if only I had been…stronger…but it is too late. It is unbearable sometimes. And no one will talk to me of her. Or let me talk about her. That is why I don't go out. It's the silence I can't bear.'

She nodded. She could understand that, in a way. Part of her just wanted to escape, but she stood there, wishing there was something she could do to ease this man's pain. Somehow she felt she had become entangled in Max's guilt and pain about Serena's fate and that imposed a degree of responsibility on her as well.

'I would be glad hear about your daughter, Lord Morecombe.'

He reached out, his hand closing on hers rather convulsively.

'I was so right, so right about you. I knew the instant I saw your face that you were kind. It worried me so. Would you come tomorrow? For tea? And please don't tell Harcourt. He won't let you come. He wants to put it all behind him like all young people and it would just drag everything up again. It will be our secret.'

Sophie agreed that Max would probably not appreciate this particular charitable gesture on her part.

'I will come tomorrow, then. If you like.'

'Yes, yes, indeed. And not tell Harcourt?'

'No, you are right that there is no need to tell him. Things are complicated enough as they are. Good evening, Lord Morecombe.'

'Goodnight, my dear.'

She turned and with a sharp kick of shock she saw Lord Wivenhoe standing at the bottom of the stairs leading up to the boxes, watching them. She hesitated, but headed resolutely towards the stairs. She had just decided she wasn't going to let fear of other people's reactions dictate her actions, hadn't she?

'Good evening, Lord Wivenhoe.'

His gaze was on the man behind her and he did not move out of her way. They both watched as Lord Morecombe moved back into the darkness of the passage, then Wivenhoe looked down at her.

'I didn't know you were acquainted with Lord Morecombe.'

'I wasn't. He introduced himself just now.'

'What did he want from you?'

She frowned at the abrupt question and breathed in.

'To talk. To have tea. He's lonely. And guilty. I think he feels he didn't protect her well enough.'

'*Her.* Her name is Serena. You talk as if you knew her.'

The charged anger in his voice clicked something into place in her mind and her conviction she had been wrong about him grew.

'You didn't give her that poison, did you?' she said slowly.

'Are you mad? I loved her! And that was my child! Of course I didn't!'

'Then why are you so guilty?'

The words, low and tense, poured out of him, his amber eyes reflecting the hundreds of candles in the chandelier above them. 'Because it was my fault she died. If I hadn't got her with child she never would have sought the potion that killed her. Of course it was my fault. I've lived with that knowledge—' He broke off. 'But if it hadn't been for Max she would have married me. I know she would have. He knew she didn't love him and he sure as hell didn't love her, but he held on to her. Out of his stupid sense of duty. If he had been a man he would have sent her packing and then there might have been a chance… If I'm guilty then he is a thousand times more so! He might as well have poured that poison down her throat himself! For all I know that is precisely what he did. He's capable of it, the bastard, just to make sure the world fell into line with him. You're a fool to marry someone who has as much emotion in him as a block of ice! I know she was spoiled… and selfish, but she was so alive. It was amazing to see her. As vivid and beautiful as a sunset.'

Sophie stood mute before his pain, pushing back at her own resentment and fears that his accusations about Max dragged up. She understood Lord Morecombe's pain. Serena was his only child after

all, yet there had also been that strangely adoring, almost impersonal passion that Wivenhoe
was mirroring. As if loving Serena was more a
religious than a human experience. It was not the
kind of love she valued or sought, but she felt
pity for these two men who had adored the vivid,
flawed girl.

'I hope you find someone else you can care for
as much one day, Lord Wivenhoe. Both you and
Max were very young then. And Serena was, too.'

She had not meant to sound condescending and
she cringed a little at her words, but contrarily he
relaxed, the passion fading from his eyes.

'So I was. Must you be so sensible? I was in full
dramatic flight.'

'I have had enough of that for this evening,
thank you,' she said primly and he laughed and
reached out to grasp her hand. After a moment of
surprise she pulled hers away, but not before she
saw Wivenhoe's eyes flicker past her shoulder and
narrow. She turned, knowing what was coming.

Max moved towards them with the swiftness
and brutal focus of a panther and without thinking Sophie moved in front of Wivenhoe. Whatever the necessity for her move, it was probably
not wise. Max did slow down, but his gaze fixed

on her and there was something there that frightened her. Her own sense of fatality and fear that he would never come to care for her, not in any way that was close to what she felt for him, fed on what Lord Morecombe and Wivenhoe had said about him. She was a fool to think she knew this inscrutable, guarded man. All she knew was that they were all tainted by Serena's legacy and that she was so tired of being in her shadow.

'Don't,' she said quietly, but she could hear the desperation in her voice. 'Nothing happened here. And I'm tired and I can't take any more dramatics. Please. Just let's go back to the box.'

She didn't know what might have happened if a large group of people hadn't come down the stairs in a cloud of chatter and laughter. It dimmed somewhat as they noticed the tense trio at the foot of the stairs but then, thankfully, Wivenhoe turned and headed leisurely up the stairs. The crowd continued outside, letting a cool damp wind into the foyer. A porter came to secure the doors, but remained standing by them, looking impassively into the middle distance.

Finally Max moved. His grip on her arm was too controlled to hurt, but it communicated tension and even disdain, holding her like something distasteful but inescapable. Sophie walked beside him, wondering if there was anything she could say to fix this. She knew that if she tried she would only get all tangled and just dig the hole deeper.

And what she really wanted to tell him would probably only earn her one of his 'that is not the nature of our relationship' answers and then she was likely to sit down on the stairs and cry. She should just keep quiet and hang on to her rickety little dinghy and hope to weather the storm. Perhaps when he calmed down she might be able to explain how she came to be standing alone with Wivenhoe, again, her hand in his, again.

She closed her eyes tightly. She had been so looking forward to coming to the theatre with him and his friends. How had she managed to ruin it so royally? He was right about her. She might mean it all for the best, but she just kept making things worse. She was paving her road to hell marvellously with her good intentions and dragging him with her. She knew he had never really wanted to marry her, of all people, but she hadn't been strong enough to turn him down that fateful day and get on the first coach to Bristol and home. But neither was she strong enough to carry these emotions buried inside her. Or to live up to his expectations. She had begun to believe she could do it, become the right kind of wife that would satisfy his needs without losing herself completely.

Yet it took no more than a simple slip on her part to ruin everything, to expose the weakness of her position. Whatever he might say to the contrary, she knew he didn't really trust her and sometimes she didn't know whether she trusted him either. When he was in these black moods, cut off and all drawbridges raised, it was easy to wonder if he had been the one to supply Serena with the poison that had killed her and if her death had been just an accident. Part of her...most of her knew this fear was nonsensical. She *knew* him. Even if she couldn't reach him, if she could never gain access to the warmth she knew was there, waiting for someone to release it, she knew him. She would not believe he had been capable of destroying that girl on purpose, no matter what the circumstances. But there was still that small, wounded part of her that had no faith in herself and her ability to ever be accepted by the world, and that part wondered if she knew him at all or whether it was all a fantasy, as maudlin as the wish that he might come to care for her some day.

They finally reached the box and she was grateful that the intermission was over and she slipped into her seat and stared straight ahead, avoiding all the curious glances directed at them and wishing she could disappear altogether.

Max had no idea what was happening on the stage. He had no idea how he managed to sit there, as if nothing had happened, as if he hadn't come across her and Wivenhoe standing with her hand in his, her face raised to him so trustingly... And the worst wasn't even the way she had come to stand in front of Wivenhoe, protecting him, a mocking reflection of that moment back in the Huntley parlour when she had stood between them in very different circumstances. It had been the sadness that had been so apparent in her beautiful eyes as she had come to stand by him once Wivenhoe walked away. She hadn't even been able to talk to him. She had returned with him to the box and sat down, as subdued and silent as a chastened schoolgirl.

He had no idea quite what had happened there, but his first savage instinct to grab Wivenhoe and drag him away from her had faded as soon as he had seen the stricken sadness in her eyes and he realised he had somehow failed her, again. He wasn't even quite sure how. All he knew was that once again he had managed to depress her joy, turn it into sadness and silence. She had managed to keep hold of her warmth and individuality despite all her family's attempts to subdue her, but he was succeeding where they had failed. It was a matter of time before she realised he had nothing to offer her beyond the physical and he would lose her, in spirit if not in body.

He should have risked it and said something, but he hadn't trusted himself to speak, to her or to anyone. Not that anyone had tried. They must have realised something was wrong. And then the second act had begun. He shouldn't have even taken her back to the box. He should have left and sent his apologies or something, because this was unbearable. She sat inches from him—he could feel the heat of her leg along the length of his thigh and it pulled at him, like a magnet, and more than anything he wanted to close that distance, feel her, even through the layers of that shimmering dress. Connect back to her at the one level he had allowed himself to break free from his controls and where she met him so openly.

He knew she wasn't watching the play any more

than he was. Her mouth drooped at the corners and her hands were held tightly in her lap and he fought against the twin urges of raging at her and taking those tense hands and twining them with his, drawing her to him, forcing her to tell him that her sadness didn't mean what he feared, that she was despairing of him and regretting their engagement. It ate at him, burning him with the same intensity of the desire that wouldn't let him go. It wasn't even the jealousy that she had stood so comfortably with Wivenhoe despite everything the bastard had done, it was something else…despair. He couldn't lose her. Sophie was *his*. She was the only thing he really wanted in this whole pathetic world.

The realisation, finally released from the confines of his control, was stunning, like a blow from Jackson's hammer-like fist. He needed her. This wasn't just lust and certainly not duty. He needed Sophie's warmth and caring and the vividness that was utterly different from Serena's draining force. He had no idea what he would do if she walked out of his life. She had dragged him out from some emotional cave and she couldn't leave him now. It wouldn't be fair. It was pathetic and selfish and undeniable. He needed her. And instead of taking advantage of their time together to try to make her truly care for him, he had been critical and unsupportive and tried to force her to behave like someone totally unworthy of her like Lady Melissa. He didn't want her like that. He wanted just the girl who talked to pugs and who laughed at life and who was interested in people for their own sake and who tried so hard to do what was right knowing she was very likely to fail. He should have had the sense to go down on his knees and tell her she could make whatever terms she wanted. If only she could come to care for him beyond the amazing physical heat that flared between them. He wanted more. He wanted everything.

The applause forced him back into the reality of the moment. He should take her apart, but he had no idea what to say. The fury that had possessed him was sinking under the weight of a corrosive ache, a sense of loss and fear. The urgent need to destroy something was already overshadowed by the urgent need to repair it, but he had no idea how or what or whether it was too late or whether there had ever been a chance. As they stood up he turned toward her, but she was already moving away from him towards Sylvie Cranworth.

Chapter Twenty

Sophie mounted the steps to the house on Manchester Square. It hadn't been hard to find it—it was the only house with the knocker covered in faded black crape, an indication of mourning she knew must have been there since Serena's death. Up close she could see the neglect in the chipping paint and the shuttered windows. These signs of obsessive grief were almost too overwhelming and she hesitated. She was unfashionably early, but she had needed an excuse to escape Aunt Minnie's oppressive house and clear her head. She knew it was a matter of time before Max came to see her and demand an account for last night and she had to clear her head before she faced him.

He had said he trusted her, but she doubted it. Not after last night. And she couldn't really blame him. She might say it was sheer bad luck that he had come across her with Wivenhoe again, but if she had been smart, she would have managed that whole situation better. With clarity and authority. She grimaced. Not her strong points. She was a leap-of-faith person and Max... Max was about clarity and authority. And from his frozen fury last night it was clear he believed she had passed the bounds of what he found acceptable. He might still want to bed her, but it was a matter of time before resentment gained the upper hand. Her foolish dream that she could reach the warm, giving inner core she believed...she *knew* was inside him would remain just that, a dream to tantalise and taunt.

The last thing she wanted to do right now was to listen to Lord Morecombe's grief about Serena, but she had promised and she clung to a faint hope that if she could clear her head she might think of a way to still make this work. And she couldn't think in that oppressive, stifling house where the one place she felt comfortable was a room overlaid with memories and images of Max that inevitably made her body flare into expectation. She would sit with Lord Morecombe for half an hour and then she would walk for a while and think.

She wielded the covered knocker with resolution and after a moment the door was opened by a middle-aged but powerfully built footman.

'I am Miss Trevelyan. I have come to see Lord Morecombe. I know I am early, but—' She broke off.

He bowed and stepped back.

'Come in, Miss Trevelyan. His lordship will be pleased to see you.'

She followed him to a musty parlour where he inched open the shutters, letting in a band of weak light, then he bowed and left the room. Dust motes shimmered in the streak of light and she looked around the almost bare room. There wasn't even a carpet to cover the floorboards which were slightly warped and mottled by ashes around the fireplace. She resisted the urge to either throw back the curtains and windows or leave before this oppressive place dragged her down even deeper into melancholy, but finally the door opened again and Lord Morecombe entered. In this dilapidated setting he looked even more pitiable and she relaxed slightly. It was no great hardship on her part after all.

'Miss Trevelyan, thank you, thank you for coming,' he said finally, reaching out to clasp her hand. His own hands were shaking slightly and she smiled reassuringly.

'Good morning, Lord Morecombe. I apologise for coming so unfashionably early, but…'

'Not at all, I told you I rarely sleep any more. I am just glad you came.' The pale, sagging face tried for a smile and failed. After a moment he turned towards the door.

'Please, come with me. There is something I would like to show you.'

Sophie followed reluctantly. She was so miserable she wondered how on earth she would find sufficient energy to be compassionate. Still, she had chosen to come and she had to complete the gesture, for this poor man's sake. He led her across the echoing hall to another drawing room. It was even mustier and the air was thick and unpleasant. She was not overly fastidious, but she wished she didn't have to sit down on one of the dingy chairs. Instead she looked around the room and stopped as she spotted the portrait on the far wall. The room was so dark she had not immediately noticed it, but now it was impossible to look away. She felt Lord Morecombe come and stand beside her, but she could think of nothing to say and just stood and looked up at the painting.

They hadn't been exaggerating—Serena had indeed been beautiful, her eyes glaring out of the canvas with an avid, demanding arrogance that would have suited a queen. Sophie tried to tell herself that Serena, too, had only been a girl, eighteen, but there was something in that face that was much older. Looking at her, Sophie had never felt so hopeless. There was something in that beauty and the intensity of her story that placed her completely beyond Sophie, taking what she had hoped might be accessible in Max with it. On all levels she realised he was beyond her. She symbolised the worst of what Serena had been—the idiosyncrasy, the wilfulness, the inability to conform, yet without everything that had drawn him to her— her beauty and voluptuousness; that coy, summoning ease men seemed to appreciate so much and which she could never emulate. Serena had left a shadow Sophie could never escape and which Max might never overcome. Even being tied to her by their experiences with Wivenhoe only confirmed the hopelessness of it all. She had known from the beginning she was swimming against the tide with him and, like tackling the waters outside the cove, she was tiring, floundering.

She loved Max so much the thought of leaving

him was a deep sharp wound each time she contemplated it, but she did not know if she could continue to live in the gap between who she was and who he obviously wanted her to become. She was used to the people she loved reflecting that gap back to her and though it had sometimes been difficult she had always tried to find it amusing. She knew they loved her anyway. Perhaps that was the difference. Max had no love towards her that might bridge that gap, the kind of mental embrace and leap that came with acceptance and tempered expectations. She had thought the passion they shared could take its place, but, as amazing and overpowering as it was, it wasn't the same. It didn't have the same healing power and eventually it, too, would succumb to that chasm.

'She *is* beautiful, isn't she?' Lord Morecombe's voice broke in on her agonised thoughts, his voice insistent, reverent.

'Amazingly so,' Sophie said.

'*He* painted this. I would not have kept it, but I thought…it is the only one I have of her. And it is so very like her. He understood her, for better or for worse. It is my fault she is dead,' he concluded and turned away, his shoulders sagging.

'Of course it isn't!' Sophie protested.

He shook his head and continued.

'I adored her, you see. I wanted to give her everything. And if she did have tantrums and was… difficult, I thought it was because she lacked a mother's touch and there was nothing wrong in giving her what she wanted when it seemed to make her happy. Harcourt…the previous Duke, that is…and I had always planned that she and Max would marry. Practically from the cradle. It is important I provide for her, you see, because my estate is fully entailed and once I pass away she will have no more than a small independence and she is quite used to receiving everything she wants. Harcourt is so wealthy they didn't mind that her dowry was modest. And when Max came down to London from school they seemed quite content to go along with our plans. She was so gay and full of life and enjoying her first Season so much it never occurred to me that they were really quite unsuited.

'When they clashed the first time it was over something quite silly—I think it was a necklace she wanted me to buy her—and he said something about her keeping to her allowance and she…well, she lost her temper. She can be quite…vocal. She said things. And he just stood there, watching her like an exhibit and I could see he wouldn't bend and that just made her worse. I told him later, it was only a necklace, and he said that it would always be "only a necklace". If only he could have been…softer with her. Perhaps they were both too young. We should have waited before we pressed for that engagement, it was just that…she was so vivacious and men were drawn to her and she…I thought it best they be married swiftly. And then she suggested having the portrait done so I could keep part of her with me when she married. She wanted *him* to paint it. I don't know if they had already…even then… My child…my beautiful, lovely, girl…'

Sophie walked up and took his hand and he clung to hers, his skin papery and insubstantial. There was nothing to say and so she just sat by him for a while until he gave her hand a little pat.

'You have such a warm heart, child. Have tea with me. Please,' he said, with such a voice of a little boy that she hadn't the heart to deny him. He wandered off and just as she was beginning to wonder if he had forgotten her he returned, followed by the same footman holding a tray with a surprisingly dainty china tea set.

'This was my wife's set and Serena loved it and

planned to take it with her. I thought it fitting to bring it out today. Under the circumstances. Here, my dear. What a blessing that you came. I have been wondering what to do about it all. I cannot sleep at night, you see. All these thoughts and memories. She won't let me sleep. And it is so much worse since I saw the notice in the *Gazette* about Harcourt and you...'

'I'm so sorry,' Sophie said, drinking her tea resolutely, wondering how they had managed to make it so sweet and still so bitter.

'I know you are, my dear. I find that very touching. I watched you yesterday, caught between the two of them. There was violence there without an act or a word, wasn't there? It's a matter of time before they destroy you as well, between them. And that would be dreadful. I watched and I thought...she will end up like my Serena. Torn between those two. They will drag her down, sully her, use her... Have they sullied you as well?'

Sophie stared at him in shock, but could not prevent colour from flooding her cheeks and he gave a queer little groan, dragging his hands over his face.

'Oh, no, I was right. I knew, watching you, that

it was inescapable. My sweet Serena, I won't fail you this time.'

She put down her empty cup, but to her surprise it missed the table and tumbled on the rug and she stared at the spreading blot on the faded carpet. He didn't seem to notice. His hands, like birds freed from a cage, fluttered and flickered above his legs. She should leave. She had not realised this about him. She had thought his peculiar comments yesterday were just those of a lonely, tragic man who needed to talk. She had not realised it was more than that.

'I really must go,' she said, or thought she did, but all she could hear was his voice, earnest and agonised.

'She said she needed a potion to rid herself of the babe and what could I do? She insisted and raged until I went and found it. Just one teaspoon mixed with water, they said. She told me Wivenhoe wanted to marry her, did you know? But she wanted more than that. She had always known she was going to be a duchess and the toast of the town and she wasn't going to give it up for an impoverished baron. She knew Max was no fool and he would soon see she was increasing and he would know she had been unfaithful and throw her over and she wasn't going to have that. She told me everything, that she had every intention of making Max adore her as much as Wivenhoe did. She wanted the Duchy and the money and both of them at her feet and she didn't see why she had to compromise.

'I tried to explain the dangers, but it was no use. One teaspoon, they said, no more. But three days and nothing. So she took more, and more, until there was no more and I could see it was making her ill and I told her it wasn't meant to be, but she wouldn't listen and then on the fourth day even though she was in pain she sent for him and went to the house where they met. She wanted him to find something more effective. But it was too late. She never came back and Max and I went looking for her and found her... I should have been strong enough to stop her from destroying herself. To stop them from destroying her. Do you see? She was my baby and I gave her poison. Of course it is my fault. But I won't let them do the same to you. I will keep you safe.'

Sophie shook her head and tried to rise, to leave, but nothing happened. She had become very small and her body very large, quite light, and he was shimmering, like a flickering candle, no, a moth, a big grey moth, yes…watching her… She had to leave, find Max. She needed Max.

'Do you feel it already?' he asked curiously. 'It's only laudanum, my dear. It is very bitter but I put lots of sugar in the tea. Still, it feels quite pleasant, doesn't it? I know, it is the only way I can sleep. You needn't worry, I will keep you safe from them. That was why I had to be certain you wouldn't tell Harcourt. They won't find you. They can't hurt you any more.'

She wondered why she was still sitting there. Except that it seemed strange to think of moving. Something someone else might do, but she was not sure how. *You must stand up*, she told herself forcefully and made an effort to push off the chair. To her surprise she found herself on her hands and knees, her eyesight clouding over and her ears buzzing. Lord Morecombe's voice washed over her, increasingly distant.

'Don't worry. I will keep you safe. Just relax, my child.'

Sophie tried to shove herself to her feet, but the effort only drained the last light from her vision and she barely felt the blow as her cheek made contact with the carpet.

Chapter Twenty-One

Max looked up. He had no idea how he had ridden that far, or why. The clouds hung low and sullen and there was very little traffic entering Richmond Park. Max checked his horse, feeling like a fool. The memory of the time they had recently spent together on King Henry's Mound was vivid but already unreal, as if it had happened to someone else. He turned his horse back towards London. The thought of seeing the park, grey and gloomy and lonely, was too painful. Nothing about the city would ever be the same, he realised. How had she overlaid so much of his world with her presence in such a short period of time? She had torn him down and built him up again with herself now rooted in his foundation. He felt dispossessed, stripped of the exclusive control that had been such an obvious part of his life. She had taken a charcoal sketch and slathered it with paint, thick and vivid and uncompromisingly alive.

And in return he had tried to force her into a mould that was totally unworthy of her. Meeting every attempt to reach him and every invitation to show human emotion with rejection or suspicion. He hadn't been brave enough ten years ago to call a halt to a disastrous alliance and he was still a coward or he would have admitted to himself that he needed her. He had never known what it was like to need someone at a level that was basic to his life, as important as his own existence. And he had never thought of someone else's joy as precious, but hers was. At some level he had known it from the very beginning. Even the stupid gesture of sending her that collar and leash had been driven by some instinctive response to her wistfulness and her thirst for life.

She was so much better than him, so much more alive and real. She deserved someone who would allow her to flourish and explore herself. Who wouldn't drag her down like he and her parents did with endless expectations to be something she wasn't. It was a matter of time before she realised just how limited he was. If he had an ounce of courage he would find a way to offer her her freedom. It was just that he didn't want to. He had no idea how he was going to redeem himself with her, but he couldn't let her go. It wasn't duty, it was sheer selfish need and he felt contemptible that he couldn't be stronger, for her. But he couldn't. There had to be some way to fix this.

It was mid-afternoon by the time he made it back to London and reached Huntley House. He stood on the familiar pavement trying to figure out what to say. The only thing he could think of was to tell her the truth and beg her to let them start over, on her terms. Because the thought that she would leave, that he would never see her again…he couldn't let that happen. He wouldn't. She was his. She had given herself to him and he was damned if he would let her go. Somehow he would atone for his mistakes.

He strode up the stairs and the door swung upon almost before he let go the knocker.

'Your Grace! You've come!'

Max frowned, his senses shifting into alert.

'What's wrong, Lambeth? Has something happened?'

'Miss Trevelyan, she's gone, sir. She left at ten this morning and didn't say where she was going.

The maid said she was wearing nothing more than a walking dress and spencer and she hadn't more than a few coins on her, she's sure of that. And then Lady Cranworth came to call seeing as they had arranged to meet at one o'clock. It is not at all like Miss Sophie to be late or forgetful, Your Grace, so of course I was alarmed. I promised I would send her word when Miss Sophie returned and then I sent James to Reeves to enquire, but she hasn't been there today. Then I went to speak with Mr Gaskell, begging your pardon, Your Grace, and he said you had ridden out and he didn't know when you would return. And finally this past hour I even sent James to do the round of the posting houses going points west, but no one matching her description bought a ticket today. I haven't yet told her ladyship, but I don't know what else to do, Your Grace… I'm so glad you have come. What should we do?'

Max's hands fisted as he listened, taking in everything Lambeth said, struggling against the shock and trying to gather his thoughts. Where could she have gone? She had been gone five hours. Five hours in a light dress and with just a few coins.

'Are you certain that it is all she had with her?'

'Yes, Your Grace. Sue was with her when she dressed and she said Miss Trevelyan just slipped a couple of coins in her reticule and left. That is all.'

'Did she say anything? Anything at all?'

'No, sir. Sue was very surprised. She said Miss Trevelyan usually has a smile and a kind word, but this time she didn't even say thank you. Sue thought she looked very…sad. She thought perhaps—'

'No.' The word whipped out of Max. 'Not Sophie. She wouldn't.'

'No, Your Grace. I quite agree, Miss Trevelyan has too much strength of character. But she is also a very considerate person. She would know her extended absence would cause a great deal of concern. She would not wilfully disappear without letting someone know.'

'Did she receive any message? Has Wivenhoe been here today?'

Lambeth's eyes widened.

'No, sir. I assure you. I have not forgotten he is not to be admitted. And there have been no notes or messages delivered either.'

Max strode back to the door. As outrageous as the thought was, it was the only one he had.

* * *

By the time he reached Wivenhoe's house on Wimpole Street his fear was stoking a vicious rage. When the butler opened the door he shoved past him without ceremony.

'Where is Wivenhoe?'

'In the library, sir, if I might...'

'This way?'

'Yes, but, sir...!'

'This is unexpected,' Wivenhoe said from the doorway and Max strode towards him.

'Sophie has been gone since this morning. Do you know anything about it?'

Wivenhoe raised one brow and stepped back warily.

'Sophie? Has she run away from you? Clever girl. But as much as I might wish she had made her way to me, she hasn't. At least not yet. You don't deserve her, Harcourt.'

Max grabbed Wivenhoe by the coat and shoved him hard against the wall.

'Let go of me!' Wivenhoe pushed back, losing some of his urbane calm. 'She's not here! And if she did come here, I'd send her packing.'

'You expect me to believe that? After those affecting scenes yesterday?'

Wivenhoe inspected him with something between mockery and pity.

'What scenes? You're a fool, Harcourt. I'm
tempted to make the most of your stupidity, but
strangely I can't quite reconcile myself to doing
that to her. There was nothing in those scenes, as
you call them, to which you or anyone could take
exception, unless you take issue with excessive
compassion, which, given your cold blood, you
might. Last night at the theatre I found her talking about Serena with Morecombe and it made me
maudlin. She was just listening to me and being
kind, damn her.'

There was, for a change, the ring of sincerity in
Wivenhoe's voice. It was only because Max was
so desperate to believe him that he held back. He
shook his head, but let Wivenhoe go.

'What does Morecombe have to do with this?'

Wivenhoe moved away towards the sideboard
and poured himself a measure of brandy, not bothering to offer any to Max.

'He was there, in the passage leading to the
foyer, talking to her. That's why I stopped. I
thought he had gone mad and disappeared somewhere. I asked her what he wanted and she said
"to have tea and talk" or something equally mun-

dane, bless her. I could tell she was hurting for the pathetic old fool and it made me angry, I suppose. At him, at her, myself, you. And she stood there and listened with those big commiserating eyes. I feel like an idiot now, but it got to me. But if you think you walked in on a romantic interlude you're the fool, Harcourt.'

Max struggled to find a stable point in this tale, while his mind remained fixed on the fact that Sophie had walked out of Huntley House hours ago and disappeared and that he needed her. Safe. With him.

'Then where could she have gone?'

It was ridiculous to be asking Wivenhoe, but he was scared and desperate.

Wivenhoe frowned, as if registering the import of what Max was saying for the first time.

'When was she last seen?'

'She left Grosvenor Square around ten o'clock. She didn't have more than a few coins with her according to the maid.'

Wivenhoe's frown deepened and he glanced at the clock.

'That's…what? Six hours ago.'

'I know that, thank you. The Huntley butler checked everywhere. Reeves, her friends, the posting houses, even though she didn't have enough funds for a ticket.'

'Did you argue?'

Max shot him a look filled with loathing and Wivenhoe shrugged, dismissing any responsibility.

'Don't lay your blindness at my door, Harcourt. So it's possible that she ran away, after all.'

Max turned away from Wivenhoe, staring at the wall. He shook his head slowly.

'Sophie isn't one to run away. Not like this. She is too honest. She wouldn't take the easy way out like Serena did.'

Wivenhoe's eyes flashed with sudden fury.

'How dare you speak of her that way? You never should have got engaged to her!'

'We agree fully on that, at least. But she could have chosen to break the engagement. I gave her every opportunity to withdraw and she didn't. As far as she was concerned she had you and me secured and she was too greedy to give anything up. Remember that when you idolatrise her.'

'Don't you dare preach at me. That was my child you killed when you gave her that poison!'

Max stared at the unveiled venom in the artist's face.

'What are you talking about? I never gave her a damn thing and she sure as hell didn't get it herself. *You* gave it to her.'

Wivenhoe's fury faded into confusion.

'No. I told her I wouldn't, that she would have to marry me. She told me she would get it from… someone who would do what he was told and hold his tongue. I thought she meant you and I *wanted* her to tell you about the child. I knew there was a limit even to your sense of duty and that you would finally break with her and then…I was *certain* it was you. I told Sophie it was you. I don't think she believed me, though.'

'You told Sophie that I poisoned Serena?! You insane bastard!' Max grabbed Wivenhoe again, all his fear and fury channelling into his hatred of this man, dragging him up against the wall as if he could shove him through it. But suddenly the significance of his words struck a chord in the corner of his brain still functioning. He let Wivenhoe go and stepped back.

'What were Serena's words? Someone who would do what he was told and hold his tongue?'

'Surely you don't mean Morecombe?'

'No wonder Morecombe fell apart when she died. She was everything to him.'

'You're being absurd.'

'My mother told me he hardly left the house or spoke to anyone after Serena's death. Why in hell would he be at Drury Lane talking to Sophie of all people and inviting her to tea?'

Wivenhoe straightened his coat, keeping his eyes warily on Max.

'I don't know. The man is mad after all. What difference does it make? Even if you're right about him getting the potion for Serena, why would he do anything to Sophie?'

Max shrugged. He had no idea if Morecombe was connected, but if she had gone there, perhaps they would know something. At least it was a something he could act on. He had nothing else. He turned to go.

'I'm coming with you,' Wivenhoe stated, marching after him.

'Like hell you are.'

'I'm coming.'

Max shrugged. He didn't care. All he cared about was Sophie.

Chapter Twenty-Two

Sophie turned over and bumped her head. The pain was muffled, nowhere near as bad as the stuttering dance of images flashing inside her eyelids without rhyme or reason; it felt like the whole Summer Exhibition had been tossed up inside her head into a chaos of shapes and colours. Finally it slowed. She saw a little girl picking up a pebble on a beach. Then someone's hand. A strong hand. She reached for it and poked something hard and opened her eyes.

The stone wall glistened slightly in the shimmering light of a candle standing on a table just at the edge of the bed. The room smelled of damp old things and added to the wave of nausea that rolled through her as she forced herself to sit up.

What a gullible fool she was. If she weren't so scared, she might even appreciate what Max might say about the stupidity of indulging in compassion without an iota of judgement. She squeezed her eyes shut. Max. How on earth would she get out? No one would find her here. She tried to stand, but the room pitched and swayed and she pressed her hand to her mouth to hold back the need to gag. Finally she heard a key scrape and turn in the lock and Morecombe stepped into the room, his arms draped with bright yellow fabrics. Behind him stood the footman who had opened the front door.

'How are you, my dear? I hope you aren't feeling too unwell because of the laudanum. I'm afraid we will have to give a little bit more before we leave for my home in Hampshire at first light. Meanwhile, why don't you change into one of your…one of these dresses? It's a pity your hair is so light. They go better with dark hair…' His voice trailed off as he looked down at the dress in his hand. 'I think you should wear the topaz dress first. It's lovely, isn't it?'

Sophie listened, trying to think, fighting her nausea and fear. This made no sense, but somehow she knew arguing with this mad, lost man would serve no purpose. He looked up and saw her shudder and frowned in concern.

'Are you cold, my dear? There's no fireplace down here, I'm afraid. Oh, dear, perhaps if you promise not to make a fuss we could move you to your bedroom until we are ready to leave. I don't want you to be taken ill. Phelps, do we still have the bedroom keys?'

'Yes, my lord.'

'Well, then. We'll wait outside while you change. I'm so sorry, but Annie isn't with us any more. It is just Phelps and I now so you will have to make do with us. Here you are.'

He laid a dress down on the bed and backed out with a tentative smile.

She closed her eyes and focused on her breathing. The thought of putting on Serena's dress was almost intolerable, but she had to humour him if she was to find an opportunity to escape. It took her a while to dress, hampered by revulsion and by the persistent dizziness that threatened to swamp her each time she moved. But when a timid knock sounded she was dressed and waiting.

The look on Morecombe's face was telling and pathetic—excitement and disappointment mingled as his eyes moved over her. Then he came and very gently placed her hand on his arm, petting it as they walked through the cellars and up the stone steps heading upstairs, with Phelps at their heels. Her nerves begged her to just run or scream at the top of her lungs, but she didn't like the look of the solidly built Phelps and she didn't want to be drugged again, and certainly not by force. Instead she leaned heavily on Lord Morecombe's arm as he cooed and tutted worriedly.

'I must have given you too much, poor thing. You are much more slight than… It will wear off, though, my dear, and then you will be right as rain, just wait and see…'

Anger was a powerful antidote to fear, she realised, and as it gathered, her compassion for this damaged and damaging man withered, replaced by a single-minded focus on getting out of that house as quickly as possible. As they reached the bottom of the stairs, she looked carefully around the hallway. Then she wavered and his arm came around her, supporting her.

'I don't think I can climb…I think I'm going to be ill,' she whispered, clinging to the balustrade and pressing her hand to her mouth. The way she felt right now, she was certain her words were believable.

'Oh, my poor dear. Phelps, do fetch…something.'

Phelps grunted and hurried towards the back stairs.

'A chair…must sit…' she gasped, sinking her forehead against the balustrade, and Morecombe glanced around helplessly before heading towards the door of the room she had been shown into before. She waited only for him to disappear into the room and then shoved herself away from the bannister, her eyes fixed on the metal bolt of the front door as if it was the exit from hell, which in a way it was. She had just reached it and shot it back when she heard Morecombe's agonised cry.

'No! Come back. Phelps! Stop her!'

She didn't even turn at the sound of footsteps thudding behind her, just grabbed the knob with both shaking hands and dragged the door open, filling her lungs in preparation to scream as she had never screamed in her life. The door opened, but she didn't make it outside. Out of the darkness a black figure hurtled towards her, raising her off her feet like something out of a tale of hell and demons coming to collect their victims.

'No!' she gasped, fighting furiously. 'No!' She wouldn't let them take her. She wouldn't. She needed to get away. Her fists were heavy and use-less like in a dream and she was held immobile, enveloped.

'Sophie...'

She didn't know if it was his voice that regis-tered, though it was so deep and shaken it was hardly recognisable, or the feel and scent of his body, but she stopped struggling. It was a trick, part of the drug's effect, it couldn't be Max. She tried to push away so she could see. It looked like him, so handsome it hurt her. But she didn't trust this apparition. They had probably given her more of that horrible drug and she was just imagining Max holding her. They would take her away and she would never escape. She felt the tears on her cheeks, hot and hopeless. She had lost Max. She should have told him how much she loved him, even if he didn't. It was too late now. That surge of energy had cost her and she didn't seem to be able to breathe deeply enough, the buzzing in her head building to an unbearable pitch. She had heard drowning was a pleasant enough way to die, if there was such a thing, but it didn't feel pleas-ant. She struggled against the downward pull of the dark, but it took her anyway.

* * *

Max picked her up in his arms as she sagged, holding her tightly, his body shaking with relief and fury as he took in her tangled hair, the trails of tears on her cheeks highlighting a faint bruise along her cheekbone. Murder rose in him and he looked up to meet Morecombe's shocked face.

'I will kill you!'

'You don't understand…I was trying to protect her. It was all my fault, giving her that potion, but she insisted. I couldn't let it happen again. I had to protect her.'

Wivenhoe stiffened at Morecombe's words, but Max didn't care about their significance.

'I don't give a damn about what you did to your daughter, you madman! But I'll have you locked in Bedlam if you come within a mile of Sophie ever again, do you understand? If you ever touch her, I will kill you.'

Wivenhoe moved past him into the hall, pulling off his gloves. The footman eyed them warily and stepped back.

'You take Sophie home, Harcourt. I'll deal with this,' Wivenhoe said calmly.

Max glanced down at Sophie's form. She wasn't quite unconscious; she was frowning, her lips moving, as if in a bad dream, and there were tears slowly streaking down out of the corners of her eyes. A vice closed on his heart and squeezed.

'What did do you do to her?' he snarled at Morecombe.

'Nothing. Nothing, upon my honour. It's just the laudanum. I might have given her a little too much. I was going to take the very best care of her, I assure you.'

Max shook his head, closing his arms more tightly around her.

'God help you.'

'I doubt He will get involved here,' Wivenhoe said. 'You really should take her home, Harcourt. You can safely leave this situation to me.'

Max hesitated, but then headed out to the waiting hackney. He held Sophie against him as they drove to Grosvenor Square, more tightly when she started shuddering. But she didn't wake, not even when he carried her upstairs to his bedroom in Harcourt House, ignoring the shocked looks of his butler and footman as he passed.

It was only when he laid her out on the bed that he noticed the gaudy topaz dress and his fury rekindled. He turned her slightly and unworked the hooks, sliding the dress off her as gently as possible. He tossed it contemptuously to the floor and pulled the coverlet over her. Then he sat down beside her on the bed and took her hand. It was cold and restless and he pressed it between his, cursing Morecombe and himself.

'No. No. I won't let you,' she mumbled and he raised her hand to his mouth.

'Hush, Sophie. It's all right. You're safe now. I have you.'

She shuddered again and she seemed to struggle to open her eyes.

'Max... What happened?'

'You're safe. That's all that matters.'

'Shouldn't have gone...so stupid... Sorry I'm trouble...'

Her voice faded and he gathered her to him, cocooning her. Her head turned against his shoulder, her body slackening.

'Stay...' she murmured and he had to physically stop himself from crushing her to him. He took her hand and pressed it to his mouth, as if that could stifle the pain, but it just grew. He hated that he had made her feel she had to apologise for an act of compassion, as if she was responsible for that madman's acts. That he could make her do that was just another sign he was wrong for her.

Finally she gave a little sigh, like a child sinking into deep sleep, her body relaxing and her breathing evening out. For the first time in his life he wished there was someone who would just take control and tell him what to do, how to make this right. How to make her stay and care for him. There had to be a way.

'Sophie. Stay with me,' he whispered, and his next words flowed almost soundlessly over her bruised cheek. 'Sophie, my love.'

Sophie surfaced from the bottom of a deep dark ocean and opened her eyes. It wasn't the basement because she could see a fireplace and the logs were snapping happy orange and red. She shifted on the bed, waiting for the nausea and dizziness, but there was nothing. Aside from being very thirsty, she felt fine, even alert. The bed was amazingly comfortable and smelt clean and even familiar. Then her memory expanded and relief and happiness bubbled up in her. Max had come for her. She was safe.

'Max...' she said it aloud, not expecting any response, but a figure detached from the shadows and moved towards her. She sat up abruptly, but then her body relaxed again. 'Max.'

He sat down on the side of the bed, the light of the fire gilding one side of his face and throwing the other into black shadows.

'What happened? How did you find me?'

'Here, drink this first,' he said, handing her a glass and she drank the sweet, tart lemon barley water thirstily.

'Now tell me,' she insisted as he took the glass from her and he hesitated, his gaze roaming over her, his expression neutral, but there was something in his eyes that made her very aware she was in a bed, in the dark, dressed in nothing more than a rather sheer shift, alone with him…

'Where am I?' she asked, to cover her confusion.

'In my bedroom.'

Her eyes widened.

'I…what time is it?'

'Close to midnight.'

'Oh, dear, have you told Lambeth? I don't want anyone at Aunt Minnie's to worry. And I was to meet Sylvie this afternoon.'

A smile softened his expression.

'I sent word to Lambeth. And not only will Sylvie not hold it against you, but she and Rob have come to stay in the guest bedroom to play propriety. Stop worrying about everyone. You'll stay here tonight and tomorrow we'll leave for Harcourt if you feel well enough. For now all you have to do is rest.'

He pressed her back gently and she complied, watching him as he pulled up the covers over her. It was such a simple but intimate act her heart and lungs constricted painfully and without thinking she sat up again and grabbed his hand before he could move away.

'Max… I did try to do this right, but this is just more proof I will never be what you need. I will always fall short, won't I? I need you to tell me, honestly, whether you want to be released from this engagement.'

Her voice wavered on the question and she bit her lip to regain control. Don't ask questions when you don't want to hear the answer, her mother had once told her. But it was too late for that. She didn't want him to feel he was trapped into this just as he had been trapped with Serena. She forced herself to look up, trying not to let the stinging in her eyes turn to tears. Max's hand tightened on hers and he sat down again.

'You are the only thing I want,' he said, his voice quiet and hopeless and it took her a moment to register not just the words but the pain that was there, the edge of despair. 'I know I did this all wrong. From that day in the gardens, when you gave me Hetty's sketch. If I had had an ounce of intelligence I would have known what was coming. You were wrong that Wivenhoe forced me, or that I offered for you because of Serena. I used him, and her, and that damn dog and whatever I could think of using in order to tie you to me without admitting that I needed you. That I was falling in love with you. Sophie...' His voice was raw and immediate with pain, reaching out to her beyond the words and the intensity in the storm-grey of his eyes. He stretched out his other hand towards her, an abrupt, almost clumsy gesture 'I need you. I'm asking if we can try again.'

She stared at him, shocked at the raw need and pain in his eyes and voice. It was so far from what she had expected she couldn't see how it could be true. As she waited the pain in his eyes intensified and he dropped her hand. She realised what she was doing and reached out, grasping his hand and holding it tightly between hers.

'Oh, God, I want to believe you, Max,' she whispered. 'More than anything. You're not just saying this? Please don't if it's not true...'

His hand turned in hers, closing convulsively, and his hand other reaching up to cradle her cheek, his touch almost tentative, as if she were a soap bubble, shimmering on the edge of existence.

'I love you. Sophie.' He moved towards her, the energy building up in him, as if her question had given him part of the answer he needed. 'I don't think I've ever needed anything in my life, not deeply. I made certain of that. But you've done something to me and I couldn't go back if I wanted to. And I don't. God help me, I need you with me. I need you to see me. It's selfish, but I can't help it. I'm sorry. But I'll do everything, anything I can to make you happy, I swear it. Just tell me what you want. I'll do whatever it takes.'

She raised his hand to her cheek, needing to feel him as she said the words.

'You just have. That's all I want. You don't understand…I loved you from the beginning. I never would have agreed to marry you if I hadn't. I'm just not capable. It's been so hard keeping it inside. I didn't want to push you away, but I rather thought it was obvious. I must be a better liar than we thought.'

He didn't move. She watched the withdrawal,

but for once it didn't threaten her. She reached up and touched his cheek gently, the line at the corner of his mouth, as if she could ease the wary tension she knew was taking over.

'That isn't a terrible thing, you know. You don't have to go away, but it's all right if you do. As long as you come back eventually. I'm here.'

The wariness was replaced by confusion and then a look of mingled joy and pain.

'Sophie…you deserve more than I can give you,' he said hoarsely.

'That's not true, Max. All I want is to be with you. As I am. I want to love you without hiding it. Do you understand?'

He nodded and pulled her towards him, holding her with infinite care. She traced her hand down his cheek, trying to smooth the tension in his jaw. She had no idea how to tell him how much he mattered to her, how much she needed him.

'You didn't tell me how you found me there,' she said after a moment, trying to give them both some time to work through what had been said. His arms tightened on her briefly and then he moved back slightly, clasping her hands gently between his again.

'You weren't anywhere we could think of so

I went to Wivenhoe. He'd told me about seeing you with Morecombe and that you mentioned something about having tea with him. We had a…a discussion and realised neither of us had supplied Serena with the poison—which meant Morecombe probably had and might be even more unstable than we'd thought. It wasn't that I thought he might harm you, but if you had gone to see him someone at his house might know something. I didn't know what else to do.'

His voice was typical matter-of-fact Max, but she could read between the lines. It must have cost him a great deal to go to Wivenhoe for help. She was curious how the two men had dealt with each other, but perhaps it was best to leave that for another time.

'I can't help but feel sorry for Lord Morecombe. I can't imagine what it must have been like for him, to know that in a way he was responsible for her death. He seemed so devastated.'

He reached out and caressed her cheek with such gentleness her eyes burned. But his next words, even though they were uttered without emotion, shocked her out of her blissful warmth.

'Wivenhoe said he told you I had poisoned Serena. Did you believe him?'

She shook her head, holding his gaze.

'No, Max. Even before we spoke I knew you would never purposely harm her, no matter what happened between you or how trapped you felt. Even if you had found that medicine for her, I knew you would never have harmed her on purpose and what happened to her must have been a terrible accident.'

'You were willing to forgive me even that?'

'Of course,' she said, surprised, and he threaded his fingers with hers and raised it to graze his mouth over her knuckles lightly.

'I don't deserve you, Sophie.'

'I told you that's not true, and besides, this isn't about deserving. Do you *want* me?' she asked, her voice hitching.

He bent forward, leaned his forehead against her hand. She could feel his tension in the way his hands pressed against hers, in his measured but not quite even breathing. She touched his dark hair with the tips of her fingers, brushing it gently as she absorbed what he was telling her without words. She was filled with joy and the need to promise him she would do anything to make him happy. But she just kept the gentle motion of her hand on his head until he looked up and then she smiled.

'I love you, Max.'

Max absorbed the words, the truth in her eyes. How had he missed it? He was a greater fool than he ever could have imagined. It didn't matter. What mattered was that whatever she said, he was luckier than he deserved and he had every intention of doing all he could to make sure she never regretted this. He touched the skin below her bruised cheek, wishing he had the power to erase it, erase anything that hurt her. It was foolish and unnecessary. She was strong enough.

'Will you let me sketch you one day?' she asked suddenly and he laughed, thrown back to that day in the gardens, to his instinctive need and even more instinctive resistance. He had been such a fool.

'You can do whatever you want, Sophie. Anything, just love me.'

'Oh, that's easy,' she said with a smile, tracing his lips with her fingers and he drew her towards him, doing the same to her, with his fingers, his mouth. She had such a beautiful, generous mouth. His, now. She was his.

'Anything else?' she asked, her breath meeting his, sliding her arms around him, drawing herself closer with the impatient need he loved in her.

'No, just that.'

'Oh, not this, too?' She drew one of his arms around her, placing his hand firmly on her behind, and something between a laugh and a growl echoed through him and he pulled her on to his lap with more urgency than grace, realising he was hard as stone under her thigh.

'God, yes. This, too.'

She squirmed on him, her cheeks heating and the languid look that tore at his control entering her eyes. He wanted to draw it out, drag her to the edge of her control just as she did to him, keep her there until she begged for release. He teased her mouth with his, sliding over her, nipping, tasting her, but slipping away from her attempts to fix her mouth on his until she moaned in frustration.

'You said I can do what I want, but you're not letting me,' she mumbled and the raw need in her voice shot such a surge of desire through him that he drew back.

'We shouldn't be doing this,' he groaned, shifting his hands to her arms, trying to regain some control. 'Rob and Sylvie are two doors down and tomorrow…I mean today we will go to Harcourt and we'll be married in a week come hell or high water and then we can do anything we want… Sophie?'

Something in the way she stiffened under his hold sobered him.

'What is it, love?'

She shook her head.

'Do we have to go there yet? I'm bound to do something wrong and your mother will hate me and whatever you say now, when it happens you'll go all duke-ish on me and then I'll be hurt and say something stupid and you'll close down and…'

His arms tightened on her.

'Stop. Sophie, I've been a fool, but I will do everything I can to do better. You come first, do you understand me? Before everything. If anyone, my mother, *anyone* makes you uncomfortable, you do what you feel is right. Or you come to me and we will deal with them together. I trust you a damn sight more than I trust myself. You can indulge your beautiful heart to its fullest and it will only do good—to me and everyone around us. And if I go…"duke-ish", then kick me. I don't want to go through life like that any more. I told you, this is pure selfishness on my part. I need you to be happy. And I want you to be happy, more than I've wanted anything in my life. So don't play by anyone's rules but your own and if we clash we'll deal with it. Together. Understand?'

Sophie nodded and leaned her cheek against his shoulder, shutting her eyes tight against the burn of tears. She loved him so much it was unbearable sometimes. She threaded her fingers through his and raised them to her lips, making a silent pact with herself to be brave enough to do precisely as he asked. There would be problems, plenty, she supposed, but she would try to be brave enough to deal with them in the open. She listened to the steady surge of his heartbeat against her, holding this moment to her as gently as possible. As amazing as it was she knew it was true, he needed her, and so much of what she had worried would stand between them had actually built this bridge of love and caring between them. Even his wary, duke-ish distance, because it was just the wall around the amazing person she loved and even that wall was beautiful. And she was so very, very happy. And becoming very, very soppily sentimental. She laughed against his shoulder and he pulled away slightly.

'What's so funny now?' he asked, answering laughter lighting his eyes, warming them, opening him to her. This was what love looked like, she realised, and she had seen it in his eyes before but not recognised it. But she knew now and she would cherish it.

'It occurred to me that I would never have met you if it hadn't been for Marmaduke.'

Max grinned at her, visibly relaxing. He brushed the hair back from her face, his hands sliding into her hair, down her neck, slow, measured caresses that were beginning to soothe away the fear and pain she had been holding inside her these past weeks. She knew this was just a prelude to the urgent heat that was gathering on the horizon, but for the moment she was content to abandon herself to his strength and love. She trusted him, she realised. Perhaps for the first time in her life, she trusted someone with her as she really was. Just Sophie.

'I never thought I would owe my happiness to a pug,' Max said, his voice as warm and caressing as his hands as they moved over her shoulders, sliding down her bare arms. 'We shall have to get him a special treat.'

'It wasn't just Marmaduke,' she murmured. She

loved it when he touched that soft skin on the inside of her arm like this…like the day he had proposed, and then—was it just yesterday?—when he had turned over her arm gently and kissed her, so light and yet it had been so powerful. 'I am very grateful you were so well trained. Otherwise you might not have stopped when I called him to heel.'

'Any other demands you want to fling at my head, my lovely little madcap?'

His voice, laughing and hoarse, filled her with a possessive joy she realised she could now set free. He was hers. She wanted to take all the time in the world to explore him, touch him, taste him until she knew every inch of him. Made him hers fully, because she could now.

'Yes. I want to touch you everywhere,' she said dreamily, without thinking, and his arms stilled and then closed on her convulsively as he shuddered, pulling her hard against him. She laughed, loving that just her words had the power to do this to him. She arched into his strength, the tingling heat rising, urgent, and her breath tightened and then released on a moan. His hands moved down her back, over her hips, gentleness replaced by a mirror of her urgency, and the sheer force of the muscles under her turned the tingling to a scalding need. She wanted him inside her, now. She didn't have to keep her love to herself any more and it was most amazing thing in the world. *He* was amazing and he was hers. She wrapped her arms around his neck, leaning back against his arm and revelled in the brilliant storm in his eyes.

'One more command, Max,' she whispered, her breath hitching as his hand curved over the soft skin of her thigh, sliding her towards him, promising everything.

'Anything...' he said, his voice as lost as hers. 'Lie down, Duke...

* * * * *

If you enjoyed this story, you won't want to miss these other great reads from
Lara Temple

THE RELUCTANT VISCOUNT
LORD CRAYLE'S SECRET WORLD

MILLS & BOON®
Hardback – September 2017

ROMANCE

The Tycoon's Outrageous Proposal	Miranda Lee
Cipriani's Innocent Captive	Cathy Williams
Claiming His One-Night Baby	Michelle Smart
At the Ruthless Billionaire's Command	Carole Mortimer
Engaged for Her Enemy's Heir	Kate Hewitt
His Drakon Runaway Bride	Tara Pammi
The Throne He Must Take	Chantelle Shaw
The Italian's Virgin Acquisition	Michelle Conder
A Proposal from the Crown Prince	Jessica Gilmore
Sarah and the Secret Sheikh	Michelle Douglas
Conveniently Engaged to the Boss	Ellie Darkins
Her New York Billionaire	Andrea Bolter
The Doctor's Forbidden Temptation	Tina Beckett
From Passion to Pregnancy	Tina Beckett
The Midwife's Longed-For Baby	Caroline Anderson
One Night That Changed Her Life	Emily Forbes
The Prince's Cinderella Bride	Amalie Berlin
Bride for the Single Dad	Jennifer Taylor
A Family for the Billionaire	Dani Wade
Taking Home the Tycoon	Catherine Mann

0817 GEN STD HB

MILLS & BOON®
Large Print – September 2017

ROMANCE

The Sheikh's Bought Wife	Sharon Kendrick
The Innocent's Shameful Secret	Sara Craven
The Magnate's Tempestuous Marriage	Miranda Lee
The Forced Bride of Alazar	Kate Hewitt
Bound by the Sultan's Baby	Carol Marinelli
Blackmailed Down the Aisle	Louise Fuller
Di Marcello's Secret Son	Rachael Thomas
Conveniently Wed to the Greek	Kandy Shepherd
His Shy Cinderella	Kate Hardy
Falling for the Rebel Princess	Ellie Darkins
Claimed by the Wealthy Magnate	Nina Milne

HISTORICAL

The Secret Marriage Pact	Georgie Lee
A Warriner to Protect Her	Virginia Heath
Claiming His Defiant Miss	Bronwyn Scott
Rumours at Court (Rumors at Court)	Blythe Gifford
The Duke's Unexpected Bride	Lara Temple

MEDICAL

Their Secret Royal Baby	Carol Marinelli
Her Hot Highland Doc	Annie O'Neil
His Pregnant Royal Bride	Amy Ruttan
Baby Surprise for the Doctor Prince	Robin Gianna
Resisting Her Army Doc Rival	Sue MacKay
A Month to Marry the Midwife	Fiona McArthur

0817 GEN STD LP

MILLS & BOON®
Hardback – October 2017

ROMANCE

Claimed for the Leonelli Legacy	Lynne Graham
The Italian's Pregnant Prisoner	Maisey Yates
Buying His Bride of Convenience	Michelle Smart
The Tycoon's Marriage Deal	Melanie Milburne
Undone by the Billionaire Duke	Caitlin Crews
His Majesty's Temporary Bride	Annie West
Bound by the Millionaire's Ring	Dani Collins
The Virgin's Shock Baby	Heidi Rice
Whisked Away by Her Sicilian Boss	Rebecca Winters
The Sheikh's Pregnant Bride	Jessica Gilmore
A Proposal from the Italian Count	Lucy Gordon
Claiming His Secret Royal Heir	Nina Milne
Sleigh Ride with the Single Dad	Alison Roberts
A Firefighter in Her Stocking	Janice Lynn
A Christmas Miracle	Amy Andrews
Reunited with Her Surgeon Prince	Marion Lennox
Falling for Her Fake Fiancé	Sue MacKay
The Family She's Longed For	Lucy Clark
Billionaire Boss, Holiday Baby	Janice Maynard
Billionaire's Baby Bind	Katherine Garbera

0917 GEN STD HB

MILLS & BOON®
Large Print – October 2017

ROMANCE

Sold for the Greek's Heir	Lynne Graham
The Prince's Captive Virgin	Maisey Yates
The Secret Sanchez Heir	Cathy Williams
The Prince's Nine-Month Scandal	Caitlin Crews
Her Sinful Secret	Jane Porter
The Drakon Baby Bargain	Tara Pammi
Xenakis's Convenient Bride	Dani Collins
Her Pregnancy Bombshell	Liz Fielding
Married for His Secret Heir	Jennifer Faye
Behind the Billionaire's Guarded Heart	Leah Ashton
A Marriage Worth Saving	Therese Beharrie

HISTORICAL

The Debutante's Daring Proposal	Annie Burrows
The Convenient Felstone Marriage	Jenni Fletcher
An Unexpected Countess	Laurie Benson
Claiming His Highland Bride	Terri Brisbin
Marrying the Rebellious Miss	Bronwyn Scott

MEDICAL

Their One Night Baby	Carol Marinelli
Forbidden to the Playboy Surgeon	Fiona Lowe
A Mother to Make a Family	Emily Forbes
The Nurse's Baby Secret	Janice Lynn
The Boss Who Stole Her Heart	Jennifer Taylor
Reunited by Their Pregnancy Surprise	Louisa Heaton

0917 GEN STD LP